Margaret Bacon was brought up in the Yorkshire Dales and educated at The Mount School, York and at Oxford. She taught history before her marriage to a Civil Engineer whose profession entailed much travel and frequent moves of house. Her first book, *Journey to Guyana*, was an account of two years spent in South America. Her subsequent books, including one children's novel, have all been fiction. She has two daughters and is now settled in Wiltshire.

# Home Truths

Margaret Bacon

First published in this edition in 1995
by HEADLINE BOOK PUBLISHING

A HEADLINE REVIEW paperback

10 9 8 7 6 5 4 3 2 1

ISBN 0 7472 4879 6

Typeset by
Letterpart Limited, Reigate, Surrey

Printed and bound in Great Britain by
Cox & Wyman Ltd, Reading, Berks

HEADLINE BOOK PUBLISHING
A division of Hodder Headline PLC
338 Euston Road
London NW1 3BH

# Home Truths

# Chapter One

The telephone rang. Seven o'clock on a Sunday morning.

'I'll get it,' he said, and did not move.

She lay still, eyes closed, pretending to be asleep. The telephone went on ringing.

He stretched out an arm, lifted the receiver, lost it temporarily among the clutter on the bedside table and retrieved it in time to hear a man's voice say, evidently not for the first time, 'Has it gone yet?'

'What?' he asked, his voice still slurred with sleep.

'I said has it gone yet?'

'I meant has *what* gone?'

'The house. *Your* house.'

He looked around. 'No,' he said. 'Still here. I think you've got the wrong number.'

'Chorfield 764682?'

He looked at the dial. ''sright,' he said.

She sat up suddenly.

'For God's sake!' she hissed. 'Give it to me.'

He relinquished the receiver and fell back among the pillows.

'Good morning,' she said brightly. 'Can I help you?'

How could she? Lying there, her hair all over her face, her nightie inside out, sounding like an answering machine. Just as well they didn't have a televised telephone. He yawned loudly.

'I imagine you're ringing up about the cottage we advertised for sale in the *Sunday Times*?' she enquired sweetly.

1

'That's right,' he heard the voice say at the other end, relieved, no doubt, to be talking at last to an intelligent fellow creature. 'We were afraid it might have gone already.'

'Not by seven o'clock, it hasn't, no,' she said rather less sweetly.

'Well, I'm sorry to ring so early, but you see we've been looking for two years and we know how quickly houses go. Could my wife and I come to view today? This morning if possible?'

'Perhaps I should tell you a bit more about it first?'

'You won't let it go to anyone else before we come?' the voice enquired anxiously.

'No, you can have first refusal,' she reassured him, and went on to give details and directions.

He lay, listening. Evidently they were called Armstrong and were coming this morning by the Green Line coach that passed the cottage gate at a quarter past eleven. At last she had finished being bright and helpful, put down the receiver, groaned and lay back exhausted.

'The contrast between how you sound and how you look is quite startling, Heather Barnicoat,' he said, settling down beside her.

'Well, honestly. You were awful. You might have lost us a sale.'

'You know I'm no good in the morning.'

'You didn't even sound sober.'

'Your nightie's inside out,' he counter-attacked irrationally.

'You know why.'

'I'll take it off for you and put it right in no time,' he promised.

'You've just said you're no good in the morning.'

'Ah, but I'm not going to sell you a house. What I had in mind was quite different,' he said, kissing her shoulder.

'No, really. They're coming at eleven and . . .'

'And it's only just gone seven now,' he pointed out, rolling her over towards him.

James appeared in the doorway.

'The telephone woke me,' he accused.

'Sorry, Your Highness.'

'Well, you two get mad if *we* wake *you* up.'

'What are the others doing?'

'Jonathan's playing with his Lego and the Ant's just lying in his cot. But he's taken his nappies off.'

She went downstairs. In the corner of the little sitting-room, the baby was lying in his cot, staring abstractedly at the branches of apple blossom that waved to and fro across the square of blue sky that he could see through the little sash window. His nappies and plastic pants lay rolled in a ball in one corner of the cot. When he heard his mother come in he looked towards her, his eyes suddenly bright with recognition, his arms outstretched, his back arched ecstatically, his whole body taut with joy. For a moment she leant over the cot, gazing back at him, her face reflecting the delight on his. It was the best moment of the day. Then he looked suddenly solemn, his eyes withdrew from hers and he gazed intently at the wall, contemplating more serious matters. A fine jet of clear liquid rose delicately from him into the air and then flowed down on to the mattress.

'You rotter,' she said, lifting him out of the cot. 'And just when we don't want washing hanging around all over the place.'

The telephone rang.

It rang eight times before they had finished breakfast. By then the two older children were grumpy and the Ant had quite lost his early morning serenity. By nine-thirty he was screaming in the pram, under the apple tree.

'If you do the washing up, Derek,' she said, coming back into the cottage, 'I'll see to the rest.'

As he moved towards the sink there was a scrunching sound of trodden plastic.

'My bridge, you've broken my bridge,' James roared. 'Don't you ever look where you put your great feet?'

'Sunday, bloody Sunday,' he murmured.

She laughed. 'He sounded just like you,' she said.

The telephone rang.

★ ★ ★

At first sight the Armstrongs were a disappointment; they seemed, as they walked hand-in-hand up the uneven brick path to the cottage door, much too young and small to be taken seriously as house-buyers.

The impression soon passed. They said disconcertingly little as they were shown over the cottage, but they obviously noticed everything. Occasionally Christopher Armstrong asked unanswerable questions about such things as the under-drawing, and, looking at the pond in the field at the back of the house, something about what he called the water table. But they obviously liked the cottage and pictured themselves living in it.

'One could build an extension,' Christopher Armstrong pronounced as they stood in the kitchen.

'We did think of it,' Derek told him, rather defensively, 'but the builder said there wouldn't be headroom. It's a lean-to already, he said.'

'Oh yes, but you'd build this way, taking off the back door,' Christopher Armstrong explained. 'Is this a load-bearing wall?'

'I've no idea,' said Derek, who had not heard the expression before.

'I don't imagine it is,' Christopher said thoughtfully, 'and anyway, we could always put in a reinforced concrete beam.'

Derek nodded knowledgeably.

Later they drank coffee on the undulating little terrace which Derek had laid at the back of the cottage.

'I'm sorry we rang so early,' Bunty Armstrong said, 'but we were so afraid of missing it. It's happened to us before.'

Heather laughed. 'You did right,' she said. 'The telephone hasn't stopped ringing all morning. We took it off the hook in the end to get a bit of peace. We'd no idea there'd be such a response to those few lines in the paper. It seems crazy.'

'There's such a shortage of this kind of house, that's why. The agents all say the same – they've never had so few on their books.'

'Well, we'd heard that, so we decided we might as well try to

4

sell it ourselves and save agents' fees, but we hadn't realized quite how desperate people are to buy.'

'And these other people who rang,' Christopher Armstrong cut in, 'are they coming to see it?'

'I said I'd let them know if you didn't want it.'

The Armstrongs looked at each other. They nodded, Tweedledum and Tweedledee, she thought. 'Yes,' they said in unison, 'we want it.'

'We'll pay the full asking price,' he said.

'Oh, well . . .' Heather began.

'Thank you,' Derek said. 'Then that's settled.'

'You see, if we make a lower offer, you could accept the full price from somebody else this afternoon,' Bunty pointed out shrewdly. She looks about sixteen, Heather thought, but she's years older than I am in the ways of the world.

Bunty caught the look.

'You think I'm cynical,' she said.

'No, of course not.'

Later, as they looked around the garden, the two women strolled over to the pram. The Ant slept, uncovered. Bunty gazed down at him.

'He's lovely,' she said, awe-struck.

'He's called Anthony really, but the poor chap gets called Ant for short. You like babies?'

'I can't wait. We've been married four years, but first we were abroad so we postponed having any, then back in England we couldn't find a house, and the basement flat we've got in Victoria is horrible, and anyway the landlord doesn't allow babies or pets.'

'Well, this place is marvellous for children. It's so safe and the garden's much bigger than you'd expect with such a tiny cottage.'

'It doesn't seem tiny after our flat, I can tell you!'

Heather smiled. 'Yes, I remember when we first came it seemed quite big. It's ideal for a couple and one child, it's a bit of a squeeze with two children, and it's quite impossible now we've got the Ant. We looked for something bigger a while ago, but we couldn't see anything to compare with this position – the shops are handy and it's all so quiet, and then Derek can walk up to school.'

'He teaches – your husband?'

'Yes, at the local school. But he saw this job advertised in Leicestershire as head of the English Department, so he applied and we've just heard he's got it. So really it's all worked out very well, because we'd have to move to a bigger house anyway, and we know there's not much around here, so we might as well move away. But it's sad all the same. We haven't told the children yet. I expect they'll be furious.'

'So when would you go?'

'He starts in September. We'll look for a house up there straight away now, but if necessary he can go into digs for a while. What does Christopher do?'

'He's with a firm of civil engineers in London. They asked him to work abroad again but we wanted to settle down and have a family, so they offered him this job at head office, doing tendering. He doesn't really enjoy it, he'd much rather be on site, but that means moving around all the time.'

'Yes, it's difficult moving once you've got kids. And what about you? Do you have a job?'

'I trained as a child's nurse, looking after healthy children, that is. I'm working at a day nursery at the moment in London. They're pre-school age, about two to five, but sometimes we have a baby to look after. I was lucky to get the job really when we came back from abroad. It's near the flat too.'

'I should think *they* were lucky to get *you*. There must be an enormous demand for people like you, especially now so many mothers go out to work. But how lovely to be an expert on children. I mean you'll know exactly what to do with your own kids when you have them, won't you? I hadn't a clue what to do with mine.'

'What sort of work did you do before you were married?'

'I was in publishing. I loved it, but I can't honestly say it was much help when it came to finding out how to put on nappies. Oh, do be careful,' she added as Bunty tripped over the uneven bricks of the path. 'I'm afraid Derek didn't get it exactly flat.'

'Don't worry. Christopher will take it up and re-lay it in no time. He's very practical,' she added, her face glowing with pride, 'and a real perfectionist.'

'You're lucky to have a tame handyman around the place.'

'Oh yes, I *am* lucky. And I'm sure he'll be a marvellous father; he'll be able to make all sorts of things, dolls' houses and climbing frames and everything like that.'

She looked around the garden, peopling it with her children and their splendid home-made toys.

'She's really very sweet,' Heather remarked after they had gone. 'In fact they both are.'

'Never mind being sweet, just so long as they can get a mortgage.'

They began to stroll aimlessly around the garden, curiously drained by the experience of selling their home.

'They look so young,' she said. 'You'd never think they'd been married for four years.'

'Good lord! I thought they were newly-weds. I mean the way she looks at him, all dewy-eyed and adoring. You must be wrong. I bet they haven't been married more than a few months.'

'Rubbish. She *told* me. Don't men ever tell each other anything?'

'Well, he was on about underpinning and foundations and water tables so I couldn't really interrupt and ask him how long he'd been married, could I?'

She laughed and took his hand.

'You don't have to ask. These things just emerge. At least between women they do.'

'Not with him, they don't. Nothing but breeze blocks emerge. And load-bearing walls, and girders and suchlike. Tell you something,' he went on, 'I don't remember that *you* ever looked at me like that when *we'd* been married four years.'

'We had two kids by then and I hardly ever looked up from the sink, if you remember.'

'Do I smell the smell of burning martyr?' he asked, putting his arm around her.

She yawned and leant up against him. 'Speaking of kids,' she said, 'I suppose I'd better go and collect them from Mary. It was jolly nice of her to take them out of the way while we showed off our house.'

'Yes. You'll miss her when we move.'

They had reached the bottom of the garden and were leaning on the fence, looking out over the field beyond. It was ringed with trees and in the foreground cattle grazed peacefully round the pond.

'Yes,' she sighed. 'I shall miss her very much. And we shan't easily get another view like this either.'

She gazed across the field, drinking it all in, as if for the last time. Then she turned and looked back at the cottage.

'Who would have thought,' she said, 'that it would be so easy to sell a house? Just a little notice in the paper and the deed is done. Soon it won't be our cottage any more. After all these years.'

He nodded. 'Can't think why anybody bothers with estate agents,' he said.

They stood looking at it in silence, she thinking of the home that they had made and would soon leave, he contemplating with satisfaction the agent's fees that they had saved.

'I've just thought,' he said suddenly, interrupting the silence, 'since it was so easy to sell, maybe we won't find it so easy to buy. I mean the boot's going to be on the other foot now, isn't it?'

In the damp hall of their basement flat Bunty and Christopher Armstrong stood and hugged each other. Then they moved clumsily into the sitting-room, still clinging together.

'I can't believe it,' she said almost in a sob. 'I mean after all these *awful* months.'

He patted her shoulder and said nothing.

She looked up at him. 'And when you didn't say anything,' she went on half-laughing, half-crying, 'I thought perhaps you didn't like it.'

'I didn't dare say much, in case they put the price up.'

She sniffed and dabbed at her eyes.

'Oh, they weren't like that,' she said.

'Everyone's like that, when they're selling houses.'

'Not true. Not everyone.'

'Well, I must admit they seemed a very nice couple.'

'Oh, we're so lucky. Such a beautiful little cottage and such super people selling it. I just feel everything's going to be all right this time.'

She began to cry in earnest.

'Come on,' he said, 'you're exhausted. Let's get something to eat.'

In a daze she went into the kitchen, which was really just a bit of the sitting-room roughly partitioned off. She scrambled some eggs, made coffee and put biscuits and cheese on a tray. And all the time she was thinking of babies.

'You all right?' he asked, looking at her curiously, as he picked up the tray.

She nodded, unable to put it into words.

He put the tray down on the table in front of the gas fire, which they had to have on all the year round to keep the damp at bay. 'What is it? Don't look like that.'

'It's the baby,' she managed to whisper. 'Now we can start a baby.'

He looked at her, surprised. 'Before or after the scrambled egg?' he asked.

'We're looking for a four-bedroomed house, preferably old,' Derek began. 'You know, Georgian or Victorian, without too much garden, in the suburbs or a village outside the town. Quiet, but not too remote. We'd like shops handy and public transport and—'

'How much?' interrupted the young man.

'How much what?'

'Your price range.'

'Oh, well, it all depends, doesn't it? I mean, what sort of condition it's in, and so on. Can't you just show us all the houses of the sort I've described and we'll think about price afterwards?'

'No. It doesn't work like that. We file them under the price. But actually we've nothing such as you've described on our books anyway. If you care to leave details on this form, we'll keep you posted.'

They filled in the form and left.

'A bit take-it-or-leave-it, wasn't he?' she remarked as they walked towards the next estate agent on their list.

'Well, we obviously struck the worst estate agent in the town for our first attempt,' he said. 'No doubt Flint & Skellow will make up for it.'

They didn't. Young Mr Flint said they only had three properties on their books, namely a flat and two mansions. They filled in another form and made their way to Namboe & Namboe.

Mr Namboe was the senior partner and took them into an inner sanctuary. He had just the thing, he said. It was a three-bedroomed house on a high-class estate. They could convert the utility into a small fourth bedroom.

'What a cheek,' she said indignantly as they walked to the next agent. 'Can you imagine? The poor Ant in a *sink*? Honestly that house was no bigger than our cottage.'

'And cost nearly half as much again.'

'It makes you realize your own home's jolly good.'

'Do you think we asked enough for it?'

'Well, we can't go back on that now. Where's the next agent on the list?'

She stood comparing the list with the town map. 'Let's give that one a miss – it's almost on the outskirts, and it's going to rain. But Soggets is only a couple of streets away.

'Do you remember,' she said as they walked, 'how we used to grumble about the centre of towns being taken over by estate agents instead of proper shops? I'm jolly glad now, aren't you?'

'Yes,' he admitted reluctantly. 'It shows how house-hunting corrupts one.'

She laughed and took his arm. 'Cheer up,' she said. '*You* were the one who said what fun it would be, a day off without the children, all on our own, choosing this dream house.'

'Well, I thought there'd be plenty to choose from. All lined up, you know, waiting for us.'

'Here we are – Soggets. Perhaps it's waiting for us here.'

'I hate this business of reciting the great rigmarole of requirements when we go in. You say it all this time.'

There was no need. Soggets was in charge of a girl who sat at a huge desk filing her nails. 'We've only got four houses on our lists,' she told them, 'and they're all 'orrible.''

They filled in the inevitable form and left her to her manicuring.

Rain was pelting down. They stood in Soggets' doorway, appalled, watching as the road turned into a river in front of their very eyes.

'There's a pub next door,' he said. 'Let's make a dash for it and have an early lunch.'

'Can't say I'm very hungry.'

'We'll have a ploughman's lunch; you can manage that.'

Soon they were sitting in the damp and gloomy saloon bar contemplating plates of dispirited lettuce leaves upon which rested lumps of dry cheese, impregnable bread rolls and tightly wrapped parcels of butter.

'Do you think,' she asked as she pursued a hard and slippery pickled onion round her plate, 'that many ploughmen actually eat meals like this?'

'No, they're all having *coq au vin* at the Hilton round the corner.'

Over coffee, she said, 'Derek, what shall we do if we don't find anything by October?'

'October? I start work in September.'

'I know. But we promised the Armstrongs we'd be out of the cottage by October.'

'We didn't sign anything.'

'Derek! We promised.'

'Oh, all right. We'll find something. We've hardly started.'

'I know, but all the same, you do get a feel of how things are, even in one morning. And I think there just aren't any houses on the market.'

'There's bound to be something, you'll see. We'll do the other three agents in town and then we'll start on the villages. At least it's stopped raining, or almost.'

As they went from agent to agent, in the fine drizzle, she noticed that their list of requirements got shorter and shorter. By the time they reached Freeman, Tucker & Son, Derek asked simply, 'Have you any houses?'

'Would you consider half a country house?' the agent asked. He was a gangling, sandy-haired youth, very keen to oblige, who introduced himself as the young Mr Tucker. 'I have a very desirable property of that nature which I know well actually, as it belongs to my cousin Susan. I have the particulars here, with a sort of map.'

He produced a piece of paper with a plan of the house and grounds. 'Lovely setting,' he said. 'In the village of Hunting-ford. Very much sought-after district, of course. It used to be the manor house, now converted.'

'Which bit is it that she's selling?'

Young Mr Tucker pointed to the north-west corner.

'So it doesn't get the sun or a view of the garden?'

'Well, no; it was the servants' wing.'

The telephone rang. 'Excuse me,' he said. 'I'll be with you in a moment.'

'Let's go,' Derek said. 'He can find some other muggins to buy the damp bit of cousin Susan's house.'

'Sh, he'll hear.'

'I don't care if he does. Come on – he said he hadn't any more houses to show us.'

They got up. Mr Tucker put his hand over the receiver and made noises at them to wait. Then he turned back to the phone and said, 'By chance, Mrs Soddie, I have a Mr and Mrs Barnicoat here at the office who might be very interested. Could I bring them along with me when I come to measure up? They've come a considerable distance. Very well. In about half an hour, then.'

It was not at all the kind of house they had intended to buy. Tall and forbidding-looking, it was in a Victorian terrace in the centre of the town.

'Faces due north,' Derek remarked as they got out of Mr Tucker's car.

'Which means that the garden, which is entirely at the back, faces due south,' the agent pointed out.

'It probably hasn't got a garage,' Derek said gloomily.

'Ample parking in the square or the back lane. This is a very good residential area, of course. The best in town, some would say.'

Mrs Soddie was tall and handsome but there was something sad, almost apathetic about her.

'My husband's in Zanzibar,' she said casually. 'They always are, aren't they?'

There was an archway across the hall beyond which the staircase wound gracefully out of sight. Mrs Soddie began to show them round the house, pointing out its disadvantages as she went, to the evident discomfiture of the agent commissioned to sell it. By the time she had insisted that they take a good look at the brown patch above the dining-room fireplace, a crack down the landing wall and holes in the bannisters which might be woodworm, young Mr Tucker could obviously bear it no longer.

'Shall I show them round, Mrs Soddie?' he suggested in tones of restrained exasperation. 'There is no need for you to worry about the viewing.'

'Well, that's very good of you,' she said and made obediently for the stairs. Half-way down she turned to warn them, 'Do mind your heads at the top of the stairs, they're dreadfully dangerous; a friend nearly knocked himself out up there. And I'm sorry about the smell in the attic. My husband thinks it might be the start of dry rot, but I don't know.'

'You see what spacious rooms they are,' Mr Tucker cut in. 'Such perfect proportions. And an amplitude of accommodation. The garden too is amply commensurate.'

Heather, who had fallen in love with the house at first sight, agreed eagerly. From the moment she had come in the front door she had felt at home. The welcome the house had given her, and her own warm response to it, took her totally by surprise. She felt a kind of joyful recognition, but it was as unexpected as that of a traveller who approaches a stranger in some remote place only to find it is an old friend.

It wasn't just the thick walls and shuttered windows, the archways and unexpected corners, it was the whole feeling of the house. She belonged here, she knew it. It would be impossible now to live anywhere else. Indeed it would be a kind of treachery. She felt quite apologetic for looking around it, for she knew, before she entered each room, that it would be perfect, so much did she trust this house.

'The stairs will kill you,' Derek remarked.

'No, they won't. The boys can have the top floor, we'll sleep on the first floor with the Ant in the other room, the sitting-room's on the ground floor anyway, and we'll eat in the downstairs kitchen.'

They had reached the top. Mr Tucker stood at the bottom of the little flight of steps into the attic. She climbed up behind him.

'Oh,' she gasped. 'Isn't it perfect up here? Oh, Derek, just the place for the boys. They could leave their train set up all the time. And it's so light and airy.'

'Close boarded, too,' Mr Tucker pointed out.

'What was that she said about dry rot, Mr Tucker?' Derek asked suspiciously.

'I can assure you there is no possibility of it. The ventilation is excellent.'

'I bet it's freezing up here in winter,' Derek said. 'In fact the whole place must cost the earth to heat.'

'I think you'll find these thick walls retain the heat very admirably,' Mr Tucker told him. 'And of course being a terraced house there is minimum heat loss through the walls.'

They turned and went thoughtfully downstairs. 'About those holes,' Mr Tucker said on the first landing. 'Certainly not woodworm. More like drawing pins.'

In the hall, he said to Derek, 'Perhaps you and your good lady would like to discuss it before we rejoin Mrs Soddie? I shall be measuring the garden if you need me.'

14

# Home Truths

'How much?' Derek said bluntly. 'You realize we don't know how much they want for it?'

'Well, as you know, I haven't measured up, but I think the figure Mr Soddie has in mind is quite reasonable. Let me see.'

He took out a pocket calculator and, muttering about gas central heating and number of rooms and garage space, did some sums. Having named his price, he tactfully left them alone to discuss it.

They stood in the hall, whispering at each other, feeling like burglars in this strange house.

'Derek, it's fantastic,' she hissed. 'You said we could afford the price of the cottage plus about a third. It's easily within that.'

'Yes, but there might be a lot to spend on it.'

'That's true of any house.'

'Not new ones. There'd be no work to be done on a new house.'

'Old houses are much better value. We've always said that. I mean, if it's stood for over a hundred years it shows it's strong. It's not going to fall down now. These new houses are ever so flimsy. They're always falling down—'

'All right, I can see you like it. I'm just being practical. Somebody has to be practical.'

'It's not practical to refuse the only house on the market. Nobody else has seen it yet. It was a chance in a million to be in the office when she rang up. Don't you see?'

'We don't want to seem too eager,' he whispered, nodding his head and looking crafty. 'We'll say we have to look at several others before we make up our minds.'

'Idiot. We'll lose it.'

'And there's no harm in offering less than the asking price. People expect you to offer less.'

'If you lose us this house for the sake of a few hundred pounds, I'll never forgive you. Never.'

'The road could be noisy.'

'We'll sleep at the back.'

'I still think the stairs will kill you.'

'I don't mind the stairs.'

'It's you I'm thinking of. There's a lot of work in these old houses.'

'I tell you I don't mind. Think how much house we're getting for our money. Compare it with that modern one on the estate, with the utility room old Namboe wanted to make into a miserable fourth bedroom for the poor little Ant.'

'And then there's that basement kitchen . . .'

'*Semi*-basement. And it's almost on ground level at the back because of the way the land slopes. The sun must stream in at the back. And did you see that dear little conservatory where she had the plants?'

'You mean that glass porch on the back door? Hardly a conservatory.'

'Oh, do stop *quibbling*, Derek. It's a super kitchen. You could put most of our cottage into it and still have space left over.'

'It's a nice big kitchen, I grant you that. But you'll still have to carry food upstairs to the dining-room.'

'No, we'll eat downstairs. There's heaps of room. We could make a dining end to the kitchen. Window seats and everything.'

'What would you do with the dining-room?' It's a shame not to use the dining-room. The nicest room in the house, I thought.'

'You could have it for a study.'

'Mm. Yes. Well. As you say, it *is* a very nice house.'

'Oh, Derek, *please*.'

They sought out Mr Tucker and the three of them returned to the drawing-room. Mrs Soddie was sitting at her desk, reading. She put aside her book, which, Heather noticed, had pictures of flowers on the cover. Heather's love affair with the house seemed to have sharpened her perceptions; though she caught only the briefest glimpse of Mrs Soddie as she sat there absorbed in her book, she saw that the face was changed, much more alive than it had been. And for a second, as she looked up, startled as the three of them interrupted her reading, Rosemary Soddie's face held its animation before being masked by the quite different expression of dutiful interest which she now turned on Mr Tucker.

'About the house, Mrs Soddie,' he said. 'Mr and Mrs Barnicoat are certainly very interested.'

'Only if we can move in by October,' Derek said. 'When are you planning to leave here?'

'You see, we've promised to leave our cottage by October,' Heather began.

'Oh, we shall have gone by then,' Mrs Soddie assured them. 'My husband opens his northern office at the end of September and we have already arranged to buy a house up there.'

Heather sighed audibly with relief. It was all working out so easily. Even the rain had stopped; sun shone through the big sash windows catching the white paint on the panelling of the shutters.

'Yes,' Mrs Soddie went on, more or less reciting the arrangements. 'The house we're moving into belongs to an old lady who is going to live in a hotel, so there's no problem of her having to find a house or anything like that.'

She spoke without real interest, as if she was managing all the arrangements vicariously.

'Ah, an ideal situation for you, no chance of a hold-up,' Mr Tucker told the Barnicoats, as gratified as if the situation was all of his own making.

'And do you like where you're going?' Heather asked.

Rosemary Soddie hesitated. Then, 'It's more convenient to like where you live,' she said, in her resigned way. 'I've always found that.'

Heather heard her with astonishment. She couldn't imagine herself not caring about where she lived. She cared desperately. She had adored the cottage. It was going to be a heartbreak to leave it after all these years and everything that had happened in it. But Mrs Soddie's flat statement showed that she didn't care about leaving here. She didn't seem to be involved, as a person, at all. She was only going through the motions of buying and selling. She gave the impression of one who would see to everything very competently, but without any relish.

'But the house,' Heather persisted. 'I hope you like the house you're buying?'

'Yes, it's a nice house we're going to. Just on two floors. You see, here you've got four floors and all those stairs and—'

'Well,' Mr Tucker cut in brusquely, 'this is a lovely house too and Mr and Mrs Barnicoat are seriously interested. I know your husband wants it settled as soon as possible, Mrs Soddie.'

She looked at them in mild surprise. 'Well, it's your decision, of course,' she said, 'I mean if you *want* to live here.'

'Do you wish to make an offer?' Mr Tucker asked them.

The Barnicoats looked at each other. It was suddenly very quiet.

Derek hesitated. Heather glared at him.

'We'll pay the full asking price,' he said hoarsely.

# Chapter Two

Bunty sipped the tea. She nibbled at the biscuit. He watched her anxiously.

'All right?'

'Yes, thanks. Much better.'

'Good.'

He stroked her forehead. God, but she was pale. You would think all that heaving and retching would bring the baby up.

'I don't mind, you know,' she said. 'And it's lucky I always get it over early. It would be awful if it went on all morning and I couldn't go to work.'

'If it did, you'd just have to stop work. We could manage.'

'Even now that we've paid the deposit on the cottage?'

'Yes, if we had to.'

She sighed and lay back, relaxed. 'You know, I feel so much happier now that we've paid the deposit. I shall really enjoy telling old Skinflint we've got a home of our own to go to, and he can have his horrible flat back. It's such a relief to know it doesn't matter if he notices I'm pregnant now.'

'I shouldn't think he'd notice for a while. You're skinnier than ever.'

'Give me time,' she said and laughed.

Her colour was coming back, he observed with relief. If things followed the usual pattern she'd be better in time to cook his breakfast.

'I don't think the rent's at all bad really,' Heather said. 'Not for nowadays. And you have to remember that it includes dinner and breakfast. And it's a nice room.'

They had spent the previous day in Leicestershire looking for lodgings for Derek to go into next term.

'Well, it's only for four or six weeks anyway,' he said.

'More like two months. From early September until we move at half-term. It's not far off, you know. We're into August already.'

She sighed and turned in the bed to look at him.

'It'll be odd being here alone just with the boys next term.'

'I'll be home every weekend. It's not for long.'

'Oh, I don't mind really. I'll be able to get on with all the sorting out and packing up in the evenings when the boys are in bed. And I shan't have to cook at night.'

'How lovely for you! What was it somebody said about a husband's exile being a pleasant foretaste of widowhood?'

'Derek! Sometimes you're absolutely foul!'

'It was only a joke, my lovely.'

'I hate sick humour.'

'Sorry. Come here.'

'No, it's time we got up. I'll go and put the kettle on. Mary'll be bringing the boys back soon.'

'No, she won't. She said she'd keep them until at least eleven o'clock this morning because she knew we'd be exhausted after hunting for digs for me yesterday. I heard her say so. She said we deserved a lie-in.'

'Well, we've had a lie-in,' she said, getting out of bed. 'Where are the cups? I know I brought them upstairs last night.'

'On the chair behind you.'

'Oh Derek,' she said, suddenly turning back to him. 'Won't it be lovely when we've got space in our room for a bedside table?'

'And more bookcases,' he said, drawing her back into bed again.

'And a room of his own for the Ant,' she said, snuggling up to him.

20

'And a study for me,' he said, kissing her.

'And an attic room for the boys' trains,' kissing him back.

'And clothes in wardrobes instead of in trunks,' he said, taking off her nightie.

'And a place for my mixer in the kitchen. And – oh Derek, I was going to make the early-morning tea.'

'It's too late,' he said, 'for early morning tea.'

Afterwards he sighed deeply and said, 'We haven't had a morning like this since James learned how to get out of his cot.'

She laughed. 'Our poor little boys,' she said. 'How you don't miss them!'

'Do you?'

'Of course I do! The house felt all horrid and quiet last night when we came home. And I kept thinking I could hear them. Really, I was sure I heard the Ant early this morning. Do you realize it's the first time they've ever been away from us for the night?'

'Of course I realize, softie. I've just told you – normally they'd be in bed with us by now.'

'Mary says she'll have them again if I need to go up to see the house. And she'll have them when we move. I suppose I'll stay down here and see the furniture off and you'll stay up there to receive it?'

'Yes.' He yawned. 'We ought to arrange for the removal men soon.'

'I was just thinking that. We should get estimates from two or three firms. They'll have to come and assess the furniture, won't they?'

He laughed. 'It's the other end they ought to worry about,' he said. 'Just think of lugging all this stuff up those flights of stairs. There's no need,' he added hastily, 'to tell them that, of course.'

'Well, I shall have to, if they ask.'

'Just don't let honesty get the better of you, that's all.'

'Like Mrs Soddie and her damp patches.'

They laughed. 'And the woodworm and the dry rot. Poor Mr Tucker. I thought he'd have a fit.'

21

'I expect she was quite disappointed when the building society surveyor gave the house a clean bill of health.'

'Oh, but she was nice. I like people like that. Uncalculating. It makes such a refreshing change. You know really, we've been awfully lucky, Derek, the way things have gone so smoothly. You hear such dreadful tales about moving house, but we've had really nice people to deal with, both buying and selling.'

'How do you know Mr Soddie's nice? We don't know a thing about him except that he's never there. First it was Zanzibar, now it's Nairobi. Anywhere except Wellington Square.'

'I have a call for you from Nairobi. Will you accept the charge?'

Rosemary Soddie wondered idly what would happen if she said no.

'Yes,' she said.

'Just rang to see that everything's all right. Have you heard from the solicitor yet?'

'Yes, Mr Blunt rang this morning to say he had just put the contract to us in the post. Then he'll be sending it off to Mrs Moon's solicitor for her to sign.'

'Excellent. So we'll get possession on the last day of this month. And the next day we hand over to the – er, what are they called, the people who are buying our house?'

'Barnicoat.'

'That's it. I can never remember.'

'It's a Cornish name, she told me. They're very nice. A pity you haven't met them.'

'Well, there's no need. Leave all that to old Blunt. Listen, I think you'd better get somebody in to tidy up the garden, do the lawns and so on. I shan't be home next weekend.'

'But what about Thursday?'

'What about it?'

'We're going to school for the open day, and they're doing the athletics that they missed when sports day was rained off last term. And we're going out to dinner in the evening, you remember?'

'Sorry. You'll have to cancel. They'll understand.'

'They?'

'Whoever we were having dinner with.'

'They're our best friends and they're called Sutcliffe,' she told him with rare asperity. 'And the open day is your eldest son's.' Then she added, for good measure, 'And he's called Simon.'

Silence.

'I've said I'm sorry.'

'He was depending on you. You promised.'

'Look, he's sixteen. He's not a baby any more. Old enough to understand. It isn't as if it's the first time.'

'Quite.'

'Look, Ro, be reasonable. It's going to be much easier when I move up to the northern office. I'll be at home much more. And I shall see much more of him and of his new school.'

'He hates the idea of changing schools, you know. He's going to miss all his friends.'

'Oh, he'll adjust. The young are very resilient.'

'It's a bad time to move. With exams and everything.'

'He's bright enough to manage that. Don't you worry. You just concentrate on your side of things. You'll have plenty to think about won't you, with the removal and the new house to do up from top to bottom? You'll enjoy that.'

Embarrassed, as she always was when he talked to her as if she was a little girl, she could think of nothing to say.

'Well, I must be off now,' he said. 'There's a chap waiting for me at the office. I'll ring again on Thursday. All right?'

'Yes, thank you,' she said politely.

'No worries?'

'No. We're all right.'

'Back early next week, I hope. Probably Wednesday. Goodbye then.'

'Goodbye.'

She put the receiver down and turned back to her gardening book. She never actually did any gardening, but loved reading about it.

★ ★ ★

Florence Moon surveyed the new mowing machine. It was a Hawker four-stroke with seat attached. She had bought it before she decided – or had been persuaded – to sell her house. She didn't regret buying the machine; she never begrudged money spent on the garden.

The house was a different matter. Nothing in it was ever changed or renewed, nor had it been decorated since her husband had died thirty years ago. There was still the same old stone sink in the kitchen and the original wireless in the drawing-room. The housekeeper, Winifred Herbert, still pushed across the same carpets the same ancient vacuum cleaner that her mother's resident maid had first pushed in the 1920s. She did the ironing on the same wooden table with the same New Model electric iron which she had to plug into the light in the kitchen ceiling, having first climbed on to the table in order to remove the light bulb.

The garden, by contrast, was full of modern gadgetry. The walls of the tool shed were hung with long-handled automated implements, advertisements for which in the Sunday papers she had found irresistible, and here in the stables where she now stood was a range of machines for cutting grass. She still had the old light cylindrical cutter and the heavier Qualcast with the roller, the Flymo which she'd given up in disgust because it didn't make stripes on the lawn, the electric mower which she hadn't used since it had mowed its own flex, and the four-stroke which she had just abandoned in favour of the one with seat attached which she had seen in use on the village games field.

It had, alas, given considerable trouble and had just returned from a lengthy adjustment at the agricultural machinery shop. Never mind, it was in time for what was probably the last mowing of the year.

It was a hazy October afternoon. All afternoons were hazy nowadays. The garden was a mass of blurred shapes and fuzzy colours. She could make out objects just to the right or left of her line of vision much more clearly than those in front, so had developed a way of swivelling her head round to get the best view of the world. Still, she thought as she struggled to manoeuvre the machine out of the stable door, she wasn't doing too badly compared with most of her contemporaries. She was still pretty good on her legs; we're only as old as our knees, her husband used to say, before disproving his point by dying of a heart attack.

Of course she had lived here so long that she hardly needed to see. She latched the stable door back against the wall now without need of eyes, her hand finding its own way to the little hook, sliding it into the old iron staple in the crumbling sandstone wall, as it had done thousands of times before.

She tipped the machine up expertly and pushed it across the courtyard, bumping over the cobbles, clattering over the manhole, steering it through the side gate and round the side of the house. She always did the side lawn first; it had more obstacles. She paused, assessing. Against the far wall a few white roses rambled. In the flower beds, dahlias and chrysanthemums lingered on with Michaelmas daisies, mauve and purple, between them. To the right she could see more clearly the red blobs of tomatoes ripening in the greenhouse. Her last autumn here. Her last autumn at all really because there weren't seasons in hotels. Something sharp, a piece of jagged ice, seemed to twist inside her. No good regretting, she told herself, giving a tug to the engine, better make a start. She'd made up her mind. No sense in living in a six-bedroomed house, particularly with Winifred fussing on about being seventy-eight next birthday.

The machine started at the first pull. She jumped on to the seat and pushed the lever into gear. It started off very fast, much faster than before. She clutched at the right-hand lever, thinking it was the brake as it had been on her old machine. It went faster. She wasn't getting off, she thought grimly, she would stay put. No machine would get the better of her. Something loomed up in front of her, she twisted her head to get a better look; the corner of the rose pergola, of course. She managed to lean out to the left, wrenching the machine over. It swerved, missing the pillar by inches. Of course, she shouldn't be squeezing the lever. Stupid old woman. She relaxed her hold. But the thing had jammed and the mower continued at break-neck speed, just missed the bee hive and then the corner of the rockery. As the greenhouse loomed up ahead she tried to unjam the lever but her fingers couldn't get behind it.

She tried to wrench the mower to the left as she had done before, determined not to leave go. But this time it had no effect. The machine crashed into the side of the greenhouse; rotten timber splintered all round her and glass tinkled and clattered. She had an impression of tomato plants, of branches which she had solicitously tied to bamboo canes with orange raffia, being flattened and bent, as she ploughed her way through the greenery. Still the machine did not stall, but continued on its way across the greenhouse and, with more splintering and crackling of ancient timber and glass, out on to the grass on the other side. Then at last the new mower grunted to a halt. Beside it, on the uncut lawn, lay Mrs Florence Moon, quite still.

# Chapter Three

'But I don't understand . . .'

The line crackled. There was thunder in the air. Also the new telephone installations at Abu Dhabi were having teething troubles.

'Well, I rang Mr Blunt, as you said, to ask why the contract was so long in coming back, and he said Mrs Moon had changed her mind about moving. That's all he knew.'

'But it doesn't make sense. She was moving because she was too old to cope with the house. Then she has this accident and breaks her hip. Right, it's very sad. I'm very sorry for her, but she must see that now she has even more reason to move.'

'I suppose she feels she just can't cope with the actual move. She doesn't feel up to it.'

'She wouldn't have to. There are such things as removal men.'

She nodded, at the same time raising her eyebrows, acquiescing in his logic, baffled by his lack of understanding. She didn't find it hard to imagine how the old lady felt: a sense of not being able to manage nor of being able to face the unknown. Of course Mrs Moon would cling, in her pain and fright, to the old familiar things.

'She doesn't want changes, I suppose.'

'Oh Christ, it's so unreasonable of the woman!'

She sensed that he included her as well as Mrs Moon in the unreasonableness of womankind.

'Her solicitor told Mr Blunt that she's bound to sell the house eventually,' she said, trying to cheer him.

'Well, at least we haven't signed away our house,' he said. 'Let's be thankful for small mercies.'

'The Barnicoats are planning to move in here the day after we leave; we'll have to let them know.'

'Not yet. They might rush off and buy something else. We don't want to lose the sale and then have Mrs Moon suddenly expecting our money.'

'Yes, Mr Blunt said we should wait a few days, just to see. And I suppose there's no point in worrying them unnecessarily. They're so nice.'

'I'll be home on Friday. Late, I'm afraid. Oh, by the way, how was the sports day, or whatever?'

'It rained.'

'Oh, well, that let me off the hook.'

'Not really. They had the indoor athletics and Simon came top.'

'Oh hell!'

Silence.

'I only meant hell that I missed it, Ro, not that he'd won. Well, see you on Friday. Goodbye for now.'

'Goodbye, Claud.'

She put the receiver down and sat for a while, her head in her hands. Oh, the pointlessness of it all, of the move, the house, everything. Once she had hoped that when they moved things between them would change. But of course nothing changed just because you moved house. Only the skies above you changed. The rest you carried with you. Claud would go on doing things in his own way, as he had always done, so what did it matter what she felt or thought or wanted? Somewhere in the course of her married life she had ceased to know what she wanted, for herself anyway.

She had been young, unformed when they were married. He was older. It was natural that he should take charge, like a father. She had been glad of that. She had let him dominate her. Oh yes, she had colluded. With a mother who had never cared for her and a father who was dead, she had been surprised and grateful that anyone should want to look after her.

With hindsight, of course, she could see now that it would have been better if in those early days she had taken a job that would have given her a life of her own, let her expand and grow up, not depend upon him so. But at the time it had seemed right and proper that she should fit into his established pattern. It would have made difficulties for him if she had taken a job that tied her down, when his work might require them to move suddenly. She didn't want to add to his anxieties in this or any other way, for he was always worried about work even as it was. Work was everything to Claud. All she wanted to do was to help and support him in his career. She had been a very idealistic young wife.

Having the children made her even more dependent on him. Somehow she had seemed more vulnerable as the years went on. She did not grow in strength. It never seemed the right moment to rebel, and it grew more difficult the longer she left it. Yet she saw what was happening and watched helplessly, unable to reach him. She knew that he grew more dominant the more she gave in to him, his appetite growing with her subservience. And she despised herself for it, for she loved him and knew it was not good. She saw him make mistakes and could not find the strength to advise him. She watched as he went into action like a well-regulated machine, cutting his way through problems, not noticing the damage he was doing on the side. Nothing checked him. She knew that she should have been the one to do it, but could not find the courage. He was so much stronger than she was and always seemed to have reason on his side, his kind of reason. She did not understand his world.

She got up now and drifted down to the kitchen and out to the tiny lean-to conservatory, her favourite bit of the house, with its Victorian cast-iron pillars interfaced with very thin glass behind which was a ledge on which she had a few pot-plants. Once she had loved gardening but Claud had decreed it was not her province, so her love was confined to this tiny space in which she now stood, her fingers moving instinctively among the plants, plucking off a dead leaf here, pinching off a straggly stem there, poking it down the side of the pot in order to take a quite superfluous cutting. She stopped herself; there was no point now even in having green fingers.

Bunty Armstrong arranged herself on the bed in preparation for doing her antenatal exercises. She did them religiously every afternoon now that she had stopped working. She had expected to miss work and the company of the children but in fact the travelling, the lifting and standing about had become so tiring that she had felt nothing but physical relief when she gave up her job. Altogether she had found pregnancy more exhausting than she had expected. Besides, now that she had a baby of her own to look forward to, she missed the other children less. Certainly, she reflected, she never felt lonely.

Some of the exercises were easy. It was the relaxation which she found most difficult. She had never been a relaxed person, she knew that. Even if she had not known it, Chris had told her so often enough. Scowling now with concentration, she tried to persuade her body to relax. It helps if you think of black velvet, the booklet said. Bunty thought of black velvet. Soon she was thinking of curtain material for the cottage. A single width would probably do for most windows, but they'd need to be long. Then there was the lining, that added to the expense. And carpets, what about carpets? Mrs Barnicoat had offered them theirs pretty cheaply, but they were very worn. She had a sudden vision of a little child tripping over a frayed carpet. No, they must get new ones, gradually perhaps. Certainly a new one in the little back bedroom where the Barnicoat boys slept, and which she would make into a nursery.

Thinking of black velvet didn't seem to be doing her much good. She re-read the instructions. Concentrate on each part of the body in turn, they said, starting with your toes and working upwards. First stretch the toes, then relax them. Relax, Bunty told her toes, but they remained obstinately sticking upwards towards the ceiling. She lifted her leg a few inches off the bed, tensed it and tried to let it flop down again of its own accord. It stayed there, rigid, until she lowered it herself.

She went back to the beginning and started on her toes again. She did better this time and had reached her thighs, tensing and relaxing them in turn, when the doorbell rang. She leapt off the bed as if a gun had gone off, snatched her skirt from the chair, struggled frantically with zips and tapes and got to the front door just as the stranger was setting off up the area steps.

It was a tall young woman of the kind Bunty found intimidating, poised, well-groomed and confident.

'I'm Jenny Pierce,' she told Bunty, smiling, 'and I'm a friend of the Roses who live upstairs. I know Elizabeth Rose through work. She told me you might be moving out of your flat, and that you probably wouldn't mind if I asked if I could have a look round it.'

'No, of course I don't mind. Come in. You'd have to ask Mr Skinner about renting it. I know Mrs Rose by sight. I've seen the name on the bell, of course. This is the main room,' she went on, talking in a rush, as she always did with strangers, who made her nervous. 'Then there's the kitchen behind that partition and the bedroom's through that door. And the bathroom's through there and there's a funny little room, a sort of coal-hole really, which my husband uses as a kind of workshop.'

As she showed her round, everything looked suddenly worse under the uncompromising gaze of this young woman. Through her eyes Bunty seemed to see with awful clarity the improvised kitchen, the damp bedroom, the old-fashioned gas fire. She felt suddenly and illogically responsible for all the shortcomings of Mr Skinner's property.

'It's not what I want,' Jenny Pierce said bluntly. 'But you've made it very pretty. I love these old curved gas fires, don't you? Does it pop?'

Bunty laughed.

'Yes,' she said. 'I'll light it and show you. I'd only turned it off while I was in the bedroom. We have it on pretty well all the year round.'

She lit the fire and offered tea and they sat and drank it by the gently popping gas fire. She felt relaxed, vaguely surprised at herself for enjoying the easy company of this stranger, she who always thought of herself as a loner.

'Why are you leaving here?' the girl asked. She had a very direct way with her. 'It must be quite convenient, isn't it, near Victoria?'

Bunty hesitated, not wanting to hurt the girl's feelings by emphasizing her own happiness, for she was so overjoyed about her baby that she felt sorry for anyone who wasn't pregnant.

She looked at her shyly. 'I'm going to have a baby,' she said.

'Poor old you,' Jenny replied.

Bunty stared at her, not sure how to take this. Perhaps the visitor was just putting a brave face on things. She was certainly much older than herself. Thirtyish. It must be awful to be thirty and childless. Not that Jenny Pierce seemed to find it so. She was looking at Bunty now with her direct and cheerful gaze and asking, 'So you've got to find somewhere to live with more room, have you?'

'Yes. And also Mr Skinner doesn't allow babies.'

'Very wise of Mr Skinner,' Jenny said. 'Neither do I.'

She laughed, a long, uninhibited, infectious laugh, which Bunty joined in.

'We've been very lucky,' she said. 'We've found this cottage in the country, in Surrey.'

'Where?'

'It's in a village called Chorfield. I don't expect you know it.'

'I do, actually. My parents live in Surrey and sometimes I drive that way, through Chorfield. It's a bit of a long way round, but it's so pretty.'

'It's the cottage on the corner, opposite the shop.'

'I know it. It's lovely. I didn't realize it was on the market or I might have made an offer myself.'

'Oh, I'm so glad you didn't,' Bunty exclaimed, alarmed.

Jenny laughed. 'It's all right,' she said. 'I won't try to out-bid you.'

'I'm sure you wouldn't. I didn't mean that. It just seems such a coincidence. It wasn't really on the open market, it was just a private sale and we were first in. So,' she hesitated, puzzled, 'really you want a cottage in the country, do you?'

Jenny shrugged.

'I don't know what I want,' she admitted. 'Well, I do, in a way. You see, throughout my career I've lived in digs, or I've shared flats, or I've sometimes lived at home with my parents and travelled up each day. I once lived in a guest house for a bit. Up till now I haven't wanted to be bothered with anything of my own. But an aunt's just left me a few bits of furniture and some money, and I thought I'm really ready now to get something more independent, so I looked for an unfurnished flat to rent, but then that's difficult to find, so I thought I might possibly buy something. Really, I want a place of my own. Now.'

'Oh, I do understand,' Bunty told her earnestly. 'I'm tired of having landlords. I'm just longing to have our own place now, to do just what we like in.'

'Oh, I always do just what I like anyway. It isn't that. I'm not sure what it is actually.'

'Perhaps its the nesting instinct,' Bunty suggested.

'The *what*?'

Bunty laughed. 'My husband says I have a strong nesting instinct. You know, like the birds, I need to build a nest to lay my eggs in and prepare for chicks.'

'Oh, I don't think it's that,' Jenny said, with some distaste. 'I can't say I've ever felt a need to lay eggs. I don't even ovulate now I'm on the pill all the time.'

'*All the time?*'

'Well, you can't be bothered with periods when you're working, can you?'

'I suppose not,' Bunty said baffled. 'I just didn't know you could do that.'

'Well, I expect there are a lot of other things you know about that I don't,' Jenny reassured her. Bunty tried to think of some, but couldn't.

'Wouldn't you find it hard to make a home on your own?' she asked. 'I mean doesn't it really take two of you?'

'But I don't want to make a home,' Jenny said. 'I just want a place for me. And somewhere to invite my friends,' she added. 'And lovers. You know how it is.'

Bunty shook her head, not knowing. She had lived with her grandmother until she married Chris, and after that they had moved around together, and now she wanted to settle down and make a home for them both and have children. It was quite simple really. She had assumed it was like that for everyone.

'I think I'll probably end up renting a place,' Jenny said. 'One is less committed then.'

She lay back in her chair and stretched luxuriously, the long body arching, taut, and then relaxing beautifully. Bunty watched her with something approaching envy. Jenny would be very good at antenatal relaxation exercises, she thought. It seemed a waste.

'Well, I'd better get back to work,' Jenny said, getting up, 'before I fall asleep over your gas fire. I'll tell you what. I'll come and knock on your cottage door next time I'm driving through Chorfield.'

'Oh, do. We'll be moving in in a couple of months. Look, here's the proper address and telephone number.'

'I'll give you mine in London, shall I?' Jenny asked, as she took the piece of paper. 'We could meet for lunch sometime. Then you can tell me more about your home-making theories. It's not for me, of course, this nesting thing, but I'm interested in a detached kind of way.'

Bunty hesitated. 'It's very kind of you,' she said, 'but I don't go out much.'

'But don't you get very bored, being pregnant in a basement flat?'

'Not really. I still have to cook and clean and everything for Chris. And of course I've lots of preparations to make for the baby.'

Jenny smiled and shrugged. 'Well, you know best,' she said. 'I didn't realize being pregnant was such a full-time job. I'll come and see you in a couple of months at the cottage. There's a threat.'

As they walked towards the door, she added, 'I do hope it's a nice baby after all this carry-on.'

It was raining, Bunty noticed, when she opened the door to the area steps.

'Have you far to go, to your office, I mean?' she asked.

'Miles, but I'll take a taxi. I really came over here because it suited the client I was taking out to lunch. He was between trains, as it were. But I must get back now. My secretary will be going mad. Thank you for showing me the flat.'

She smiled and was gone. For a moment Bunty wished she had taken her address or suggested she should come to the flat again. Chris was always saying she should make more friends. Then she turned off the gas fire and went back into the bedroom, clutching the relaxation instructions tightly in her hand.

'Of course the flat wasn't her style at all,' Bunty told Chris that evening, as they had supper. 'But it was fun talking to her. Her life's so different from mine. I mean she had her own secretary and had been taking a man, a client, out to lunch.'

'Envious, were you?' he teased.

'Oh, no, I'd hate it,' she exclaimed, alarmed. 'I wouldn't *dare*. But she was very nice, all the same, and so friendly.'

'You ought to make more friends, Bunty. You'll need them now you've stopped work.'

She shrugged.

'It's not worth it,' she said, 'when we're moving so soon. Besides, I'll be busy with the baby, and then later on I expect I'll make friends through the children, won't I?'

Later, as they sat drinking mugs of coffee by the popping gas fire she said casually, 'Isn't it about time we had the contract back? It's ages since we signed our bit.'

He hesitated. He put down his mug and said carefully, 'Now

I don't want you to start getting worried.'

She looked at him in sudden anguish. People never tell you not to worry unless there is something dreadfully wrong.

'Don't look like that.'

He took her hand.

'I rang Bowman's this morning. Just because, like you, I thought it was time we'd had the contract back.'

'Well?'

'All right, keep calm. Apparently there's a slight hitch. Nothing serious. Nothing to worry about. It's just a delay because somewhere further up the line there's a spot of trouble.'

'You mean Barnicoats have changed their minds?'

'No, no. They're keen to move. In fact he's gone ahead already. He's started work up there and he's in digs, so obviously they want to move house as soon as they can.'

'Well then?'

'It's the house they're buying. The people can't move because their own purchase is held up. I don't know why. George Bowman said he'd try to find out more, but the other solicitors have assured him it's just a question of waiting.'

'I don't think I could bear it if we lost the cottage.'

'We won't lose the cottage. The Barnicoats are longing to move. It's just a question of delay. I wish I'd never told you now.'

'I'm not a child,' she said, flaring up. 'I knew there must be something wrong when we didn't get the contract back. It's nearly three weeks since we signed.'

'It's not the end of the world. We may just have to accept there'll be a delay of a month or so.'

'Old Skinflint knows about the baby. He'll make us leave. Where shall we go?'

'We'll just have to find something else to rent if necessary.'

'But you know what it was like looking for rented places. Besides, how can we afford it?'

'We'll manage,' he told her. 'In a few days we'll probably hear that the houses are moving, contracts have been signed all along the line. Just leave it to me and don't worry.'

She smiled bleakly, trying to believe him, trying to ward off foreboding, clinging to the vision of the little pink-bricked cottage, so safe in its leafy garden, with the pram under the apple tree.

'Do you realize we're the last couple left in this restaurant?' Jenny remarked. 'Let's go, or they might make us do the washing up.'

He laughed. 'I'm not going to be hustled,' he said, and filled up their coffee cups. 'What was the flat like, by the way? I forgot to ask you. The one at Victoria, I mean?'

'Hopeless. But there was a nice girl in it who gave me coffee. Preggers, she was, very domesticated.'

'Not your type of woman, I'd have thought.'

'Oh, I like all types of woman.'

'And men?'

'Oh, men are all right for sex, but I prefer women as friends.'

He took her hand and gently kissed the palm of it. 'Once upon a time I'd have argued with you,' he said, nibbling the fleshy base of her thumb.

She laughed.

'How boring of you to give up arguing with me!' she said. 'Now I can't explain all about women being more interested in people and relationships, as well as all the other things men care about. That's why I enjoy women's company. Yours too, of course.'

'Are we going to enjoy each other's company tonight at your place, or mine?'

She hesitated. Such a bore, these choices were. His place was nearer, hers would be more convenient for her in the morning.

'Yours,' she said.

Later, as they lay on the big divan that half filled his bed-sitter, he said, 'It would be so much simpler if you'd marry me.'

She laughed. 'I'm not going to get married for simplicity's sake,' she said.

'Don't be provocative. You know what I mean.'

He stroked her gently. She lay, sometimes stretching like a cat, sometimes moving under his hands, relaxed in a way which Bunty might have envied.

'Other things wouldn't change,' he went on, talking inter-mittently, 'not really. You'd go to work just the same as you do now. I wouldn't try to alter your precious life-style in any way. You know that.'

'I tell you it wouldn't work. No, don't stop doing that. It's nice.'

There was silence, his tongue occupied with other things.

Then he looked up. 'Besides,' he said, 'I love you.'

She reached down to touch his face. She rubbed his head gently between her knees.

'I know,' she said.

'And you?'

'I'm not going to say it. Not yet.'

'Why not?'

'It makes you rush.'

He grinned at her.

'That's what I love about you,' he said. 'You're so honest.'

'Or just uninhibited, maybe.'

She lay silent, thinking that she did love him, or anyway it felt as if she did. Certainly she couldn't imagine life without him now. How long had she known him? Two years at least. But then if she really loved him, wouldn't she want to marry him? Wouldn't she know for sure? Perhaps she just enjoyed his company, perhaps it had more to do with enjoying the flicker-ing tongue and the tantalizing fingers than with having a settled life together for years and years and years. Perhaps it was just that lying here with him was so very agreeable, more agreeable than it had been with other men.

No, it wasn't true. It was more than just agreeable, it was compelling. She broke the silence with little sounds. It wasn't fair, but she did love him. Yes, she did. Yes, but she didn't want to. That was it, or rather, she didn't want to be married to him. Or did she? Yes, she *did* love him. Yes, now, because it was intolerable not to love. Yes, that was it. Intolerable. 'Yes,' she heard herself saying. 'Yes, yes, yes.'

Then she burst out laughing.

'Why do you laugh?' he asked afterwards.

'Because it's funny. Do you mind when I laugh?'

'No. I don't mind. It's just that most people don't laugh.'

'They should. I think sex is the funniest thing ever thought of. I think it was intended to be utterly ridiculous.'

'And the people involved?'

'Oh, no. They're not ridiculous. Just the things they get up to.'

'Ah, that's a relief.'

'Good,' she said, laughing again. 'I thought it was.'

'Idiot,' he remarked, kissing her. Then he lay back and stroked her hair off her face. Soon the flush would fade from her face and breasts. Soon she would sigh and move back into his arms. Then he would make love to her again. He had never loved anyone like this. They were right for each other, he was sure of it. He was thirty-four, he told himself, and he knew.

He kissed her with little tiny pecks and bites.

'You're my obstinate love,' he pronounced. 'Anyone with any sense would have given in and married me ages ago.'

'If I hadn't been obstinate,' she told him, 'I'd have had no success at work at all. All the men I've competed with have been obstinate and nobody criticized *them* for it.'

'Well, maybe it helps at work. But if obstinacy stops you getting married when you really want to, it's not doing you much good, is it?'

'But how can you know I want to, when I don't even know myself?'

'I do think you want to, but current bloody stupid fashion dictates some rubbish about it not being your life-style.'

She thought about it.

'No, it's more than that. Honestly, I don't have a nesting instinct.'

'A *what*?'

'It's a thing Bunty Armstrong has. The one whose flat I went

39

to. It means women want to make a nest and lay eggs in it and all that. Babies anyway.'

'Men too.'

'Yes, I suppose so. Some men, anyway. But it's women who get lumbered with the consequences.'

'Well, I think you *do* have this instinct. Otherwise, why are you now deciding, at thirty years of age, that you want to have a place of your own?'

She shrugged. 'Just for my own convenience, I suppose. I don't see it as symbolic of wanting to marry and raise a family. It would just be a place to house my belongings, to contain my life in material form, that's all.'

'Nothing more?'

She sighed deeply. 'And somewhere to make you welcome,' she added, curling herself up small, so that she could fit nicely into his arms again.

'But you promised, you promised,' James shouted. 'You said that if we were good about having to leave here, we could have a lovely attic room for the trains and we could leave them up all the time and—'

'I know, James, I'm sorry. It's not our fault. It's just that we *may* not be able to go and live in that house. Daddy and I may have to look for another house.'

'But you said—'

'Could we stay here then?' Jonathan put in timidly. 'We don't mind staying here, do we, James?'

'No, we don't mind.'

'Oh, please, can't we stay here?'

'No, darling. Daddy's started work already up there. We must move to join him.'

'Why? He can go on living up there and we'll stay at home.'

'No, Daddy can't go on living in digs. It's horrid for him.'

'You said Mrs Peck was nice.'

'Yes, of course she's nice, and very kind, but it's not right for him to live away from home.'

'It's his own fault. We didn't ask him to go and get a job in

Leicestershire or wherever he is.'

'It's all his fault,' Jonathan chimed in.

'Look, boys, even if Daddy hadn't decided to get a job in a different place, we'd still have had to leave here. The cottage is just too small for us. Poor Ant can't go on sleeping downstairs. It was too small before and much too small after the Ant was born.'

'We didn't ask you to have the Ant,' James put in indignantly. 'You didn't have to have another baby. People don't have to have babies now like they used to. Dad said that.'

'James, that's enough. We have to move to a bigger house and we have to move to be near Daddy's work. So we won't argue about it.'

'I'm not arguing,' he shouted. 'You said if we were good we'd have a lovely place for our trains. And we were good and now you say we can't. And we've wasted all that goodness. It's not fair.'

Suddenly she knew she either had to hit him or get out. She got out.

She was standing under the leafless winter boughs of the apple tree, clenching and unclenching her fists, when she heard the gate click. Mary was coming up the drive, carrying a bottle of sherry.

'If you've got the glasses,' she said, 'I've got the stuff to put in them.'

'You don't know what good timing this is,' Heather told her and her voice was shaky.

'Oh well, I know Monday's always a bad day for you.'

'Yes, and it seems to get worse each week.'

'Any new developments?' Mary asked, as they walked slowly back towards the cottage.

'No, they seem to think we'll be able to have the house in the end, but I don't know, when things begin to go wrong like this – well,' she shrugged. 'I just don't know. It might be for another term, or it could drag on for a year. I wouldn't mind if we just knew for sure that we'd get the house in the end. It's the uncertainty that's so awful. Sometimes I think we're kidding ourselves, living in a fool's paradise, and we ought to give up the idea of Wellington Square and start all over again.'

They were in the kitchen now. She took glasses out of the cupboard.

'It's only bulk sherry, decanted,' Mary said, pouring it out.

'Is there any other sort?'

'What does Derek feel about it all?'

She shrugged. 'Oh, he's philosophical. And of course he's very much bound up in his new job. I seem to be the one who can't adjust.'

'You will.'

Heather shook her head.

'I don't seem to be very good at adjusting,' she said.

'Rubbish! You adjusted to not having a career, didn't you? You adjusted to being a mother. I bet you'll adjust to this situation better than Derek in the long run,' she added shrewdly.

'Oh well, I suppose it'll all work out in the end. I just wish I knew where we'd be living a year from now, for the boys' sake as much as anything. They get so upset and they can't really understand, so they just blame me. You'd think I'd got us into this mess out of cussedness.'

'Well, to be fair to them, Heather, we do organize our children's lives, don't we? If we give them the impression we're in control of everything, we can't be surprised if they blame us when things go wrong. It's our own fault for playing God.'

'And if we didn't get the impression of being in control, they'd grow up without any sense of security and we'd be to blame for that too, for being rotten mothers who didn't give them a nice safe feeling. We can't win, can we?'

'We'll drink to that,' Mary said. She looked around the familiar kitchen. 'You know, from my own selfish point of view,' she admitted, 'I'm glad you'll be here a bit longer. I can't bear to think of anyone else living here.'

'Oh, but they're poppets, the Armstrongs. Real Tweedledum

42

and Tweedledee. You'll like them. I can just see you mothering her!'

'No, I shan't. I shall hate her for being in your house. I shall walk past with my eyes closed.'

Heather laughed, moved by this display of uncharacteristic childishness in her sensible friend.

'We'll always keep in touch,' she said. 'And there'll be holidays together.'

Mary sighed. 'It won't be the same,' she said.

Heather looked at her. There was no point in contradicting. Theirs was a friendship too bound up in the daily round to survive separation. They both knew it.

'Have some more of your own sherry,' she said.

A November gale blew the leaves wildly across the common, twigs and dead branches fell to the ground, whole trees bent and swayed in the wind. Simon Soddie ran among them, weaving his way between the trees, leaping over bushes and torn branches, tripping and saving himself again and again, as he rushed into the wind, nearly crazy with delight.

'We don't have to go, we don't have to go,' he shouted with joy, bawling the words into the wind, his voice blowing back at him, inaudible in the noise of the storm, but loud and clear inside his head. He paused for a moment in a clearing to draw breath and then, still shouting the same words, set off again at a gallop, charging in and out between the windswept trees, dipping beneath the swaying branches. At last he fell exhausted against a tree, letting his long, thin body collapse against it, his head rolling forward so that his pale, flushed face was almost covered with the thick, dark hair.

He was safe. He hugged himself as he lay back, still panting, against the tree. Safe. He would stay at school, stay with his friends. Not even his sod of an absentee father would make him leave in the middle of A levels. 'God bless Mrs Moon,' he shouted suddenly, and laughed aloud. Even if they found another house now it would be Easter at least before all the legal business was settled. Lawyers don't hurry; he had often heard his father say so. To think how he'd been scheming and planning and worrying and trying to persuade his father, trying to work on his ineffectual mother to get them to see reason and just leave him where he was, not tear him away and dump him down in some strange school where he'd be an outsider. And all the time fate was arranging that out of the blue, quite suddenly, this marvellous old lady would change her mind and solve everything so simply, just like that. *Deus ex machina*, old Pullein would say. Except that she was a *dea*, she was a saint, old Mrs Moon, and he would love her for ever.

His father had expressed a hope – disguised as a fear, of course – that the old girl might snuff it as a result of the accident and then they'd get possession of the house immediately. But she was made of sterner stuff. Actually he had himself prayed for her survival. He laughed as he remembered. Well, maybe it had done the trick, never mind why, so long as she came up trumps and survived and refused to budge, at least for a few months more. After that it didn't matter. School would step in and stop his father moving him at the end of his first year in the sixth form, bang in the middle of his A-level course.

He glanced at his watch. Better get back. God, he'd have burst if he'd stayed cooped up indoors. Sometimes he'd felt the joy trying to break out of him as he heard them grumbling about house-hunting, his mother sighing down the telephone when his father rang, groaning over the rubbish the estate agents sent her at breakfast time. It was all music in his ears. He sympathized of course, pretending to care whether she went to view their rotten houses or not, tut-tutting with her over their shortcomings when she returned home afterwards disenchanted with what she had seen. And all the time he was rejoicing inside, hugging his joy to himself for safe-keeping. Besides, it gave him a sense of power to go around looking morose when he was so pleased with himself inside. His mother, who understood perfectly how he'd felt about leaving school but was utterly incapable of doing anything to help him, worried about him a lot. He'd seen to that.

It was getting dark; he braced himself to set off again into the storm. Only this time he did not run wildly among the trees, just kept up a steady jog as he made his way home, contented with his lot.

# Chapter Four

He brought her poinsettias. Poinsettias in a round, ochre-coloured, fluted bowl. For a moment she looked at the brilliant leaves and thought they couldn't be real. She touched them surreptitiously.

'Not plastic,' he said, laughing at her dubious expression.

He came up behind her as she stood at the cooker stirring the soup, and put his arms around her, his hands over her stomach. He loved to feel the baby move. He looked down at her fascinated.

'It's amazing the way he kicks,' he said. 'I wish we could see him.'

They always called the baby him, not that it mattered either way, so long as they had a healthy baby. It was just that Chris seemed to think that only boys could kick like that and she still thought of all babies looking like the Barnicoat baby as it lay in the pram under the apple tree at the cottage. Her own baby and the cottage where she and Chris would be living when it was born were inextricably entwined in her imagination.

She rested her hands on his. Now she could feel them both, her husband's hands on her body and at the same time the baby moving inside her. It was magical; the three of them so close. She seemed to be filled with a very special, positive kind of peacefulness. It was going to be a marvellous Christmas, she thought, as she looked at the poinsettias glowing on the table.

'I saw old Skinflint today,' she said. 'And he asked me about the cottage, so I told him there was this slight delay, but nothing to worry about.'

47

She smiled confidently up at him; she was really rather proud of the way she'd conquered anxiety. Of course it was only because she trusted him so completely, that she'd been able to still her fears. If Chris said there was nothing to worry about, then there could not be.

He hesitated. Then he said, 'Good, that's my girl.'

It lacked conviction, the way he spoke. She looked up at him sharply.

'Something's happened?'

'Nothing really. Just that George Bowman rang me at the office today and said he thinks that we ought to ask for our deposit back.'

'But we don't want it back. We want the cottage.'

'Of course. It doesn't alter that, but it's ridiculous to have all that money sitting there doing nothing for two months when—'

'But to take it back!' she interrupted. 'He must think we won't get the cottage.'

'It makes no difference legally. The deposit doesn't bind them to sell. Only signing the contract does that. The situation isn't altered.'

But it is. Disaster is officially recognized.

'And we shan't lose the cottage,' he went on. 'And if we did there are always others.'

'But there aren't. Not that we can afford anyway. We looked and . . .'

'Well, there's nothing we can do about it over the holidays, so let's just enjoy Christmas. You may be having indefinite time off now, but I'm not and I'm going to enjoy this break.'

'Oh, I'm sorry,' she exclaimed, horrified at the thought that she was spoiling his holiday. 'Of course I shan't worry. I promise I shan't say a word about it for the whole of Christmas.'

'That's the way,' he said, kissing her. 'And just to help you forget your worries, I've asked the Feathers over for the day on Sunday. I saw Tim this morning and I suddenly thought it would be a good idea. A bit of company'll help distract you.'

'Do you mean you've asked them for supper?' she asked. She had done all the Christmas cooking and preparing. There had been a lot, for they were having friends in on Christmas Eve and Christopher's parents on Christmas Day. She got so tired nowadays that the prospect of more hours to be spent standing in the kitchen filled her with dread.

'I suggested lunch and tea,' Christopher said, 'but I expect they'll stay for supper.'

The Feathers had two large, hungry, adolescent sons. She would have to go shopping tomorrow morning and cook all the afternoon.

'You look tired,' Chris said. 'Early bed.'

She thought the Feathers would never go. It was a huge effort to force herself to keep cheerful and polite. She just wanted to lie down, fade out, not to be bothered with anything. She stood in the kitchen, propping herself up against the corner of the table. Her body felt leaden. On the other side of the partition she could hear them talking and laughing. The effort of bending down to take the scones out of the oven was beyond her. She took the oven glove, knelt down on the floor and opened the oven door. As she slid the hot baking sheet out, it caught the underside of her wrist and she dropped it. The scones cascaded on to the floor. She could have lain down among them and cried with weariness.

Instead she picked them up and hauled herself upright. The floor was all crumbs. She stood, buttering the scones, fighting back tears, feeling as if the baby might fall out of her at any moment.

She gathered up cups and saucers, put scones and cakes on plates, brewed tea. She had just finished when Christopher came through the door.

'Something smells good,' he said. 'Can I do anything to help?'

Christopher slept late the next morning. She lay beside him, relaxed. At this time of day she always felt better nowadays. It was only when she'd been standing for an hour or two that the leaden feeling settled on her, the awful weight seemed to drag her down. Perhaps she would go on feeling well today, perhaps the heaviness would not set in. Perhaps they would hear that they could have the cottage and the burden of hidden anxiety would be lifted. She hoped all this every morning.

'I'm going to get on with making the playpen,' Christopher said.

He'd seen instructions on how to make various pieces of equipment for children in his 'Do It Yourself' magazine and had bought all the necessary materials the day before. In the disused coal house in the basement, he hammered and sawed, while she baked more cakes and puddings for his parents' visit, the Feathers having eaten all that she had prepared in advance. The heaviness descended on her as she cooked. She wasn't a very tidy cook, she reflected guiltily as she started mixing up sponge cakes before she had cleared up the debris from making an apple pie. She remembered her grandmother, who had brought her up, cooking in the immaculate cottage kitchen, the sleeves of her dark dress protected with little starched cuffs. Dear, trim little Gran; she wouldn't have approved of all this mess, nor of this horrible, damp, basement flat.

She piled the mixture into the tin and slid it into the oven. Biscuits next, she thought, reaching for the recipe book. But first go and spend a penny. Always having to go nowadays. Micturition, the book called it. Natural at this stage, baby pressing on the bladder. It was a good baby book; she had consulted it constantly ever since she first knew she was pregnant.

She stared, shocked. A spot of blood. A little spot, but blood undoubtedly. It was a warning sign, the book said; never to be disregarded. For a moment she felt faint with fright. Then she went to find the book, make sure she'd remembered it right. Lie down, the book instructed. Get somebody else to call the doctor.

She must get Christopher. She went out to the back. She

could hear him sawing. She had to call a few times before he heard. 'Coming in a minute,' he said. 'Just finishing the bars.'

He appeared at last, shaking sawdust off his hands. 'What's wrong?'

'I'm bleeding.'

'Well, I don't expect it's anything to worry about.'

'I think,' she hesitated, not wanting to make a fuss. 'I think it might be.'

'Come here, give us a kiss and stop looking as if you've seen a ghost.'

He kissed her. 'There, that's better. You actually smiled. Reminded me of a girl I married. Come on, into the bedroom and let's have a look.'

She showed him. He laughed.

'Oh Bunty! Really, you had me worried. I mean, I thought you meant a deluge. That's nothing. It's just a dot.'

'I think – I mean *any* blood is a danger sign.'

But she was already less sure of herself. Especially since he had laughed.

'Well, if you think that, have a rest this afternoon. Coddle yourself. Why not?'

'Oh, no, it's all right.'

She wasn't one to coddle herself. Her grandmother had brought her up never to make a fuss. And Chris always said he was glad she wasn't the sort of woman who made an illness out of pregnancy. Feeling rather foolish, she went back into the kitchen, where the sponge cake was beginning to burn.

The playpen was nearly finished by the evening, the cooking was all done. By the time she had finished clearing up the mess she was too tired to stand and the bleeding had begun in earnest. At six o'clock she decided to consult the doctor.

She only meant to ask advice. She was surprised when he told her to go to bed and wait until he visited her that evening. She was so much better when she was in bed that she felt a fraud lying there. 'How long should I stay in bed?' she asked the doctor.

'Well, perhaps a week. We'll see.'

'A *week*?'

She could hardly believe it. It was awful, at Christmas too. Spoiling Christopher's precious holiday. Yet it was a relief. Such a relief, her body felt.

'Well, you've got everything you want here, Mrs Armstrong. You enjoy it. Just lie there and relax and I'll pop in tomorrow. Don't move out of bed, whatever you do.'

'No, I won't, thank you. It's just that I thought nothing ever went wrong after three months. And it's nearly five now.'

'There's nothing to worry about, but we must take every precaution.'

She wanted to ask more, but he was obviously in a hurry.

'Worrying won't help,' Christopher said when the doctor had gone. 'What's for supper? You tell me what to do and I'll bring it to you, when I've finished off the playpen.'

'I don't really want anything.'

'Nonsense. I need a meal even if you don't,' he said, sitting down on the bed.

She tried to think what he could manage to cook. It was a great effort to think about it. 'I was just going to use up all the bits and pieces,' she said wearily.

'I'll get a piece of paper and you tell me the recipe,' he said.

So she roused herself out of the pleasant lethargy that had set in once she'd given in and gone to bed, and concocted some sort of menu for him. He went off with it and she heard him sawing and banging, then cooking. After he'd eaten and taken his tray away, he came back and said, 'I've run a nice hot bath for you.'

She was about to say she didn't think hot baths were very good if you were in danger of miscarrying, but he went on, 'Nothing as relaxing as a hot bath. Up you get. You mustn't let all that lovely expensive hot water get cold.'

So it seemed ungrateful to raise objections.

Next day was worse.

The doctor came again and examined her. Afterwards he stood for a moment by the bed looking down at her, and she knew, beyond a shadow of doubt, what he was going to say.

'I'm afraid, Mrs Armstrong, that there's nothing I can do. You must go into hospital immediately. The baby could be born any time, the cervix is almost fully dilated. I'm afraid there's no chance of the baby surviving. It's too soon for that. I'm so sorry.'

'Thank you,' she said.

She was left alone while arrangements were made. She lay unmoving. She never doubted that he was right; it was as if she had always known. One day she was told not to worry, the next it was too late for worrying.

The baby was still moving inside her. Nobody had told the baby. The baby did not know. She laid her hands protectively over him. He was no different. It was impossible to believe that he only had a few hours to live, he wasn't ill, there was nothing wrong with him. Only her body had let him down. But soon he would not be there, kicking and turning inside her. She knew it was true, but couldn't grasp it, couldn't believe that he would not be there, that there would be nothing left. She would never hold him in her arms, never feed him, never lay him down gently in the pram. She would never be able to do anything for him, just go on loving him as she did now.

Christopher came back into the room. He was brisk and business-like.

'The ambulance will be here shortly,' he said. 'They're expecting you at the hospital. I'm going to pack your case. Tell me what you want. You just lie there like a lady and give me orders.'

Now that it doesn't matter, you tell me to lie here and give orders. When it did matter you laughed, went off and did carpentry, imposed extra work upon me, made me have a bath. And I thought you were so wonderful, so knowledgeable. And you didn't know anything. And I was weak and silly and didn't trust my own instinct. So between us we killed our baby.

Hot tears of guilt crept from under her eyelids.

'We can't have that,' Christopher said bracingly. 'Chin up. You'll be in good hands in the hospital.'

Behind him, on the dressing table, the poinsettias shrieked at her from their fluted bowl.

# Chapter Five

Mrs Florence Moon set off across the drawing-room. She was managing her crutches extremely well now. She'd be shot of them next month, she reckoned.

Samuel Vereker, her eighty-year-old solicitor, watched her apprehensively.

'Do take care, Florence,' he warned. 'You'll come a cropper over that rug if you don't watch out.'

'Oh, I've been crossing this floor on crutches for weeks now,' she told him airily, 'and I've not fallen over once. There's no need for you to worry your poor old head about me.'

She paused by the window and looked out over the garden, still white with last night's frost. Her head swivelled to and fro, trying to make something out. She gave up.

'What is that, Samuel?' she asked. 'That pillar-box thing in the garden?'

'It is Mrs Herbert,' he told her, 'wearing a red coat. She is standing by the bird table, observing, I imagine, the pleasure that the birds are taking in her recent contribution to their diet.'

Mrs Moon pirouetted round on her right crutch and set off back across the room.

'I quite enjoyed Ethel's funeral last week,' she remarked inconsequentially. 'They gave her a jolly good send-off.'

'*You* gave her a jolly good send-off,' he corrected her. 'Funeral expenses come out of the estate of which you are the sole beneficiary.'

'Ethel hadn't much option,' she told him, shrugging her

shoulders lopsidedly. 'It was me or the dogs' home she had to leave her money to.' She stared thoughtfully into the fire and then added, 'Funny to think that out of seven of us in the family there's only me left.'

'Like a river,' Samuel Vereker intoned solemnly, 'your fortune has been swelled by the tributaries flowing into it from the hills of your siblings.'

Only about money did he ever wax lyrical.

'You mean, being the youngest, I was bound to clean up in the end? But you know, Samuel, what puzzles me is that none of us was ever rich. I mean, take poor old Ethel. She was widowed early on, like Ada. They always had to struggle, both of them. Yet now you tell me Ethel's left me a small fortune.'

'It mainly derives from the sale of the house.'

'And when she bought that house for £800 before the last war, we thought it was a crazy price to pay for a little place like that in the middle of nowhere.'

'Well, it probably was overpriced, at the time.'

'And think of Silas and Edith,' Florence Moon said, setting off again restlessly towards the window, 'poor as church mice and going off to live cheaply in Cornwall. We were so sorry for them because they had to buy that row of damp cottages on the creek as part of the job lot at the auction when all they really wanted was the bungalow farther up the hill.'

'We did very well out of those cottages,' Samuel Vereker said with satisfaction. 'Of course, it was the moorings that people wanted, that's what put the price up.'

'And Arthur!' she went on, unheeding. 'Poor old Arthur. How we laughed at him when he spent his gratuity on buying that field at the back of his house in Devon to safeguard his privacy! We told him it would be cheaper to put up a fence.'

'Your brother-in-law's field has thirty houses on it now, and you are many thousands of pounds the richer.'

'Yes,' she said. 'I'm glad he didn't take our advice about the fence. Still, poor old Arthur.'

'My dear Florence, forces quite outside your control have

inflated the price of houses and land. There is no need for you to feel guilty about it.'

'Oh, I don't feel guilty. Arthur can't appreciate the view any more. Nor the money, come to that. Mind you,' she added, 'the money isn't much use to me either. I'd swop the lot for a new set of legs.'

The remark gave him the opportunity he had been waiting for.

'I really do think, Florence,' he told her, 'that you should consider very carefully your plans for the future. Surely the recent inclement weather has made you consider the wisdom of moving into a nice warm hotel where everything is seen to?'

She laughed. 'Take no heed for the morrow,' she said, 'like the birds and the lilies which don't spin.'

It worried him. Her mind was undoubtedly strong enough, but somehow out of focus since she'd been in hospital.

'It won't *do*, Florence,' he said. 'This house is far too big, your housekeeper is nearly as old as you are yourself and—'

'And we're both younger than you are,' she concluded for him.

'That's different. I don't try to manage a big house on my own.'

'No, you were shrewd enough, taking a wife fifteen years younger than yourself. She was the best investment you ever made, was Mabel.'

He sighed. There was no arguing with Florence in this mood, yet he felt he owed it to their long friendship at least to try.

'And there's your eyesight to consider.'

'Oh, there's nothing much wrong with my eyes. I'm a bit near-sighted, maybe, but not blind yet. And I know my way about here. I know this house like the back of my hand. I know exactly where everything is.'

'You didn't know where the greenhouse was.'

'Indeed I did!' she contradicted indignantly. 'It was all the fault of that stupid machine. It had nothing to do with the position of the greenhouse.'

'Well, we'll not argue about it.'

'Anyway, I'm quite glad to be rid of it. I still have the other two big glasshouses in the kitchen garden.'

'But the point at issue isn't one of greenhouses or—'

'As for cutting the grass I shall go back to using the old four-stroke.'

'Florence, no! And you on crutches.'

'Oh, I'll have got rid of them long before the first cutting of the summer, don't you worry,' she said waving her right crutch at him.

He tried a new line of attack.

'There is another thing to consider, my dear,' he said. 'This house is not only your home. It is also a very important asset. At the moment it is an asset you can very easily realize. You could have the purchase money from the Soddies tomorrow. But it may not always be so. The house market changes. Who knows but in a year we could have a buyers' market? The Soddies could find someone else – they are looking – and you could find yourself quite unable to sell, just when circumstances force you to.'

'Circumstances,' she told him with dignity, 'have never forced me to do anything. I shall sell if and when I choose.' Then she rather spoiled the effect by adding, 'So there.'

'If you stay, Florence, you'll have to spend money on this house. There are things which will have to be done. The winter will show up all the weak spots.'

She looked at him kindly. What a worrying old duffer he was, she thought. He knew about money, she granted him that. She wouldn't have been nearly so rich if he hadn't seen to her investments all these years. But he didn't really understand much about anything else.

'I'm very sorry for the people you promised to sell to,' he began.

'Samuel Vereker,' she said sharply, 'you yourself told me I was at liberty not to sign that contract.'

'Of course, my dear,' he agreed soothingly, 'that was my professional advice. And, of course, all the way down the chain, the contracts were returned. Nobody doubts the legality

of that. All I am saying is that as a fellow human being I am
sorry for the Soddies.'

'Humph. You've never let being a fellow human being
interfere with your business advice before, as far as I can
remember. If you think I don't realize that you're developing
all these feelings in order to force me to leave my home you
must think I'm very foolish.'

'Then there's that great big garden,' he said, ignoring the
tirade and strolling over to the window. 'Gardeners are expensive. And in my experience it's almost impossible to get help in
the garden anyway.'

'I don't need help in the garden. I can manage the garden,'
she said, coming across to him and looking out over the great
front lawn.

'Oh, Florence.' He shook his head at her hopelessly.

'I shall get one of those little tractor-mowers that they're
advertising,' she told him.

'But I don't see how we can put pressure on her,' Rosemary
Soddie said, 'even if we wanted to.'

Across three thousand miles the sound of her husband's
tongue clicking irritably against the roof of his mouth travelled
very clearly into her right ear, as she sat gripping the telephone
receiver in the hall at 10, Wellington Square.

'I'm sure I don't know why you say *even if we wanted to*,' he
said. 'Don't you want the house now? Have you seen something better that is vacant?'

'No, nothing. I only meant that it can't be right to put
pressure on an old lady.'

'Even when it's in her own interests?'

'But, Claud, imagine it was *your* mother.'

'What?'

'I mean if we had an old mother like Mrs Moon.'

'God forbid!'

'Imagine she'd been in hospital,' she persisted, 'and some
outsiders tried to bully her into selling her house. We'd hate
that, wouldn't we?'

'No. I wouldn't mind a bit. Not if she was eighty and the house was too big for her. In fact I'd be grateful to them for making her see sense. You have to consider the feelings of the people who badly need to buy a house as well as those of the owner.'

'You didn't say that when Martin Stokes died.'

Martin Stokes was the man who should have taken over from Claud as overseas director last summer but had died suddenly of a heart attack after an exhausting tour of the oil sheikdoms.

'I may be a bit slow, Rosemary, but I don't see how the demise of poor Martin Stokes affects the argument.'

'You remember that somebody wrote to his widow and said that if she was selling the house they'd like first refusal on it? You said it was disgusting when the poor man wasn't even buried yet.'

'That was different. This is not a bereavement situation.'

'No,' she agreed, suddenly too weary to argue any more.

There was silence.

'So what do you suggest I do?' she went on. 'Ring Mr Blunt tomorrow and ask him to speak to Mrs Moon's solicitor again?'

'No. That's produced no results so far. What I had in mind was our own personal intervention. We'll make it clear to her that she's put us in a very awkward situation.'

'But she hasn't really, has she? I mean with Martin Stokes dying you couldn't have moved up there anyway.'

'Well, that needn't concern her. The point is that we want to move now. What I suggest is this; you write to her and say it just so happens that by chance you and I will be in the area on, say, the first weekend of May, and that we'd just like to call and see her. Then we'll be able to see how the land really lies.'

'How do you mean?'

'Well, if it strikes us, from what she says, that she might still be thinking of moving, but not yet, we can issue an ultimatum and say our offer holds firm but only until the end of the month. We can always say we've seen something else, you know the sort of thing.'

'She doesn't sound like the sort of person who gives in to blackmail.'

'Oh, really, Ro! It isn't blackmail. We're just going to lean on her a bit. She's had things her own way for far too long. It's time someone made her see reason. I don't think Blunt has been nearly forceful enough. She's bound to sell eventually, we're only helping her to make up her mind to get on with it now.'

'You don't think that, before we do this, I should go and have another try at finding another house?'

'Your last house-hunting expedition wasn't exactly a roaring success, was it?'

'There just wasn't anything available, Claud. I don't think you realize how few houses the agents have. I'm sure the best ones never get to the agents anyway. I think they just get sold by word of mouth.'

'Quite. All the more reason to shift Mrs Moon. I really am serious about moving by June, Ro.'

'Even if I saw another house immediately I doubt if we'd get the contract through and everything signed by June.'

'That's what I'm trying to make you understand,' he said, with thinly veiled exasperation. 'If we can get Mrs Moon to move there'll be no legal delays. Everything's seen to, the searches, the surveys, the lot. With any other houses we'd have to start all over again. So do pull yourself together, Ro, and co-operate with me in trying to work on the old lady, there's a good girl.'

When she did not reply, he went on emphatically, 'Well make July our absolute and final deadline.'

'July was our deadline last year,' she remarked inconsequentially.

'Yes, and as things turned out, it didn't matter, as you have just pointed out. But I'm depending on you now, Ro. It really is up to you. If I'd been able to get home sooner it would have been different, of course. I'd have found another house by now, but with the Brazil contract suddenly being awarded to us and then all the delays with this job in Ethiopia, it just hasn't been possible for me to come and see to things myself.'

'But you will be home for that first weekend in May when we go to see Mrs Moon?'

'Yes, I'll make a point of it. By then this job should be well under way. We've just got a new rig out from Canada and a very good drilling team is due next week from New Zealand. They've had experience with geothermal wells in their own part of the world, of course, so I've every confidence in them.'

'So, it's going smoothly, the drilling and everything like that?' she asked vaguely. She understood nothing of his work and enquired politely after its welfare in much the same tone of voice as his fellow directors enquired politely after her children, of whom they likewise knew nothing.

'Oh, yes. I shall certainly be able to hand over to my successor by May or June without feeling I've landed him with any serious problems on any of our overseas contracts.'

'It's settled then, I mean who is to take your place as overseas director?'

'It's still a bit hush-hush,' he said, 'but yes. It's going to be somebody from outside.'

She realized she had been indiscreet.

'Of course,' she said.

'Well, I must go now,' he said briskly. 'You won't forget about contacting Mrs Moon, will you? After all, think how delighted those poor Barnicoats would be if we could let them know they can move into our house after all.'

She knew that he didn't care at all about the poor Barnicoats and was only using them to put pressure on her. But it was an argument that moved her all the same. The Barnicoats had rung up two or three times in the early days to see if there was any hope. They had been so hesitant, so fearful of seeming to press her or be a nuisance, yet so anxious to have the house. It was true; it would be wonderful if she could delight them with the news that they could move into this house after all.

'All right,' she said. 'I'll write to Mrs Moon this evening.'

Derek Barnicoat arranged his books carefully on the shelf and collected his papers together on the table which served as a desk. It was very quiet in his lodgings. He sat, savouring the calm, contrasting it with the racket that went on at home when he tried to mark books and prepare lessons. There were no sudden shrieks here, no fights going on in the background, no likelihood of the door bursting open, no toys to be mended urgently, no horrid discovery, as he settled down to marking, that his red biro had been borrowed. A place for everything and everything in its place, as his mother used to say.

In fact this room was very like the one he had had when he lived at home with his mother before he was married. Sparsely furnished, scrupulously clean, it had the same kind of dark veneered furniture, a wardrobe which was so narrow that you had to hang your jackets at an angle in it, the same lack of decoration or clutter of any kind. He felt curiously at home here. His own mother, like Mrs Peck, had cleaned the room every morning after he left, but had nonetheless found it necessary to wipe away odd specks of dust on the polished surfaces as she stood talking to him, duster in hand, her eye flickering round the room in search of anything amiss. His mother, he remembered suddenly, had spring-cleaned his room every Wednesday. It was part of her routine, like washing on Monday and baking on Thursday. Everything had its day, and even its appointed hour. However hot the weather, the Sunday roast was on the table at half past twelve and he had grown up in the belief that if tea wasn't served at four o'clock the world would come to an end. Even after his father had died and there were only the two of them to organize, his mother would refuse any outing or invitation that might possibly cause the routine to be disturbed, or a meal delayed. 'We can't have that,' was how she dismissed the possibility that something might not be done at the right time or on the right day. Mrs Peck was a widow too. Her only son had left to get married recently, so she had advertised his room to let. She didn't speak of him much. Perhaps she didn't approve of her daughter-in-law, he reflected, or perhaps it was just that, like his own mother, she didn't talk much about people, mainly about arrangements. He had been lucky really, in fact they both had. It suited her to let the room and it suited him to stay here until they found another house.

It was a pity about Wellington Square, of course; nobody could have been more genuinely disappointed than he was when the sale fell through. On the other hand, there were compensations. He wondered sometimes how on earth he would have managed if he had had to spend his first months at his new school harassed by all the problems of moving house, his evenings decorating, laying flooring, trying to make things fit. There was a lot to be said for not moving until he had really settled in at work. They would find something later on. There would be more houses available in the spring, the agents said. People put their houses on the market in the spring because they thought their gardens looked better.

Poor Heather, though. He had thought she was showing signs of stress during the Christmas holidays. Still, she'd be better now that term had started and the two older boys were out at school all day, and she was left at home with just the Ant. It was idyllic for her really, if she would only see it that way. She took things to heart so, that was her trouble. It wasn't as if she'd been left high and dry, stranded away from familiar faces and places, on her own. She should really try to make the most of her last few months in Chorfield, enjoy the cottage and her friends and everything. After all, he was making the best of things up here, positively enjoying the peace and quiet of his lodgings, deprived, as he was, of his family.

There was a knock at the door.

When he called for her to come in, Mrs Peck opened the door and stood discreetly in the doorway. She was dressed, as always, in brown. She was stouter than his mother, but had trim legs. Her hair was neatly plaited round her head, her brown eyes were bright and watchful behind the gleaming spectacles.

'I am sorry to disturb you, Mr Barnicoat,' she said, 'but Mrs Barnicoat is on the telephone.'

Somehow it put Heather in the wrong. He apologized on her behalf, and then preceded Mrs Peck down the stairs and picked up the telephone on the hall table.

'Hello, darling. How are things?'

'Well, I thought I'd give you a ring, since I hadn't heard.'

Lord, of course, he'd promised to ring, just after six. He glanced at his watch. Half past seven.

'I'm sorry, darling, I was going to ring you later.'

The door into the drawing-room shut quietly but firmly. It was Mrs Peck's discreet way of letting him know she was no longer within earshot.

'I was wondering if anything possible's turned up?'

'Possible?'

'*Houses*, Derek.'

'Oh yes, I mean no, I'm afraid there's been nothing in the post.'

'But don't you keep going to the agents to remind them?'

'Not really. They've got all the details already.'

'Oh, *Derek*.' She sounded exasperated. 'We'll never get anything if we just sit and wait for it to arrive on the doormat. If they get anything good they'll offer it to someone on the spot, in the office, or who's been in that day. Remember what happened when we heard of Wellington Square? We were there. That agent didn't keep quiet and then post off details a week later to all his other customers.'

'All right, I know. But I don't get away from school until the agents are almost closed. Really it isn't as easy as you think, Heather.'

'I know, I'm sorry. But you did keep saying how much easier it would be when you were up there on the spot. And you are up there now. And if you can't do anything there, there's much less I can do from down here.'

'You could come for the odd weekend.'

'And bring the boys?'

'God, no! Mary'll have them.'

'No, I can't keep imposing on Mary. They're really a handful, Derek. You've probably forgotten,' she added sharply.

'That's not fair.'

'Sorry. I know I'm edgy.'

'Look, why not spread the boys around a bit? The older ones could go to their separate friends, and then Mary would only have the Ant to look after.'

'Ye-es, I'll try. I'll see what I can do later in the term, shall I?'

'Do that. It'll give you a break. You sound better already.'

She laughed. 'It *is* a lovely thought, Derek. Let's stay at an inn somewhere outside the town. You look around and find a village that might be possible to live in, and book us in at the local pub. Then we can enquire for houses there as well. Word of mouth, you know.'

'I'll find somewhere really good, I promise. You just arrange about the children and I'll see to things this end.'

'And get round those agents in the week ahead, then make appointments to view for the Saturday and Sunday, so we won't waste any time.'

'Yes, ma'am.'

'And Derek . . .'

'Yes?'

'I know I've been grumpy, but I do love you.'

He would have responded more warmly but Mrs Peck chose that moment to emerge from her drawing-room and cross the hall in the direction of the kitchen. So he just said casually, 'Same here,' and rang off.

'Everything is well at home, I hope?' Mrs Peck enquired, hand on knob of kitchen door.

'Yes, thank you, Mrs Peck. Splendid. My wife's hoping to come for a weekend soon to help with the house-hunting, so we shall stay somewhere nearby. I'll let you know nearer the time.'

'Oh, there's no need for that, Mr Barnicoat. Mrs Barnicoat can have the little bedroom. I know it's small, but you won't be in much, will you?'

He hesitated. 'Well, that's very kind,' he began.

'Not at all. I shall be very glad to welcome Mrs Barnicoat. The room is always kept ready, but I shall of course give it a thorough clean before she comes.'

'Well, perhaps you should wait until we've settled . . .'

'Don't worry, any time. You don't want to go wasting your good money on hotels.'

'Well, actually we'd thought of something like a village pub. Nothing grand.'

'Oh, they're all the same, these places,' she told him knowledgeably. 'Daylight robbery. We can't have that, can we?'

She sounded so like his mother that he agreed automatically that they couldn't have it. It was only when he was back in his room that it occurred to him that Heather might not agree with his landlady's view of life any more than she had agreed with his mother's.

He could still remember the shock he had felt at the casual way Heather, when they were newly married, said heretical things like, 'It's too hot to cook, let's just have a sandwich,' or didn't wash the clothes because it was raining, although it was Monday, nor iron on Tuesday, nor bake on Thursday. Evidently it wasn't true that you couldn't have that; you could have it, and often. It made the early days of their marriage extraordinarily heady and exciting, for their whole way of life seemed to be immoral. Every day they broke the rules. He knew his mother was shocked by the lawless way they lived. But she said nothing, she had kept her lips discreetly closed. Sometimes he thought that their life-style had hastened her death. After a particularly chaotic weekend staying with them in their first flat, she had rushed home to restore her morale in a great campaign of cleaning, in the course of which she had taken a damp cloth to the electric wiring.

'Well, now let's make a start on the papers, shall we?' Christopher Armstrong suggested briskly, lifting up the pile of newsprint and carrying it over to the table.

It was their Sunday morning ritual. He went out before breakfast and bought all the Sunday papers from the stand in the square. They already had all Saturday's papers, as well as the local weeklies which Christopher had arranged to be sent to them from any area he thought they might possibly live in.

They spent their Sunday mornings going through the advertisements of houses for sale and marking anything at all suitable. Then he rang up the ones that were private sales and sorted out the rest with the various agents during the following week. It was a pretty good and comprehensive system, he reckoned. So far it had produced absolutely nothing, but, as he said, one had to do something and anyway it was good therapy for Bunty.

'Which ones would you like?' he asked her now.

'Oh, it doesn't matter. Just dole them out.'

He dealt them like cards: *Surrey Mirror* for her, *Kent Today* for him, *Express* for her, *Mail* for him and so on.

'Want the *Observer* or the *Sunday Times*?' he said, at the end. 'There, you have the *Observer*. That's the one we saw the Barnicoats' cottage in, after all.'

Actually, it had been in the *Sunday Times*, but she didn't correct him, couldn't bring herself even to think the name of Barnicoat anyway, with its memories of the pram under the apple tree and of everything else. Was it herself, that hopeful girl pictured there in her memory of that garden?

'Just a minute. I'll get you a marking pencil. What colour would Madam like?'

He had taken to addressing her in this breezy way, hoping to jolly her along. She did her best to co-operate. 'I'll have purple,' she said brightly.

He handed it to her, noticing that she was staring at nothing in particular. She did a lot of staring nowadays; it worried him. The shock should have worn off by now. After all, it was two months ago. Time to start looking ahead, planning for the future. It was a pity the doctor thought that they should wait a bit before trying again. Another baby would have been the answer. At least she didn't keep talking about it all the time, the way she had those first awful two days after she came out of hospital. He had had to be firm and tell her it did no good to harp on the past. Certainly she had been better since then, scarcely mentioning it. All the same, he didn't like this staring, this lack of interest in anything. After all, there were other things in life besides babies.

'Keep your eyes open for jobs too,' he told her. 'You never know, something may crop up.'

The day nursery where she used to work had been closed through lack of funds, and others that she had applied to were reducing staff as a result of cuts in government spending.

'I don't really feel ready to go back to working among children,' she said hesitantly. 'I mean not little ones.'

'Nonsense,' he told her brusquely. 'You're good with kids.'

She did not reply, and he went back to looking for houses.

'Ah, this is possible,' he remarked. 'No, too big, dammit. But the right situation, forty mins Victoria.'

Although it was too big, he read its description aloud. She held the paper in front of her in order to have something large to hide behind, to be able to dream and relive the past, not to have to talk or pretend to listen.

The newspaper was like a screen around her. They had put screens around her when she went into hospital. She had been taken into the women's general ward, but they had made this little enclave in one corner and the sister who looked after her was a midwife.

Sister was business-like, capable. 'It won't be long,' she had forecast immediately Bunty was put in her charge.

She had felt panic as the first pain approached and engulfed her, but afterwards, as it ebbed away, she was suddenly calm. It wasn't true that there was nothing she could do for him. His birth would be the only event in his life. She could at least give him a good birth. Suddenly all that mattered was to keep calm and brave and give him this one gift.

A young doctor arrived at the bedside. He was officious. She wanted to be left alone with the midwife, but he hung around. 'Do you, er – have you been told?' he asked.

'Yes,' she said quietly. 'I know that there is no hope.'

She was aware that he was disconcerted because she was so calm. He thinks I don't care, she thought, percipient in her desolation. It didn't matter what he thought. Nothing mattered except to give the baby a good birth.

Time passed, labour progressed. A young trainee midwife came to help. She stayed with her when Sister had to see to the other patients in the ward.

'They're being very good,' she heard Sister say after one such absence. 'All my old ladies are. Sitting round the telly, good as gold.'

The pains were intense. Determined though she was to make it a good birth, she couldn't help screaming.

'What about out there?' she heard the trainee ask, nodding towards the ward.

'They're all more or less deaf,' Sister said. 'But go and turn the telly up, just in case.'

The trainee disappeared.

'They're watching all-in wrestling,' she reported when she came back.

'We're in luck. It's their favourite programme.'

So that explained the strange sounds she had heard, the groans of wrestlers, slaps of bodies, squeals from the old ladies, a crazy background to the terrible thing that was happening to her.

'It will be born the next time,' Sister said. 'It must be.'

But she was exhausted.

'If I could just have a rest . . .' she pleaded.

'No. Next push,' Sister said firmly, and it seemed like an order that could not be disobeyed.

A huge pain had overwhelmed her. She felt him leaving her, suddenly the little slippery limbs between her giant legs. After so much agony it was with great gentleness that he blessed her as they touched and parted, their one brief meeting in this world. She gave a sob of joy and recognition. She heard a tiny answering cry.

She tried to sit up, struggled to see her baby, but they held her down against the pillows. She was too weak, she lay back exhausted. Then there was bustle and talk of placenta trouble and everything became hideous. She was pushing and heaving without sense or rhythm and the young doctor said threateningly, 'If you don't push that placenta out, *we'll have to take you downstairs,*' and the terrible unknown menace of *downstairs* made her panic and struggle and it seemed like hours before she succeeded. It was a terrible travesty of the birth.

It was dark now and silent and she was alone. She was frightened. Something seemed to taunt her from the bedhead, a demon with burning eyes. But it didn't occur to her to ring for help; she was paralysed with fear. She lay unmoving and the thing watched her, glaring, gibbering. It seemed to go on for years. She had no sense of time.

A nurse put her head round the screen. 'All right?' she asked.

She wanted to ask her to stay but couldn't find the words.

'Sleeping tablets, perhaps?' she requested instead.

'Oh, no dear. It's half past two and we don't give them after two o'clock. Besides, you've had lots of drugs already, you know.'

At least the demon had gone.

She lay still, remembering everything that had happened. Was this real? These were her hands lying on the bedclothes. She put them under the sheet, slid them down on to her stomach. It was flat. So it was true. It couldn't be true. Not after all these months. She would wake up soon. Everything would be all right.

'You don't seem to be marking many houses,' Christopher said now, from the far side of the screen of newspaper. She jumped. Then she lowered the paper and smiled at him.

'There's nothing this week,' she said. 'Absolutely nothing worth marking. Shall I make some coffee soon? I'll just do one other local paper first.'

He nodded approvingly, glad she was showing initiative.

'That's my girl,' he said.

Idly, behind the newspaper, she wondered how he would feel if she said things like, 'That's my boy.' Would he have minded being addressed like a pet dog?

She had known she would have a boy. Yet she had needed to be told and to know if he had been all right, though she had been sure of that too. So the next morning she had tried to ask, but Sister had always managed to elude her. 'Mr Clayton, the gynaecologist, will be in soon,' she had called from a safe distance. 'He'll have a talk with you.'

Mr Clayton arrived, and visited several beds, but hers was not one of them.

The little trainee brought her some coffee, but she decided it was unfair to question her. Instead she asked her if Sister could possibly come and see her. Sister came reluctantly.

'How are you this morning, Mrs Armstrong?' she enquired. 'Your husband has been ringing. He'll be in to see you soon.'

'Please, tell me about the baby.'

'Well, Mr Clayton says you can go home tomorrow. You can have a bath this morning. We'd like you back for a check-up in six weeks' time.'

'Was it a boy?'

Sister looked at her and didn't reply.

'And was he – all right?'

'I've known all the morning,' Sister said, suddenly unbending, 'that you'd ask me. I've seen your poor eyes following me everywhere. I told Mr Clayton, I said, "She's going to ask me." Do you know what he said? He said, "Tell her you didn't notice." I said, "I can't treat another woman like that. I can't tell her a lie. She's a right to know." '

She took Bunty's hand.

'You had a perfect little boy, my dear,' she said. 'There was nothing wrong with him at all. It was just that he was too small to live.'

At the words Bunty started to cry. Sister stayed, holding her hand.

She didn't want to cry, didn't want them to think it was wrong to trust her with the truth.

'Why didn't he want me to know?' she asked at last.

'Well, dear, his idea is that you should try to forget, shouldn't personalize the foetus, as they say. Some of the old school think you'll get over it better if you regard it just as an unfortunate event, and that once you start thinking about the baby as a person, it makes it harder for you to bear.'

'But that's silly,' Bunty said, baffled. 'He's been a person for months. I can't not know him, can't not love him just because he's been born early. It wasn't his fault.'

'I know, I know. I understand. But they have their theories.'

Some bleakness in her voice made Bunty look at her sharply.

'I lost my first baby,' Sister said, 'at seven months. She was a perfect little girl. She would have been twenty now but it seems like yesterday that she was born.'

For a moment they held hands, the vulnerable young woman and the older one, still vulnerable, and they both wept. Then Sister bustled back to see to her old ladies in the ward and Bunty went to have her bath.

But in the dreary days that followed, turning with agonizing slowness into weeks and then months, she remembered that moment as the one that gave her most strength, as if she had glimpsed a community of suffering which somehow sustained its citizens.

Her balance was all wrong; she nearly fell over as she crept through the ward to have her bath.

'Yours was my first midwifery case,' the little trainee told her as she ran the water and helped her to get into it. 'I know it ended badly for you, but I thought it was the most exciting thing I have ever seen in my life. I stayed awake half the night thinking about it. I'd been told that the first birth you ever see is like that, but I'd no idea what it would be like. Oh, I'm sorry, I shouldn't remind you, but—'

'It's all right,' Bunty said, shaking her head. 'I like to hear you talking about it.'

She couldn't explain that it warmed her to think that somebody shared the memory of him, could talk thus of his birth. Later, when she had to bear the cheery dismissiveness of friends and even of the baby's own father, she thought of the little trainee, who had found his birth so special that she had stayed awake half the night, and was comforted. Why had Chris thought it morbid to remember? If the baby had lived they would have celebrated his birthdays, all of them. Why shouldn't they dwell just for a little while on the one birthday their son had been allowed?

The trainee left her to enjoy her bath on her own. She stared down at her stomach, a drooping, empty little bag. But the breasts were hard, engorged with milk. They throbbed and ached. Oh, for a baby to suck them dry. Anybody's baby. She began to sob and cried until she felt quite relaxed. Then she got dried, put on her nightdress and dressing gown which were far too big now and hung about her in folds, and made her way down the ward.

'How long are you in for?' asked one of the old ladies, sitting round the table in the middle of the ward.

'I'm going home tomorrow.'

'Ooh, aren't you lucky? Did you hear that, girls?' she asked the other old ladies loudly. 'This young thing's going home tomorrow and look she's been crying.'

'I wouldn't cry if I could go home tomorrow,' a fat old party gobbled at her. 'I can't go home for another ten days and I'm not crying.'

It was all a nightmare. She climbed back into bed and turned her face to the wall. The screens had been taken down so she was exposed to their inquisitive eyes.

From behind her screen of newspaper now she heard Christopher asking in his new, teasing voice, 'Didn't I hear a certain person mention the making of coffee?'

Painfully she dragged her thoughts back into the present, for nothing was real now except the past and she seemed only to be alive when she was reliving it, which she did over and over again.

'Oh, yes,' she said. 'I'm sorry. I'll get it now. I got absorbed in the advertisements.'

Hastily she encircled in purple ink a highly unsuitable house in Oxshott, put down the newspaper and went into the kitchen. It didn't matter at all to her now if they moved house or not. Like everything else, since the catastrophe, it seemed of quite monumental insignificance.

# Chapter Six

Heather Barnicoat did not just enjoy the journey to Leicester-shire; she wallowed in it. To be on her own, even to walk along the train to the dining-car, unencumbered by children and their belongings, was a luxury. It was heavenly just to sit and drink coffee, looking quietly out of the window, without having to produce bottles of orange juice, wipe sticky fingers, issue boring and repetitive reprimands, answer equally boring and repetitive questions, resolve arguments. Would she ever have believed, in her childless days, that it was possible to revel in such little freedoms? She wriggled indulgently inside her coat, as if establishing her own contours, her own inde-pendent being.

The sunshine reflected her mood; spring was not far away now, and spring was the time when houses bloomed. They would find a house this weekend, she and Derek. She was sure of it. By the time the train drew into the station she had convinced herself that they would find something just as good as 10 Wellington Square, better even.

To confirm her optimism, Derek was clutching an impres-sive bundle of particulars about houses.

'Come on,' he said. 'I thought we'd just have lunch here at the station buffet to save time. I'll tell you about the houses while we eat.'

He showed her the two best ones first.

'This is The Limes,' he said, handing her the description. 'On the Dursley road. Dursley's a village about four miles outside the town.'

'Derek, it's lovely!'

She put down her soup spoon and gazed at the photograph. 'It really is a beautiful old house. About the same age as Wellington Square, I should think, but detached, and you can see from the photograph that there aren't any other houses near it.'

'Yes. And it can't be too remote – it must be only a couple of miles out of town. It's an ideal position. We'll get the best of both worlds, town and country on the doorstep. It's the right size, too.'

'When are we going to see it?'

'Not until five. That was the earliest they could do. I've made us appointments to see two other houses before then. I don't think they'll be any good, but the agents were pressing, so I thought we might as well have a look at them; it does no harm to get an idea of what's on the market.'

'And the other good one?'

'Ah, just you wait. Crayswick is something different.'

He shuffled the papers around and finally produced The Old Rectory at Crayswick. He held it out, tantalizing for a moment, and then let her take it.

'I thought you'd drool,' he said, watching her face.

It was a four-square Georgian house, clad in Virginia creeper.

'We're going to view it tomorrow morning,' he said. 'Apparently there's quite a bit to do to it, but you'll see the price is reasonable. Anyway, you read it, while I get the coffee. Note the good local primary schools, by the way. When the boys are older, of course, they can travel in with me.'

'Oh, Derek,' she said when he came back. 'Aren't we lucky? I mean two such lovely houses to choose from? Both the right size, both near villages, both handy for the town. What shall we do if we like them both equally?'

'Take the cheapest,' he said. 'Drink up and we'll be off.'

The two houses they visited after lunch were, as he had predicted, no good. One was on an estate and had huge picture windows which looked directly into the neighbour's huge picture windows. The other, by contrast was all by itself in the middle of a piece of scrubland outside the town. Described by the agent as 'a house of character' it consisted of a pre-war pebble-dashed bungalow which had had bits and pieces built on it by a succession of do-it-yourself owners. It had a ramshackle, prefabricated look and reminded Heather of the kind of houses the boys built with their Lego sets, rooms leading off rooms and corridors leading nowhere. The kitchen, described by the agent as 'vaulted, an interesting feature of this characterful house', turned out to be a Nissen hut left over from the war.

'Never mind,' she said cheerfully, as they set off to look for The Limes. 'We weren't expecting much of those two anyway. Left at this roundabout, Derek. It's sign-posted Dursley.'

He didn't reply, preoccupied with the traffic. Then he said, 'I loathe this roundabout. The traffic's awful even now, but on weekdays when the juggernauts are on the roads it really is a nightmare. Did you notice all those warehouses and factories? During the week they all have lorries turning in and out, snarling up the traffic that's coming on and off the roundabout. It's crazy.'

'Yes, it's very built up for a roundabout, isn't it?' she said absently, peering out of the window, looking for the house. It was beginning to get dark now and was drizzling.

By the time they reached Dursley it was raining in earnest.

'Well, we must have passed it, that's all,' Derek said.

'We can't have missed it. I looked at every house.'

'It says it's on the Dursley road out of the town, so we must have done,' he insisted, reversing up somebody's drive and turning in the road. 'Back we go.'

They stopped at every house they saw, getting out of the car to look at anything that seemed remotely possible, checking it against the agent's photograph. Thus they made their way, in heavy rain, slowly back to the roundabout.

'We need petrol,' Derek said. 'So I'll ask at the garage if they know where The Limes is.'

There was a garage among the warehouses and factories that

fringed the roundabout. They pulled in and asked the attend-ant if he knew the whereabouts of The Limes.

'Well, it's here,' he told them.

They looked around, bewildered.

'Next door,' he said.

And so it was. Squeezed between the garage on one side and a factory on the other, with traffic rattling its front windows, was an old stone house with *The Limes* cut into the stonework by the front door.

'They sold off the garden to make this forecourt,' the garage attendant told them. 'Nice old house, though. Must have been in a lovely position once, before all these buildings and the roundabout came.'

'But look, here's the photograph, and you can't see any buildings. I mean I can't understand how they took it.'

'Oh, well this chap came from the agent's and he climbed up on to our back wall to take that picture. If you want to see the house looking like that photograph you'd best climb up there yourself,' he added, nodding towards an eight-foot wall.

'No, thanks,' Derek said.

'I'm sorry for the bloke really,' the garage man went on. 'It's been on the market a year and nobody's wanted to buy it.'

'But I had the impression from the agent that it was new on the market.'

'New to *that agent*, maybe. All the other estate agents in the area have had a go at selling The Limes.'

'Well, thank you,' Derek said, turning back to the car. 'I suppose we've got to go and look at it, since we made an appointment.'

'We might as well leave the car here,' Heather said, 'while we're viewing the house.'

'Bloody waste of time,' Derek grumbled, locking the car door.

'And how have you got on today?' Mrs Peck enquired politely as they sat in her immaculate, darkly polished dining-room. 'May I pour you some water, Mrs Barnicoat?'

Heather thanked her. As the water broke the silence, tinkling coldly into her glass, she had a sudden vision of how it might have been. If only they had been allowed to have what would have seemed like an illicit weekend in a pub, they would have been sitting now by a roaring log fire, with a carafe of wine between them, recovering from the disappointments, sustaining each other. But Derek had been quietly adamant that they should accept the kind offer of his landlady, who was, to be fair to him, no doubt within earshot at the time. So, instead, they were sitting decorously here, weary and making conversation.

Derek was recounting the experiences of the day. 'At least we hadn't made an appointment to see that house, "nestling into an embankment",' he told Mrs Peck. 'We just drove past to have a look because it sounded nice. It turned out it was up against a railway embankment – main line to London, with trains roaring through every half hour. And the other two sides of the plot were bounded by busy roads, so it was on a traffic island really.'

'It's quite funny, the phrases they think up,' Heather remarked. 'We couldn't help just sitting in the car and laughing when we realized what "nestling into an embankment" really meant, could we, Derek?'

'Well, I think it's no laughing matter,' Mrs Peck reproved her. 'It is downright dishonest to mislead people so.'

She wiped her mouth severely on her starched table napkin, and then went on. 'I'll tell you what I'll do. I shall enquire among my friends. They may know of somebody who is thinking of selling their house. Between them I think my friends cover most of the good residential areas of this town,' she added with satisfaction.

An alarming vision of being forced to buy some awful gloomy house just because it belonged to one of Mrs Peck's friends filled Heather with such panic that she exclaimed, without thinking, 'Oh, please don't bother,' at which Mrs Peck looked momentarily put out, but quickly rallied and said sanctimoniously, 'It is no trouble, Mrs Barnicoat. After all, we are put on this earth to help each other, I always say.'

'You needn't have brushed her off like that,' Derek said afterwards, as they sat upstairs in his room. 'She meant well.'

'I'm sorry. But . . .' she shrugged. 'Anyway, she's pretty thick-skinned. She'll recover.'

'I don't know why you think that of her. And remember I do have to go on living here. It is my temporary home.'

'Oh, don't be so stuffy,' she said, laughing.

'Since when have good manners been stuffy?'

She looked at him, surprised. He sounded just like his mother.

She got up. 'Come on, let's go out for a drink.'

'What *now*? Heather!'

'Why not? It's an hour to closing time.'

'Well, if that's what you want. But we shall have to tell Mrs Peck on our way out. It's a bit awkward really, she's a teetotaller.'

'Surely you don't have to tell her where you're going when you go out?'

'It's only common courtesy,' he said defensively. 'Besides, she might lock us out.'

As they set off to drive to an inn in a village outside the town, he yawned loudly and remarked that he was exhausted.

She laughed and put her hand on his knee.

'Well, *I'm* going to enjoy an evening out,' she said, determined to recapture the hopeful mood of the morning. 'It's a treat for me to be able to get in the car and go.'

'Heather, really! We discussed the matter of the car very thoroughly. I was quite happy to leave the car with you. I still am. It was you who insisted I'd need it for house-hunting.'

'I'm not complaining. I don't need it in Chorfield, and everyone's always offering me lifts. There's no problem. It's just that it's nice now and then to be able to go off on the spur of the moment. That's all I meant.'

'You are quite free to have the car,' he insisted. 'You can drive home in it tomorrow if you like.'

'Don't be silly. I've got my return train ticket.'

'You can cash it in.'

'I've said I don't want to take the car.'

'All right. No need to get cross.'

'Oh Derek, for goodness' sake, what are we quarrelling about?'

'I'm not quarrelling,' he said, parking the car outside the pub and getting out.

If only they hadn't been staying in his gloomy digs pervaded with the spirit of Mrs Peck, she thought resentfully, how different it would have been. Never mind, go on trying, she resolved as she went over to the log fire. The logs, it turned out, were electric and gave out light but no heat.

She had in her bag the details of various houses they hadn't even gone to view. She took them out and began sorting through them while Derek queued at the bar.

When he came back with the drinks, she said, 'Let's cheer ourselves up by reading about the awful houses we haven't bought.'

She raised her glass to his.

'Here's to estate agents,' he said, trying to respond to her mood.

Loud pop music suddenly burst forth from an amplifier just above her head. Somewhere somebody must have fed some money into a machine.

'Look at this,' she shouted above the din. 'We asked for a four-bedroomed house and Hawthorne & Hicks have sent us this hairdressing business with a two-bedroomed flat above. Why do you think they did that?'

'Because it's in the same price range,' he told her. 'And apparently people are quite funny in the way they ask for one thing and end up buying something quite different, one of the agents told me.'

'You'd have to be *very* funny to buy a hairdressing business instead of a house,' she said, laughing. 'And look at this one – "Abattoir, ripe for conversion".'

'I bet the boys would love to live in a converted abattoir.'

' "Useful stunning device included in the sale",' she continued.

'There are times when I could do with one of those for use on your eldest son.'

'Come on. You don't really feel like that about him.'

She shook her head. 'Not really. Well, sometimes. I expect he's all churned up with the move and not having a father around and all that.'

He looked at her with sudden exasperation. 'We've been into all that, Heather,' he said. 'It was a joint decision about the job.'

'Oh, I know. I'm not being critical. Just trying to understand how it is for the boys.'

He didn't reply. They drank in silence. It was too exhausting trying to shout above the noise which issued forth from the amplifier. She had so looked forward to this weekend, she thought miserably. Second honeymoon. Tears pricked her eyes.

When they got back Mrs Peck was waiting for them with a hot milk drink, which they consumed together in her sitting-room.

'She's very kind,' Derek said after they had bidden her good-night and gone upstairs. Heather, who had not really enjoyed swallowing cocoa so soon after alcohol, did not reply.

'It's a bit awkward,' he said as they stood in his bedroom. 'Being over her sitting-room, I mean.'

So she kissed him good-night and went to wash in the chilly bathroom. There was a frost that night. It was cold rather than passion which made her creep back to him later, across the passage from her own little room. He was not, she thought, particularly pleased to see her. However, he did his best, which wasn't much good. Then he apologized and she said it didn't matter and then she went back to her room and cried herself to sleep.

She woke to sunshine. The Old Rectory at Crayswick will make amends, she told herself. This is going to be the house for us. She kept herself determinedly cheerful throughout breakfast, warding off the feeling that she was an intruder in Mrs Peck's dining-room and that Mrs Peck and Derek would settle back with relief into their quiet routine when she had gone.

It was a pretty-looking house, The Old Rectory. Even the peeling paint and cracked window panes and the junk yard of a garden could not spoil it. Its proportions were just right, it had a kind of gentle dignity and the sunlight fell softly on its honey-coloured stone. Derek managed to park in the drive, squeezing his way between the rusty remains of five or six other cars.

'My husband will move those, of course, if he sells the house,' Mrs Tuttle remarked as she opened the door to them.

She was a dishevelled-looking lady, slow of speech and given to hopeless shrugs and despairing glances. She padded ahead of them in her fluffy, woollen slippers.

'Well,' she said as they stood in the hall. 'This is the hall. And those are the stairs to upstairs. This is the dining room,' she went on, opening the door and surveying lugubriously one dining-room table surrounded by chairs. They nodded and followed her across the hall to the sitting-room. 'This is the sitting-room,' she said.

She led them from room to room, pointing out the self-evident.

All the time there was a great yapping and barking and scratching coming from the kitchen which she did not show them. At the end of the tour, she said, 'That noise is the dogs. There are seven of them. It's always like that, isn't it, when the children go away? Off they go and get married and live in a flat and leave you the dog.'

'Could we look in the kitchen?' Heather asked.

Mrs Tuttle shrugged. 'If you want,' she said. 'Only the little one bites.'

In the end they didn't open the door, but went outside and peered through the kitchen window. It gave them a chance to talk to each other alone.

'It's a lovely house,' Heather said. 'Honestly, every room is just about perfect. This kitchen could be lovely. And what a view! But she's so vague!'

'Yes. I wonder where Mr Tuttle is?'

'She reminds me of Mrs Soddie in a way.'

'I thought that too!'

'Not a very good omen, is it?'

'Never mind, the business side will be done by the agent and solicitors. Let's go in and tell her we want it.'

'Full price? When you think it's only a couple of thousand more than The Limes.'

He hesitated. 'All right,' he said.

Mrs Tuttle looked a bit put out when they said they wanted to buy the house.

'You'll have to speak to my husband about that,' she said. 'I'll go and ring him.'

'That's a bit odd, isn't it?' Derek remarked, when she had gone out leaving them alone in the sitting room.

'Perhaps he works on Sundays.'

'A vicar, you mean?'

'He'll be here in ten minutes,' Mrs Tuttle said, coming in so quietly on her woolly feet that they jumped. 'You can look around some more if you like until he comes.'

They wandered from room to room to the accompaniment of loud and frantic barking from the kitchen. The more they saw of Mrs Tuttle's house the more they liked it.

'That's him,' Mrs Tuttle said, as a car drew up outside the house.

Mr Tuttle was a disagreeable-looking man, red-faced and aggressive and smelling of whisky.

'My name's Frank,' he said. 'Frank by name and Frank by nature. Honest Frank Tuttle, that's what they call me. My word's my bond, so we'll shake on it.'

They seemed to have bought the house remarkably quickly. It was somehow hard to believe that any of this was real.

'Where are you going to live?' Heather enquired, trying to get down to facts like removal dates.

'Taunton,' Mrs Tuttle said. 'I've always wanted to live by the sea.'

'But . . .' Heather began, and then decided it was better not to say anything which might put the Tuttles off leaving.

'You're moving for your husband's work?' she asked instead.

Mrs Tuttle laughed. 'Goodness no! He only works nearby.'

'I see,' Heather said, not seeing at all.

'She needs something smaller,' her husband cut in belligerently.

'You see, there's only two children left at home now,' Mrs Tuttle said. 'So I only need four bedrooms.'

But you've only got four bedrooms here, Heather thought, and again refrained from pointing out anything that might make Mrs Tuttle change her mind about selling the house.

They didn't seem to be making much headway. Derek glanced at her. She nodded.

'Well,' he said, 'we'll contact the agent tomorrow and make all the arrangements with him. Thank you for showing us round and agreeing to sell us the house.'

'You haven't been round the garden,' Mrs Tuttle said. 'We should have shown you round the garden.'

'They can see it from the window,' her husband pointed out from deep in his chair, clearly disinclined to move.

Mrs Tuttle led them over to the window. From here, it was true, they did get a very good view of the garden. They could see the drive, overflowing with abandoned cars and the uncut grass of a neglected lawn thick with leaves. Giant weeds in what might once have been flowerbeds had stood the winter well: their seed heads waved tall among the rubble. The three of them stood at the window, gazing out at this scene of dereliction. Then Mrs Tuttle broke the silence. 'We're not gardeners,' she said, unanswerably.

Afterwards, they drove through the village. It was bigger than they had expected.

'I'd no idea there'd be so many shops,' Heather said. 'I shan't need to go into town except for special things. Then I can always get a lift in with you.'

She sighed. He glanced at her.

'It's all so odd,' she said. 'I just find it hard to believe. I mean, why are they leaving? It's not for his work and the house isn't too big for them. There are still four of them at home.'

'Well, you meet odd people when you're buying houses,' he told her knowledgeably. 'You have to accept that. And it's no concern of ours. There's no need for us to worry about their motives.'

'Well, I don't know. Their motives could affect us. I wish we'd got a date, even a rough one, out of them. I mean they must have thought about it, Derek, mustn't they?'

'Look, if it worries you, we'll go back and ask them. We'll have lunch first in the village pub and then we'll go and ask the Tuttles if we can talk about dates.'

'You don't think they'd mind?'

'Why should they? Dammit we are buying their house. I reckon they're lucky to have a firm offer so quickly.'

But when they went back afterwards there was nobody there. Only the abandoned cars in the drive and the frantic barking of dogs issuing from the house.

They were turning to walk back down the drive when a man, sweeping leaves in the adjoining garden, called to them over the wall.

'If you're wanting the Tuttles,' he said, 'they've gone out. Left about an hour ago. Can I help you perhaps?'

They hesitated, then walked across to him and explained that they were hoping to buy the house. The man looked at them thoughtfully.

'Come round,' he said. 'We're just going to have a cup of tea. I'm Bill and my wife's Sally.'

They sat on a bench at the back door, looking over a garden whose neatness contrasted strangely with the Tuttles' garden.

'It's funny to think we could soon be living next door to you,' Heather remarked.

'Well, it would be nice to have you as neighbours,' Sally said carefully, as she poured out the tea, 'but . . .'

She glanced at her husband. He nodded.

'It's a bit awkward, really,' he said.

'You see, we don't want to seem like gossips, but we

wouldn't want you misled like the last people.'

'Last people?'

'The people who wanted to buy the house the last time.'

'Oh.'

'Go on,' Derek said.

'We don't really know the Tuttles,' Bill said, 'but we do know that he hasn't lived there for a year. It seems he wants to sell the house and she doesn't. He lives in town with another woman.'

Heather looked from one to the other, shattered. But it made sense now, everything was explained.

'I don't think Mrs Tuttle knows if she's coming or going,' Sally said. 'She's very strange.'

'So really he's trying to sell the house over her head?'

'That's right. He puts it on the market, people think they've bought it, then she doesn't go. We were very sorry for the last people. They missed getting another house because they thought they'd got The Old Rectory. That's why we're telling this to you, but of course it's up to you whether you go ahead or not.'

'No,' Derek said. 'We're better out of it. We've had one house fall through already.'

'I'm sorry we've had to give you bad news,' Sally apologized. She offered more tea, as if in consolation.

'I think we should go,' Heather said. 'I've a train to catch this afternoon.'

They thanked them for the tea and information and left miserably.

'I'll check all this with the agent,' Derek said as they drove to the station, 'but it has the ring of truth. In which case we're well out of it.'

'Yes,' she sighed. 'Poor Mrs Tuttle. What a situation to be in.'

'Never mind poor Mrs Tuttle,' Derek said. 'What about Poor Bloody Us?'

It was a gloomy journey back. The Sunday train was slow and dirty and had no buffet car. She had achieved absolutely nothing by this long-awaited weekend of which she had had such hopes, she reflected as she stared out of the window and tried to recapture some of the hope and excitement she had felt yesterday. But it was no good. She was a different person now in a different world, drained, exhausted and comfortless, for there had been no comfort from Derek.

The train arrived late in London and she was afraid of missing the last Green Line, so took a taxi she could ill afford and reached Victoria with only two minutes to spare. It was an elderly coach; whenever she dozed off it shook her awake. Once she caught a glimpse of her reflection in the window and did not recognize herself; perhaps it was a trick of the shadows, but she looked quite an old woman.

When the coach stopped at the cottage gate she saw that all the lights were on. Mary must have brought the boys home and put them to bed and stayed to baby-sit. At the sight of those cheerful windows Heather seemed to leap back into life. Excitement filled her at the thought of seeing the boys again. How contradictory it all was, she thought as she climbed down from the coach. Yesterday it had been wonderful to be without them and now they seemed to make everything worthwhile and to be her only comfort. In her eagerness to see them again she almost ran down the uneven path, pushed open the back door. All the familiar sights seemed to wrap themselves round her, welcoming her, reassuring, safe. 'Oh, thank God to be home,' she thought, dropping her case down on the kitchen floor.

At that moment Derek, who was marking books in his room, heard a tap on his door and Mrs Peck came in with a hot milk drink.

'We must keep your strength up, Mr Barnicoat,' she said. 'In all this trouble. There is nothing more wearing on the nerves, I always say, than moving house.'

'Yes, it's been a pretty tiring weekend, I must admit, Mrs Peck.'

His landlady made a clicking sound with her tongue. 'Never

mind,' she said. 'Back to normal tomorrow, Mr Barnicoat.'

They bade each other good-night and Derek returned to his marking, his drink on the table beside him, the house quiet and everything in order. Methodically he rearranged his papers on his desk and settled down to work, comforted by the peace and orderliness of it all.

# *Chapter Seven*

'I know what you need,' Christopher said. 'A holiday. That's what you need. The papers are full of advertisements for mini-breaks at this time of the year.'

They were in the middle of their usual Sunday morning house-hunting ritual, the papers spread out between them, coloured pencils at the ready.

'Tell you what, when we've done this we'll go through the travel pages. No harm in seeing what's on offer.'

So they sat surrounded by newspapers, the silence broken only by the sound of pages turning or pencils scratching as they marked first houses and then holidays for sale.

She left most of it to him, content to sit behind her screen of newsprint dreamily reliving the past as she always did when she got the chance. She had a curious sense nowadays of existing in limbo, of waiting for something to happen. Sometimes she thought that once the date had passed when the baby should have been born, she would get back into time again. Perhaps it was always like this. Perhaps nature so attuned a mother's body to the rhythm of the expected birth date, that it couldn't adjust when everything went wrong. After all, hadn't she spent all that long autumn and early winter just counting the months until April? It had seemed as if the world would stop, or a new one start in April. After April, they used to say. When April comes. Everything in her life had been geared to April. And it wasn't just her, she thought defensively. Chris had been just the same in those days when he had been so involved with her and their baby. She remembered how he had stood behind her on that first evening of his Christmas holiday with his arms around her, his hands on their baby as he kicked, the three of them together, all three of them alive then. And now there were just the two of them and she didn't seem to belong to Chris's world any more. Yet once they'd been so close, so interdependent. Tears pricked her eyes at the remembrance of it.

She made a great effort to pull herself together. She turned to the property pages in the *Observer* and told herself firmly that everything would be better after April. It seemed a frail hope, but it was all she had. There will be a May, she promised herself, and a summer and years of life ahead, and it will all be real again, as it used to be. It was just that she couldn't grasp it now.

The next evening he came home laden with travel brochures. 'I went to three travel agents,' he told her. 'Made a pleasant change from estate agents, I can tell you.'

Later he shared the brightly coloured magazines between them.

'I've been thinking,' he said suddenly, looking up from one of them, 'it's not really worth going abroad for a mini-break. I reckon we might as well go for a whole week. After all, I'm due for a week's holiday at the end of April. And the sooner we go the better, in case we find you a job later on.'

She was frightened. It wasn't just the thought of all the organizing that would be needed to get them abroad, though that was bad enough. She had suddenly realized that she couldn't bear to be out of England for the week when her baby would have been born. But there was no way she could explain an illogicality like that to Christopher.

'We could have a mini-break in England,' she said. 'They do advertise them. Train fare and hotel all included. Or we could just go hiking for a long weekend.'

'No,' he said firmly. 'You're going to have a real change. And sunshine, that's what you need.'

He began looking at lists of temperatures in different parts of the package-holiday world.

'To be sure of being hot at this time of the year,' he said, 'you really have to go somewhere like the Canaries. Let's see. Good Lord, places like Lanzarote cost about a month's salary – and that's only half board.'

She smiled at him, suddenly moved that he should even consider spending such huge sums of money for her sake. Something touched her, a reminder of how she had once felt towards him: beholden, that was it. Involuntarily she stretched out her hand towards him but he was busy with the brochures and did not notice.

'Well, let's look at some of the others. France, Italy, all too chilly. How about Portugal? It says here that on the Algarve it would be about 70°F. Not bad eh? Let's look at prices. Hand me the Sunglobe brochure, would you?'

She picked out the one he wanted from the collection of brochures depicting sand, sun and nakedness. She handed it to him and he looked through its pages.

'Here we are. Praia da Rocha, Algarve. Fairly obviously designed for tourists, I'm afraid, but I suppose we must expect that. Look,' he held up for her to look at a photograph depicting sea in the foreground, and beyond it a sandy beach and beyond that a row of huge concrete-and-glass hotels. 'But it says there are old towns and villages inland. So we can always explore on our own. We may not want to, of course, if the weather's good. And it's more within our price range. Nearer two weeks' salary.'

'It's still an awful lot. I mean we weren't planning to spend all this on a holiday.'

'No, I know,' he shrugged. 'But we were saving every penny to buy the cottage,' he said, 'and then when that fell through I thought we might have to leave here and rent something even pricier, but of course old Skinflint won't be chucking us out now. And we haven't had all those other expenses we were expecting,' he added vaguely, not wanting to be tactless and remind her about the baby.

She did not answer.

'Anyway,' he said, 'I'll call in at the agent's tomorrow and make further enquiries about the Algarve, shall I?'

She nodded, unable to think of anything to say. Nothing that would make sense to him anyway.

But she was lucky. 'They've absolutely nothing left for April,' he said when he came home the next evening. 'So it will have to be May. But I've checked at work and there's no problem about taking a holiday then. One thing, it'll be a bit warmer.'

'Yes, that's true.'

'Now we've this form to fill in,' he said. 'Let's do it together.' He spread it out on the table and began filling in details. 'Number of nights? Seven. Departure airport? London, Gatwick. Meal arrangements? Half board. Do you want a room with a balcony? Let me see, there's a supplement. Turn to page—'

'It's not worth it,' she interrupted. 'We'll probably be out all day.'

'Well, I don't know. Let's do the thing properly. I rather fancy breakfast on the balcony. Maybe picnic lunch on the balcony; evening drink on the balcony.'

'It sounds as if you don't need the room,' she remarked.

He laughed, glad to think she was getting back her sense of humour.

'Well, I'm going to tick balcony. There. That's odd.'

'What?'

'It says all the balconies have sea views. But you can see on the photograph that there are balconies on three sides of the hotel. They can't all face the sea.'

'They could, if the hotel was well back from the beach,' she pointed out, determined to take an intelligent interest. It was the least she could do if he was going to invest all this money in giving her a good holiday to make her better. 'Look, the balconies on the sides are at an angle.'

'Good girl. So they are. Cantilevered out. Well done. I hadn't noticed that myself.'

We humour each other, she thought, observing their relationship in the detached way that had become a habit with her

94

since she lost her baby. We who were once so close.

'But they can't all face south, the way they say they do,' he went on.

'No, they can't all face south,' she agreed.

'I'll write a note saying we've rumbled that one and we specifically want a balcony that faces due south. Then we'll get the morning sun on one side of the balcony and the evening sun on the other, as well as full sun for most of the day. Right. Now then, insurance.'

He was in his element. She watched as he filled in the form, making quick decisions, writing it all in neatly and accurately. She was hopeless at form-filling.

'I'll make a photocopy of this tomorrow,' he said. 'Make sure we know what we agreed to.' How good he is at the things he understands, she thought. She had expected too much of his understanding, that was all.

'My egg tastes funny,' James said, pushing his plate away.

'Nonsense, darling. Scrambled egg's your favourite.'

'Not today, it isn't.' He poked at it with his fork. 'You've put something in it,' he accused.

'Don't be silly, James. And hurry up and finish your breakfast. You've only five minutes.'

'I don't feel like going to school. I hate walking on my own.'

'You won't be alone this morning. It's one of Jonathan's play school days, so we'll all go together.'

James sighed at her stupidity.

'I don't want *you*,' he said. 'I want to walk with Dad the way I used to. And if it rained we went in the car.'

'Dad needs the car up there, James.'

'Why?'

'To get to work and look for houses. Besides he couldn't get back home so easily at weekends without it.'

'I don't care if he doesn't come home at weekends.'

'That's enough, James.'

'Well, I don't. He was horrid in the holidays. All grumpy. *And* he didn't mend my Lego box. He said he would and he didn't.'

'I've said that's enough, James. Just finish your breakfast and get ready for school.'

He muttered something and fumbled with his knife and fork. Suddenly his mug was upside down and his scrambled egg was floating in orange juice.

She slapped his hand hard.

He stared at her in disbelief.

'You hit me,' he said with such amazement that it was more a question than a statement.

'Yes,' she confirmed. 'And if you spill anything else on purpose I shall hit you again.'

'It was an accident,' James said. 'You hit me for an accident.'

She realised what he said was true.

'We'll not argue about it,' she said, getting up from the table. 'Off to school now.'

'I hate you,' James said with quiet conviction.

Jonathan, in tears, was shovelling his egg into his mouth. She knew he was trying to placate her, to make up for James. Jonathan was very pale and almost choking on the food. She longed to take his plate away, tell him not to worry about eating it up, but how do you treat different children differently without seeming unfair?

At least the Ant was happy, she thought, lying there in his pram, all clean and ready. She leant over him for a moment while the boys got on their wellington boots and raincoats. Make the most of him, Heather Barnicoat, before he learns to argue.

As they were leaving, James suddenly stopped and said. 'Oh, I forgot, Miss Hawkes said we'd to take a cork this morning, and some yellow thread and three flowers of any sort, wild or tame.'

'It's too late, James. You should have told me last night.'

'But I can't go without them.'

'Of course you can. She'll understand.'

'She said bring them *without fail*,' James shouted. '*Without fail*, she said. We need them for this thing we have to make.'

'I'll explain to her,' Heather said firmly. 'And next time she asks you to take something you must tell me straight away when you get in from school.'

'I can't go without them.'

'Yes, you can,' she said, shutting the door behind them.

'I can't,' he repeated and began to cry.

James crying. She could hardly believe it. Then he set off up the path, small and hunched and miserable.

She ran back into the kitchen, snatched the cork out of the vinegar bottle, a reel of yellow cotton from the sewing box.

'We'll get the flowers as we go,' she said, letting off the brake of the pram.

'Dutty,' the Ant said, and she saw that his face was flushed with exertion from emptying his bowels.

'You'll just have to put up with it until we get back,' she told him, as the pram bumped along the uneven brick path. 'No time to go back and change you.'

The Ant began to yell. He hated being left dirty.

Jonathan watched him sadly, very sorry for the baby, but evidently not daring to say so to a mother who had earlier displayed such wrath.

It was raining hard as she picked the last crocus, the first daffodil bud and an indeterminate weed. She put them with the cotton reel and the cork in a plastic bag under the pram cover.

'There,' she said, 'They'll be safe there out of the rain.'

James, mollified, walked alongside, his hand helpfully on the pram handle.

'What are you going to do when I'm not there today?' Jonathan asked.

'I'm going to finish decorating your bedroom. I've done the ceiling and today I'm going to stick the paper on the walls.'

'I liked the old paper,' Jonathan said.

'I know, but it got all marked when the water came through the ceiling.'

In January, just after Derek had gone back to school, the overflow had frozen and the tank had leaked into the boys' bedroom, staining the ceiling and walls.

'We hoped it would dry out and not leave marks,' she said, 'but it didn't, so I have to decorate your room, you see.'

'I didn't like that mark on the ceiling,' Jonathan said. 'It was horrible.'

'I liked it,' James said. 'It looked like an elephant.'

He seemed better now. There had been worse starts to the day, she thought as she watched him run across the yard and into school. Not many, thank God, but some. It was only when she got back home to the cottage and lifted the Ant out of the pram that she realized that the offerings for Miss Hawkes were still lying in their plastic bag under the cover. She put them carefully to one side, but she knew that by tonight James would probably have forgotten all about them.

The Ant played contentedly as she cleared the breakfast and washed nappies. Then she carried him upstairs with her and he crawled around her feet as she pushed furniture out of the boys' bedroom and piled up all their bits and pieces on to her own bed. It was always the same, she grumbled to herself, as she pushed Jonathan's little bed on to the tiny landing, nowhere to put anything if you needed to clear a room. Oh, for more space. Oh, for Wellington Square.

She had propped a looking-glass against the wall by the door and caught a glimpse of herself in it now as she shoved the bed through the doorway. She was putting on weight with Derek away. She drew her stomach in, pulled her shoulders back. She must stop nibbling. It was only out of loneliness, especially in the evening when the boys were in bed. She must start cooking a proper evening meal again even if it didn't seem worth it just for herself. She had taken to eating up the left-overs from the boys' tea. Today, she resolved, she would buy salad vegetables, however expensive at this time of the year, and make herself a healthy, slimming supper. She had had a good figure once, she reflected, and her basic shape couldn't have changed. It was just that she was plumper and everything seemed to sag a bit. She put up an improvised trestle made of a piece of hardboard balanced across two chairs and went downstairs, carrying the Ant and holding her stomach in.

She put the Ant in the playpen while she prepared to mix the wall-paper paste. The Ant hated the playpen. He sat angrily in one corner bawling at her. She ignored him and tipped half a packet of paste into a bucketful of water. The Ant stopped yelling and watched, fascinated, as she sprinkled and whisked and then stirred the thickening liquid with a stick. She carried it upstairs and spread a length of wallpaper on her trestle and began to slap the paste on to it with a wide-bristled brush, shutting her ears to the Ant's protests as he demonstrated against his imprisonment in the playpen by roaring and banging his toys against the bars.

'It's no good,' she called down to him. 'There isn't room for you up here. You might as well shut up.' The Ant continued his noisy protest. She thought longingly of the days when he had had a morning rest. Never mind, he would get resigned soon and settle to playing. Meanwhile she sang to herself to keep out the sounds from downstairs.

Actually she quite liked papering. It was just as well, she thought, since she always had to do it. Derek was no good at such tasks. She hadn't been either, come to that, when they got married, but somebody had to do it. Thank goodness the cottage ceilings weren't too high, she thought now, reaching up to press the first length of paper up into the corner by the door. It would be a different matter at Wellington Square. If they ever got to Wellington Square.

She was poised there, stretching up, pressing the paper very carefully into the ceiling joint, keeping the sides parallel, when the telephone rang. She swore. She thought of leaving it to ring. She went to answer it.

'Mrs Barnicoat?'

'Yes.'

'It's Miss Hawkes here. James's teacher.'

Oh, God, not an accident. James lying white and cold, James with blood trickling out of the corner of his mouth.

'James isn't very well. It seems to be a feverish cold. He said he had a sore throat before coming to school. I think you should come and collect him, if you could. Besides, we don't want to spread infection among the others, do we?'

'I'll come straight away.'

She left the paper half stuck to the wall, picked the Ant out of the playpen and set off for school. James was waiting, pale and red-eyed, clinging to Miss Hawkes's hand.

'You can see he isn't well,' Miss Hawkes said, nodding significantly down at James's head. 'We were surprised really that you sent him in this state. You of all people.'

She smiled to soften the words, but Heather felt crushed all the same as she hurried with James through the cold March afternoon wind, wishing that she had a car to take him home in.

'I'm afraid your room's all upside down, darling,' she said. 'You'd better get into my big bed. I'll just clear these things off it.'

He was obviously feeling too ill to care. She left him to get into bed and went downstairs to fetch aspirins and a hot drink. The Ant was playing quietly with Jonathan's Lego.

When she got back into the bedroom James was almost asleep, looking tiny in the double bed. She drew the curtains and went and sat on the side of the bed and read him a story while he swallowed his aspirin and sipped his hot drink.

'We'll soon have you well,' she said.

He nodded.

'Mum?'

'Yes?'

'Nothing.'

He lay back, flushed.

'We don't hate each other one tiny bit,' she remarked casually. 'In fact we like each other quite a lot, don't we, funny face?'

She put a finger gently on his nose, squashing it. He pulled a face at her, but it didn't disguise the relief in his eyes. Light-hearted with relief at being at peace with James again, she drew the curtains and left him to sleep.

On the landing she skidded and nearly fell downstairs.

There was something slippery on the floor. She was standing in a great slimy patch of it. She put her finger into it, testing. Sticky it was. She looked up at the ceiling, whence disaster usually came. Nothing sinister there. Then she saw that a great slimy trail, like the track of a giant snail, was clearly visible across the landing and down the uncarpeted stairs. Puzzled, she followed it, clinging to the rail and treading gingerly, keeping well in to the side of each stair. At the bottom the trail led through the hall, making a detour into the sitting-room, back into the kitchen and across the polished tiles to where the Ant was sitting in the corner by the back door. Then she understood. The Ant had sat in the bucket of paste and tipped it all over himself. Then he had shuffled along on his padded, glue-soaked bottom down the stairs and around the house, leaving this glistening silvery trail.

She stood, horror-stricken. The whole house was sticky. She would have to get hot soapy water and wash the stairs, the sitting-room carpet, the kitchen floor, all the furniture he had touched. The Ant, grinning joyfully, began to bounce up and down and then leant forward, putting his hands to the ground, ready to crawl off again on his travels. Suddenly she wanted to pick him up and hurl him out of the house. She was hot with rage against him. How could he, how could he? She lunged at him. He didn't make a sound, but his expression changed instantly, the joy wiped out by fear. She had never known him look so frightened before. Horrified, she stopped herself just in time. She stood looking down at him, her eyes filled with tears of misery and a kind of self-disgust. Her heart was thumping. She couldn't move, but just stayed very still, gradually getting control of herself. Oh, poor little Ant, so trusting always, to be so scared. Of his own mother too. That was what was so awful. And none of it was his fault, and she couldn't explain it to him.

All the same, she'd have to get on with the practical matter of clearing up the mess. Nobody else would. But what was the point of cleaning up the glue when he would just make everything sticky again? Oh, for two pairs of hands, one to cope with the house, the other with the baby. She sniffed. Then, 'Come on, you,' she made herself say cheerfully, scooping up the Ant. 'We'll deal with you first, my lad,' and she began to strip off his glutinous clothes and dropped them into the kitchen sink. 'Then into the bath you go.'

By the time she had cleaned him and washed most of the house it was too late to go back to the decorating. She prepared the tea and put a rather chastened Ant into the pram ready to go and collect Jonathan. James was sound asleep. She stood in the bedroom doorway. It seemed crazy to wake him and take him out into the cold wind. All the same she felt very guilty as she locked the back door, leaving him sleeping alone in the house.

Most of the parents collected their children in cars. She was quite glad to be standing alone, not feeling like making conversation. Too late she observed Mavis Jones, mother of Charles Jones aged twenty and the Jones Twins aged three, approaching from the other side of the road. The enormous gap in her family, Heather had sometimes reflected uncharitably, was the only interesting thing about Mrs Jones.

'I hear you're leaving us, Mrs Barnicoat,' she said now in her nasal, mother-knows-best voice.

'Well, we're trying to,' Heather said. 'But we're having problems getting a house. Derek's up there already in digs and the rest of us will follow when we find a house.'

Mrs Jones's finely plucked eyebrows rose in the carefully made-up face.

'Surely you can go and join him. Can't you rent a house while you look?'

'No. They're not available and anyway it's an expensive way to do things. Besides, we think it's better now for the boys to see the year out here and start at a new school in September when there'll be other new pupils.'

'Oh, you should never put your children before your husband, my dear,' the knowing Mrs Jones told her. 'That really is a mistake. After all, I always say, your children will go off and leave you, but your husband will still be with you after they have flown the nest. Put hubby first, if you want to keep him, that's my advice.'

Fortunately Jonathan appeared and spared her the need to reply. He was clutching a piece of grey paper with a bright pink and mauve painting on it.

'Oh, that's lovely and colourful,' she said. 'What is it?'

'You,' he said.

'Where shall I sleep?' Jonathan asked at bed-time, surveying the half-decorated bedroom anxiously. 'With James, in your bed?'

She hesitated.

'No. We don't want you to catch whatever he's got, do we? I think I'll put your little bed in the sitting-room tonight with the Ant.'

'Where will you be, Mum?'

'Upstairs somewhere. If I've finished the papering I'll sleep in your bedroom. Otherwise I'll creep in with James. But don't you worry. I'll be safe and sound somewhere or other. Now off to sleep with you and no worrying, eh?'

She hadn't, of course, had time to buy ingredients for her slimming supper. Besides, there were jam sandwiches left over and some cottage pie and banana custard. She ate the lot, washed down with a mug of coffee, then she forced herself upstairs to get on with the papering.

God, but she was tired, she realized as she carried the second bucketful of paste into the bedroom. She was yawning as she passed the mirror. Her face looked drawn and pale and her hair was dry and untidy. How had she got to look like this? Stop it, Heather Barnicoat. Turn on the transistor. Might be a good play to make the time pass. The radio made strange wooshing sounds and went silent. She'd forgotten, of course. One of the boys had left it on and she had meant to get new batteries for it. Wearily she leant on the trestle as she dipped the brush into the glue and began to slap it on to the paper. Resentment grew with physical activity. The more she thought about it the more it seemed unfair the way everything was left to her to see to. Never mind what it was, broken fuses, leaking pipes, bedrooms needing decorating, she had to deal with it. She was at the receiving end of all the blame too. Miss Hawkes blamed her for being a rotten mother who sent her son to school when he was poorly, and Mavis Jones blamed her for being a foolish wife who left her husband to rot in lodgings because she was too selfish to join him. And of course she blamed herself for everything. How guilty she had felt this afternoon about leaving James asleep in the house on his own. If there'd been a fire and he'd been burnt to death it would have been all her fault. Even Jonathan's pale little face reproached her this evening, though he said nothing. She knew how he hated losing the security of his own bedroom, even for a couple of nights. But she couldn't have left those awful stains. Apart from anything else who would want to buy the cottage if it looked as if it was coming out in damp patches?

Nobody blamed Derek for anything, she thought furiously slapping paste on to paper. He didn't feel guilty the whole time, like she did. While she was here coping with everything, he was up there being fussed over by that old bag of a landlady, having his meals prepared for him, being waited on hand and foot, treated as if he was fine china. At least if he'd had to go on ahead of the family, he shouldn't be enjoying it. Bloody smug he's been from the moment he went into lodgings. She worked herself up into such a rage that she finished the papering in record time.

Dammit, she thought as she prized open the paint tin in readiness for finishing the woodwork, they were his boys as well as hers. Moreover, it was his fault they'd had James so soon. They'd meant to wait four years before they started a family. If he hadn't been so careless they'd have had time to save and everything would have been much easier. They might even have been able to pay someone to decorate, she thought as she lifted a lump of skin out of the paint tin with a screwdriver and plopped it on to a piece of newspaper.

She had finished the door and window frame and just

started on the skirting board when she heard someone knocking at the front door. Frightened that they would wake the boys, she dropped the brush and ran downstairs and out of the back door.

'Could you come round to the back?' she called into the night.

She heard footsteps on the path and then there appeared in the shaft of light from the back door a tall young woman of about her own age and height, but oh, how different.

'I'm so sorry,' she went on, 'but you see the front door opens into the sitting-room and the boys are asleep in there. Do you mind coming into the kitchen?'

'No, I don't mind,' the woman said, following her indoors. 'I'm looking for Bunty Armstrong, actually.'

'Bunty Armstrong?' Heather repeated, bewildered.

'Yes, she told me a while ago that she was coming to live here.'

'Oh, *those* Armstrongs. Yes, of course. I mean no, they're not here. Look, do sit down and I'll explain. I'm Heather Barnicoat, by the way.'

'And I'm Jenny Pierce,' the woman said, perching herself on a stool. She was beautifully dressed, moved effortlessly, and now entwined long elegant legs around those of the stool. Heather was suddenly very much aware of her own shabby painting dress, decrepit sandals and unkempt, dusty hair.

'The Armstrongs *are* buying the cottage,' she explained. 'But the house we're buying isn't available, so we couldn't move out of here. Are you a friend of Bunty's?'

The girl shook her head. 'No,' she said, 'I just went to look at her flat in Victoria, and we arranged that I'd call on her here one day on my way to see my parents. I'm sorry I've barged in on you like this.'

'Oh, that's all right.' A sudden thought struck her. 'Oh, dear, I suppose we're holding up your move into the Armstrongs' flat because we can't let them have the cottage yet?'

Jenny laughed. 'No need to worry about that,' she said. 'I didn't want their flat.'

'Oh, what a relief.'

She was so glad that there was at least something she didn't need to feel guilty about, that she added, 'Let's have a drink to celebrate. There's some sherry in the kitchen cupboard.'

Jenny laughed.

'Do you always take everything to heart so?' she asked.

Heather, rummaging in the cupboard to get at the sherry, looked round at her, surprised. 'Oh, I don't know. Well, yes, I suppose I do, really. You get into the way of feeling responsible for everything and everybody when you have children.'

'How awful. I'd hate that. Thanks.' She took the glass and went on, 'I just feel responsible for me,' she said. 'And for my work, of course, but even that wouldn't spill over into the rest of my life. Look, I can see you're busy. Be honest, I am stopping you, aren't I?'

'Yes.'

'Do you mind?'

'No. I'm glad.'

'I thought so.'

They laughed. It was true, Heather thought; she was glad to leave all that mess upstairs and to be distracted from the clutter in her mind of resentments, fears, guilts and frustrations. Just to talk to another adult made her feel better.

'And how was Bunty?' she asked.

'Pregnant.'

'Oh, good. When's the baby due?'

'I've no idea. I didn't think to ask.'

'You haven't kept in touch with her since?'

'No. I felt she didn't particularly want to. But surely *you* must keep in touch with them if they're buying your cottage?'

'Well, the solicitors do, on our behalf, but they don't really like too much contact between clients. At least our lawyers don't seem to. You know how it is when you're buying a house.'

'No, I don't. I've never bought a house.'

'But you're looking? I mean isn't that why you went to the Armstrongs' flat?'

'But that was just to rent.' She twisted her glass round in her hands reflectively. She looked at her watch, knowing that it was one of those moments when you must decide either to go on your way fast, or stay and get involved. 'I'm approaching the house market very tentatively,' she said. 'One step forward, two back. Just dipping my toe in the water. I suspect I'm really a career woman, plain and simple, and don't want to be bothered with anything domestic.'

'Where do you live now?'

'In rented, furnished accommodation. I can leave at a month's notice. It suits me fine. At least it did. Now I'm thinking I might rent something unfurnished and have more of my own things in it. But I don't want to buy, that's too tying. I mean I'd like to be free just to push off if work required it. Not that it's likely to, but I don't want to feel that I'd be tied down by bricks and mortar if it did.'

'What is your work?'

'I'm in publishing. I'm an editor with Frobishers.'

'Oh.'

It was a long, drawn-out sigh. Heather put down her glass.

'Tell me about it. How did you get to being an editor?'

'I started on magazines,' Jenny told her, surprised at the intensity of her interest, 'and worked my way up to being fiction editor with *Women Now*, then I moved on to books and was very lucky to be in the right place when Frobishers needed another editor.' She paused and then, 'Why are you so interested?' she asked suddenly, in her direct way.

'I had a career in publishing too. Well, I was going to have one.'

'Tell me.'

'I came to it by a different route from yours. After I'd taken my degree, I did a secretarial course and looked for a job in publishing. It was very hard for women then.'

'It still is.'

'I was living at home with my mother,' Heather went on. 'She's a widow and not at all well off, and I kept not applying for ordinary office jobs because I was afraid that if I took one

I'd get stuck in it, get used to the money and security, and give up the search for what I really wanted. Mother was marvellous about it, but I know that some of her friends thought it was selfish of me. And then in the end I did get an offer of a job with Slater & Slater.'

'Well done. You did right not to take any old secretarial job, despite your mother's friends. Then what happened?'

'Then I had a marvellous bit of luck. After a year I was made secretary to the chief fiction editor, Peter Blakeman, and he was wonderful to me. He really loaded responsibility on to me. It was terrifying in a way, but it was exactly what I needed. He used to give me the manuscripts with the readers' reports and let me edit them. He said that unless you were in on a book right from the start you never got the feeling of helping to create it. I suppose he would have interfered if I'd made any disastrous decisions, but I never got the feeling of being supervised. I really did feel responsible for each book. You know that feeling?'

It was years since she had talked about her work. She was amazed at how vividly she remembered it, the excitement of it even now after all this time. It was wonderful to talk about it to somebody who really understood.

'There's nothing like it,' Jenny said. 'That feeling of taking a manuscript and helping to make it into a book.'

'Yes. I've talked to writers who feel that once they've parted with the manuscript, the whole thing is over. For us it's only beginning. Isn't it strange? It must be sad for them, after all that work. They just don't feel any interest in it after they've handed it over. Like having a baby and giving it away!'

'Ah, but then they've had the initial excitement of writing it. And they've done their job really when they've finished the manuscript.'

'Yes, but that's such a hard, lonely business. It seems awful not to have the compensation of actually enjoying the finished product.'

'Some of them do. The author I had lunch with today told me that whenever he gets stuck with a book he goes to his bookshelves, takes out all his past books, fondles them lovingly and tells himself that if he could do it then, he can still do it now. He's about seventy and he got so worked up about it I wasn't sure if it was sex or writing he was on about at one stage.'

She laughed her full, uninhibited laugh.

'But go on telling me about your work at Slater's,' she said. 'What happened next?'

'After three years I got an assistant editorship, which sounded grander, but really I was doing much the same thing. Then I met Derek and we got married. I went on working and in fact was in line for the job of a fiction editor who was leaving in six months' time. Then I found I was expecting James. So I left.'

'How dreadful!' Jenny exclaimed. 'What a cautionary tale!'

She stared at Heather, horror-stricken, the wide blue eyes full of dismay.

'Really, Heather, your story ought to be written up, like some government health warning, over the portals of register offices and above the altars of churches!'

Her outrage was so genuine yet so exaggerated that Heather burst out laughing.

'Just like they do for cigarettes,' Jenny went on, disregarding her, 'it should be writ up large for all women to see: "*Matrimony is dangerous. It could ruin your career.*" Or words to that effect.'

'Oh, it's not as bad as all that,' Heather told her.

'But it *is*. It's worse. I mean, to have such a struggle and then to get an editorship so young, and a woman too. And you obviously loved the work and were good at it. Then to give it all up, just for a baby. Couldn't you have had an abortion?'

'No,' Heather said coldly. 'I preferred to have James.'

'Have you kept in touch with Slater's?' Jenny asked, unabashed. 'Could you do some reading for them at home? They could send you manuscripts.'

Heather shook her head. 'I've too high a regard for writers,' she said, 'to risk having their precious manuscripts in the same

109

house as my three sons.' She sighed, then went on, 'But obviously yes, I do think about it sometimes. I'd like to be involved again one day in publishing, but now that we're leaving the London area it's going to be more difficult.'

'Where are you going to live?'

'Leicestershire.'

'It can be done from there. A colleague of mine, a fellow-editor actually, commutes from Leicester. Mind you, it's a long day, but he decided it was easier than trying to move house in these hard times.'

'Yes, but I don't expect he has three children to get off to school before he leaves home and to be back at half past three to pick them up.'

'No. That's true. Oh, isn't it bloody unfair? I bet you were every bit as good an editor as he is. Yet he can be married, have kids and keep on doing a job you might be doing better than he does.'

'It's no good thinking like that,' Heather protested. 'You just have to accept that it's the way things are for women. And there are compensations, great compensations. Normally I'm quite happy with my lot,' she added defiantly, needing to convince herself as much as this confident stranger, who had come here, casting doubt on all her assumptions, mercilessly spelling out everything that she had lost, fuelling resentment that she didn't want to feel. What help is that to me, she thought, staring with accusing eyes at this young woman who might have been herself had she chosen the other road.

'Oh, I'm not criticizing you,' Jenny explained. 'I'm on your side. I mean I know how you feel about the work you gave up.' She paused, shook her head, and said, 'And you're probably right. I mean having got yourself into this ghastly situation, it would only be frustrating to think too much about getting back to work at the moment. You're probably right to try to cultivate resignation and acceptance of your lot.'

'But I don't feel it is a ghastly situation,' Heather insisted. 'I enjoy it usually, really I do.'

Jenny looked at her hard.

'Really?' she said. 'Honestly?'

'Until somebody like you comes and reminds me,' Heather said with a sudden bitterness that surprised herself as much as Jenny. 'I'm sorry,' she added miserably. 'I didn't mean that.'

'Oh yes, you did.'

They sat in silence, Jenny poised yet relaxed, her white hands with their tapering fingers and perfectly manicured nails painted pale pink, folded on her lap. Heather sat tense at the table, gripping her empty glass tightly in hands that were chapped and splashed with paint.

'Normally,' Heather forced herself to say matter-of-factly, 'I enjoy the kids and everything, but it hasn't been easy being left on my own here while Derek's gone ahead. There's a lot to see to. And I miss him. All the time I'm just longing for us to get a house and all be together again. And today's been one of those days. James had to come home from school because he wasn't well, and I just felt I was letting everyone down somehow. The last straw was a chance remark by one of the mums at school. She said that wise women put their husbands before their children and that I shouldn't have let Derek go into digs and—' To her horror she heard herself choke and could not go on.

'She sounds a really silly old cow,' Jenny commented. 'As if you weren't the sort of person who would think it all through very seriously and weigh everything up and do what was best for everyone. Any fool can see that.'

Heather looked at her, surprised. If a friend like Mary had said such a thing, she would have dismissed it as mere kindness, but if a stranger, especially such a forthright stranger as this one, could make such an assumption about her, well, perhaps she wasn't as hopeless as she'd thought, after all.

'I'm sorry about being so gloomy,' she forced herself to say. 'More booze required,' she added, pouring sherry.

'Do you know what I think you should do?'

'What?'

'Ring up Derek and pour it all out into his defenceless earhole.'

'His landlady hovers.'

'Write it all down then. I don't expect she steams his letters open. Actually a letter would be better. Writing helps you sort it out in your own mind.'

'Oh, but he's busy with his new job – teaching's very wearing, you know. There's no sense in worrying him.'

'Why not? Why should he escape worry? He's a father as well as a teacher. They're his kids, aren't they, as well as yours?'

'Nobody else's, as far as I can remember. I was reflecting on that fact only this evening as I decorated the boys' bedroom.'

Jenny laughed, her long, uninhibited laugh. Heather joined in. She felt better.

'You're right,' she said. 'I should have shared all the worries with him. And you're right about Mavis Jones too. She *is* a silly old cow. She's the sort who always has theories about everything. She trots them out ready-made for every situation. I suppose she finds it easier than thinking.'

'That's the way,' Jenny said cheerfully. 'Get nasty. Fight back.' Then she went on, more seriously. 'Heather, tell me, do you think it would have been easier if you'd left getting married until later? I mean got yourself really established as an editor before you left? So that you'd be able to go back with your reputation made, as it were?'

Heather felt her heart sink at the prospect of having to go all over that again, then she realized that it was her own predicament Jenny was talking about.

'I mean,' Jenny went on, 'I don't think I want to miss out on the family thing, but on the other hand I couldn't bear to give up my job now. I've only been an editor for eighteen months. I could do with at least five or six years to consolidate. I reckon I ought to get married when I'm thirty-seven or so.'

How naïve she is, Heather thought, shaking her head. 'Life isn't like that,' she said. 'You have to make choices, if you're a woman. Besides, if you leave it too late you'll be rather an old parent, won't you?'

'I know quite a few women who have had children in their mid and late thirties.'

'Yes, but the children. Think what elderly parents they'll have when they're teenagers.'

'That's their problem. It's me I'm thinking about at the moment. I think what would be ideal would be to get well established, then chuck up work temporarily and have a family quickly before I'm forty, and that way I'd get the best of both worlds.'

'Well, good luck to you. You may be lucky, I suppose. Some people are.'

'I'd have to do some brief training, I imagine, to find out about kids and all this,' she waved an arm around the kitchen.

'Oh, that comes. Children train you. They make you have some sort of routine, you see.'

'What do you mean?'

'Well, when they're babies they have to be fed every four hours.'

'Good God!'

Heather laughed. 'Well, it breaks you in,' she said.

'It sounds awful to me.'

'Then you would be wise to avoid it.'

'Yes. Perhaps.'

She sighed, all the same.

Heather saw that she was troubled. Part of her was glad of it; evidently choosing the other road had its problems too.

'What really and truly made you decide to give up your career?' Jenny asked suddenly.

'Falling in love with Derek. The rest followed. Until then I hadn't wanted a home or children.'

'Mm. Maybe there should be a warning about that too. Oh dear, well, I must go. My parents will think I'm not going to turn up tonight. Thanks for the drink and the talk. And I hope he gets better soon, the one who's ill.'

'James? Oh, he'll be all right. It was only a bit of a cold. Children run temperatures easily. He'll sleep it off, bless him.'

She thought suddenly of James looking tiny in the big bed this morning and of the relief that had settled on his face when she had made sure that they were good friends again. Of her own relief, too, the swift, warm, reassurance that she'd made a good job of that, at least.

Jenny, looking thoughtfully at the tired, rather worn version of herself sitting opposite to her at the kitchen table, noted the warm smile that suddenly lit up the face and made it beautiful, and was puzzled by it.

'Penny for them?' she said.

'Oh, I don't know. I was just thinking about the boys, really. The sudden storms you get in a family and the tiny, terribly important crises in their lives. Then the unexpected peace that breaks out now and then.' She shrugged. 'I suppose it all adds up to something worthwhile,' she said. 'I hope so, anyway.'

At the door Jenny hesitated. 'Don't forget to write that letter,' she said.

'All right. I'll do it tomorrow.'

'Tonight.'

'Very well. I'll write it when I've finished the decorating.'

'Oh, poor you. I'd forgotten you'd still got that to finish. I've really wrecked your evening, haven't I?'

'No. I've enjoyed it. Come again next time you're driving this way.'

'I will. I'll just take pot luck whether you're here or the Armstrongs. But I hope for your sake that it'll be the Armstrongs.'

'Thank you,' Heather said. 'I know what you mean. The sooner we all get settled up there the better.' She sighed. 'If only the Soddies could get into their next house. I could bear the waiting if I only knew we'd get that house for sure in the end. I really love it, and it's got so much space.'

'*Soddies?*'

'They're the people we're buying from. Odd name, isn't it?'

'The only Soddie I've ever known was a parrot,' Jenny remarked inconsequentially.

After she had gone, Heather sat at the table for a while, staring blankly at the empty glasses. Jenny's scent hung on the air, making the kitchen smell expensive. Strange to think that her own life might have been like that, that she might have

114

been driving her own car round the countryside, that she might even have been wearing expensive scent and fashionable clothes, able to spend a good salary entirely on herself, instead of toiling away in the house, shabby and getting plump, somehow managing so that five of them could live on Derek's salary. It was a queer old world, she thought without bitterness, getting up and yawning. Then she stretched and made her way slowly upstairs to where the half-finished skirting board awaited her attention, and the brush, its bristles stiff with drying paint, still lay where she had left it on the bedroom floor.

# *Chapter Eight*

'You won't forget to buy me some more games socks, will you, Mum?' Simon said as he sat down to breakfast. 'The very thick ones, I mean.'

'I'll get them this morning as I go through town on my way up north,' Rosemary Soddie promised. 'It's size nine, isn't it?'

'Yes. I'll write it down to remind you.'

He took one of the long brown envelopes that lay in a pile beside her plate and printed on it the particulars of his socks.

'Got many houses to see?' he enquired. 'Anything possible?'

'The one you've just written on is the most hopeful,' she said, taking the paper out of the envelope, and reading the particulars quickly.

'Sounds posh,' he said. 'What exactly is a Georgian up-and-over garage door?'

She shrugged. 'The main advantage of that house is that it's up for auction,' she said.

'I thought you hated auctions?'

'I do, but you see now that it's so difficult to find a house they do have the advantage that if you buy a house at an auction it's definitely yours. The people selling it can't just stay put.'

'Like we are,' he commented meanly.

'Not from choice, Simon,' she reproved.

'Actually,' he said, 'your best bet is to buy from somebody who's dead.'

'Simon!'

'It's true. Executors' sales go through very quickly, Mr

117

Francis said, because the deceased can't change his mind and doesn't have to worry much about the price because he doesn't have to buy another house. My advice to you—'

'I thought Mr Francis taught religious knowledge?'

'He does. But he teaches economics as well now. He's jolly good too. Much better than old Snodders.'

He reached for more toast.

'As I was saying,' he said, buttering it emphatically, 'my advice to you, Mum, would be not to bother with the estate agents, but go round the undertakers. They're the ones who really know which houses will be coming on the market.'

She took the particulars back from him and put the envelope in her bag, and began clearing the table.

'Mrs Perkins will be in soon,' she said, 'and will leave everything ready for your tea.'

'And come to think of it,' he said, getting up, 'why bother with undertakers? What you should be doing is going round the doctors up there and finding out who's likely to snuff it.'

He went out laughing and banging the door behind him.

The Pillars was, as Simon had predicted, very posh. Its name derived from the Doric columns that flanked the front door. They were painted brilliant white and made of polystyrene filled with concrete.

Mr Higgs, who was selling the house, was in the building trade himself so everything, as his wife explained to Rosemary Soddie, was built to the highest specifications, just as if he was going to live in it himself. The kitchen had been fitted by kitchen experts and had every gadget the modern housewife could dream of, she explained pulling out an ironing board unexpectedly concealed under the sink. The kitchen and all its fittings were in brilliant and unalterable red.

The two bathrooms had likewise been seen to by bathroom experts. One had a sunken, square bath, which, Mrs Higgs said, could take two.

'We nearly made a big mistake,' she said, shaking her head, 'We nearly chose avocado. Of course we realized just in time that was last year's colour. So we got the camel.'

Rosemary Soddie looked at her, startled. Mrs Higgs added to her bewilderment by saying, 'By the way, the camel bidet is round the corner.'

She led the way into the main bedroom which, like all the other bedrooms, had been fitted by bedroom experts.

'We've assumed of course that the purchaser will buy all the fittings. You will see that the bedspreads match the curtains which match the wallpaper which blend with the carpets. Everything blends,' she added with satisfaction. 'We had the colour experts in, of course, to do the entire house.'

'But,' Rosemary objected, 'people may find that their furniture doesn't quite go with your colour scheme.'

'Oh, we're quite happy to sell the furniture. They'd be stupid not to buy it because it was all chosen to blend in, you see.'

'You don't think people might prefer to choose their own?'

'Oh, no, dear,' Mrs Higgs told her. 'Definitely not in our experience. People like to have these decisions made for them by experts. The rising young executive and his wife have other things to worry about than choosing curtains.'

She led the way downstairs and through the kitchen to what she called the outdoor offices.

Claud will like this house, Rosemary thought with sudden fear, as they gazed at the well-designed triple garage. He will say it is instantly available, requires nothing to be done to it and is a good investment.

The garden, which ran parallel to those of the other three houses which Mr Higgs had put on the plot, was surrounded by a timber and wire fence.

'Sixty foot by forty,' Mrs Higgs said. 'The ideal size.'

She led the way out of the french windows and on to a newly laid concrete terrace.

'We've altered the levels to create more interest,' she said, leading the way down the garden.

The top soil had evidently been scooped off the far end of the plot and used to raise the top end, an arrangement which clearly did not suit the plants at the deprived lower end. Turf had been laid on the upper part and a small concrete pool installed with a fountain driven by a circulating pump. Literally hundreds of trees and shrubs, Rosemary noticed in amazement, had been squeezed into the garden. Cupressus leylandi had been planted round the borders no more than six inches apart. Silver birch, weeping willows, flowering cherries, conifers, all the ornamental trees were there, crowded together by the dozen.

'You've certainly put in plenty of things,' Rosemary said, looking in amazement at what seemed a fairground of little yellow garden-centre labels.

'Oh, we didn't stint on the garden. My husband says it's not commercial sense to do that. He reckons you must spend ten per cent of the value of the house on the garden. So we got the experts in to landscape it and plant everything. We told them how much money they could have, then gave them a free hand to plant what they liked. It looks a bit bare now, maybe, but they'll grow. It'll be nice and bushy in three or four years' time.'

In three or four years' time, Rosemary thought, this will be a dense forest, sixty foot by forty.

'The roses were lovely last summer,' Mrs Higgs told her as they stood by the large diamond-shaped bed which had been cut in the lawn and which contained dozens of straggly rose bushes planted almost on top of each other.

'Of course they don't look so good now,' she conceded.

'Perhaps they need pruning,' Rosemary suggested.

'Really? Pruning?'

'Yes, it's usually done in March.'

'Well, I'd no idea,' Mrs Higgs said, evidently flabbergasted. 'They never said anything about that. You'd think,' she added indignantly, 'that after charging so much money for installing these plants, they'd at least have come back to service them.'

Florence Moon stood in the kitchen garden and surveyed the plot. It had been dug, but the wintry lumps of soil awaited the hoe and rake to turn it all into a fine tilth ready for planting.

120

The whole half acre of it. Well, she would just tackle it a strip at a time, as she always had done. Out of the capacious pocket of her gardening apron, she produced, from among the packets of seeds, secateurs, string and various other useful objects, an apple: she rubbed it against her thigh and began to munch. Nice it was, a russet from the tree at the bottom of the orchard. They stored well.

Suddenly she pulled a face and spat out a mouthful of rotten apple. The centre of the russet was brown and bad. Codlin moth, drat it, she said to herself. She should have put the greasebands on. She'd bought them last September but what with one thing and another she had never put them on the trees. It was a job she hated, but she would do it now, she decided and walked, limping slightly, from the vegetable garden to the orchard.

Fixing greasebands round apple trees is not an easy task at the best of times, but with arthritic fingers, poor eyesight and a damaged leg it is well-nigh impossible. Florence Moon pulled off the first sticky band from the roll and began to cut. It stuck to the scissors, it stuck to her fingers, and, worst of all, it stuck to itself. She unravelled it and bent towards the tree. Suddenly the wind whipped it up out of her fingers and it attached itself firmly to a branch, and hung there like fly paper. After one or two unsuccessful leaps, she cut herself another strip and this time lowered herself carefully and knelt on the ground on an old plastic bag marked John Innes No. 3. Her head on one side to catch the best view of it, her palms all sticky, she managed to get the greaseband round the trunk. Then she remembered the string. With sticky hands she groped in the pouch until she found it and cut off two lengths. By the time she had done so the greaseband had fallen off the tree and was lying on the ground covered in soil.

It was then that she heard the front door bell. Through the side gate, she could make out the outline of somebody standing on the front steps. Probably some woman collecting for something, she thought, keeping very still. Let them ring.

Winifred had gone out shopping and nobody would answer.

The figure moved from the front doorstep and reappeared at the side gate and walked towards her. Florence struggled to her feet.

'I'm so sorry,' the intruder said. 'My husband has been detained in Addis Ababa and has asked me to come and see you on my own instead.'

Florence Moon looked anything but welcoming. Although a little woman, she was a formidable sight as she stood there in her wellington boots, wearing a sackcloth gardening apron over her tweed skirt, scowling under a hat that seemed to be made of felt and cardboard. She had forgotten all about the Soddies. She glared at Rosemary, as if she was some garden pest like codlin moth or sawfly. Fit only for spraying.

'Well,' she said at last. 'As you can see, I'm busy.'

'Yes,' Rosemary said. 'I'm very sorry I've interrupted you. Shall I come back later? Or would you like me to help you with that?'

Florence looked at her suspiciously. Coming here, all dressed up, making out that any fool could fix greasebands round apple trees. Serve her right if she let her try.

'Yes,' she said. 'Here you are,' and handed Rosemary the equipment.

Inexplicably relieved at not having to start bullying poor Mrs Moon about selling the house, Rosemary knelt down on the plastic bag and set to work. Deftly she snipped string, cut bands, contrived to hold them on with two fingers of one hand and tie the string with the other. She moved swiftly from tree to tree. Mrs Moon followed, silent, and grudgingly impressed.

'You've done greasebanding before,' she pronounced when Rosemary had finished.

'Yes, my father showed me the trick of it years ago,' Rosemary said. 'It's funny how these things come back to you. It's a job I haven't done for twenty years.'

It was amazing, she thought, how little she had noticed the garden last time. It had been a pouring wet day, she remembered, when they came to view the house, and they had only seen the garden through the window. Mrs Moon led her now to the kitchen garden.

It was a walled garden. Mellow pink brick enclosed it. It was so like the garden she had been brought up in that, as she followed Mrs Moon through the archway, she seemed to re-enter her childhood. She knew that there would be peach trees and nectarines, plums and greengages on the south wall and that pear trees and apples would be trained along the west side. In a dream she followed Mrs Moon past the asparagus bed and the soft fruit cage to the strawberry bed. When she was little it was her task to peg down the runners until they made new plants and then later to dig them up very carefully and plant them out. It was a fiddly job, her father said, suitable for her little fingers, and besides, wasn't she the one who ate most of the strawberries? She didn't mind. She was happy to let him get on with the boring old spraying and staking and pruning while she made new plants.

There was a bush of southernwood on the corner of Mrs Moon's herb garden, just like the one at home. She took hold of it gently as she passed, and let it slide through her fingers. Then she held her hand up to her face. The smell brought back all the hot summer days of her childhood: the herb garden where she used to sit for hours when she was tiny, basking in the sun, leaning against the wall so that she crushed the branches of the rosemary bush, her father's favourite herb, after which he had named his only child.

Mrs Moon was waiting by the main vegetable plot.

'Before you came,' she told Rosemary brusquely, 'I was just going to break the soil up ready for planting.'

'You've a lot to do,' Rosemary remarked, looking at it aghast. 'Can I help you with it?'

'What, in those shoes?' Mrs Moon queried ungraciously.

Rosemary thought for a moment. 'There are some boots of my son's in the car,' she said. 'Far too big, but they'll do.'

They went back together to the car to find the boots. The new socks were on the passenger seat. She put them on.

Then Mrs Moon produced from the potting shed a long coat

of mouldering leather, which had belonged to her husband, and a pair of gardening gloves. They selected more tools from the enormous range in the toolshed and walked back together to the vegetable plot.

They worked methodically, side by side, each tackling a strip about two yards wide. They didn't talk. The only sound was the chipping of the hoe breaking up the lumps of soil and the little scratchy sounds of the rake. Then they trod the soil level and hoed and raked it again.

'It's good soil,' Rosemary remarked as they stood on the path and surveyed their handiwork with satisfaction: a strip four yards wide, of fine soil ready for planting.

'You've done yours better than mine,' Florence said generously. 'A finer tilth. No bumps either. I do hate it when people drag the soil about with the rake and make it all uneven.'

Rosemary smiled. It could have been her father speaking.

Mrs Moon gave her an upward, sideways glance. 'It's quite professional,' she said, 'the way you've done it. Have you got a big garden of your own?' She had completely forgotten that the Soddies were trying to buy her house.

Rosemary shook her head. 'No, it's just a town garden,' she said. 'But you see my father was a market gardener and nurseryman.'

'Really?' Mrs Moon looked at her with new respect. 'So he trained you?'

'Yes, I suppose you could say that. Nothing official you know. I just grew up with it. I learned as I went along and I worked with him. But somehow, after I was married . . .' her voice trailed off. She couldn't explain to Mrs Moon how her interest in gardening, as in much else, had waned after she married Claud. They had kept moving in their first few years of marriage, Claud always insisting that the garden was his department and she should see to the house, Claud deciding that growing vegetables was uneconomic if you costed in your labour, Claud turning the growing of things into industrial production, spoiling it all, so that it wasn't any longer a matter of soil and roots but of terrible business jargon. She didn't really understand how her love of gardening had been eroded or at least been made redundant and lain dormant all these years, so she couldn't explain to Mrs Moon.

Instead she shook her head and said, 'But I love this garden. I really do.' Then she added suddenly, 'Nobody would stop me working in this garden.'

Mrs Moon looked at her, surprised by the sudden firmness of tone. She'd underestimated this woman, she realized. She was as determined as she was herself. A real gardener too. With a bit of luck she'd get her to help with planting the seeds.

'Coffee,' Winifred called from the house.

'Bother,' Mrs Moon said, afraid that this would remind the visitor of the passage of time and put her to flight.

But Rosemary Soddie was enjoying herself. She hadn't promised to go and look at any other houses today. No doubt Claud would think she was mad wasting her time like this when she should have been house-hunting, but she didn't care. The air was fresh on her cheeks, the sun getting warmer. The two of them drank their coffee standing in the doorway of the potting shed, out of the wind.

'I'll take the mugs back and tell Winifred you're staying for lunch,' Florence said.

'Oh no, don't put her to any trouble.'

'No trouble. We only have sandwiches and tinned soup. I like the tomato sort best myself.'

'Well, thank you, then I'll stay. Where's the string line? I'll start preparing for a row of seeds while you're indoors.'

'I don't bother with a line,' Florence admitted, put out. 'I just sort of scratch a line with the back of the rake.'

'I'll make a line for you,' Rosemary said. 'It's better really.'

She found a ball of string and two strong stakes. By the time Florence Moon came out again she had made the line and fixed it down the vegetable plot.

'What are you putting in first?'

From her capacious pouch Florence produced packets of lettuce, carrots, broccoli and spinach seeds. She dug further and brought forth a bundle of white stakes for labels and a gardening pencil.

It was lunch time when they had finished. Rosemary had just pushed the last label into the soil when Winifred called to them. Florence Moon observed with approval that this woman did the labels in the correct old-fashioned way, putting the variety of the seeds, the date of planting and the name of the seedsman on the label.

It was warm enough to have their soup and sandwiches outside. Winifred did not join them. 'She's an indoor person,' Florence Moon said. 'She'd rather do housework than gardening,' she added with disbelief.

'What else have you got to plant?' Rosemary asked.

Florence Moon emptied all the seeds packets out on to the bench.

'Too soon for those,' Rosemary said, rejecting the French beans and scarlet runners, 'but the beetroot and the parsley could go in. Oh, and you've got onion sets,' she added, emptying a little string bag marked Stuttgart Giant, out of its paper wrappings. 'I was going to ask if you grew onions. And I've been thinking,' she went on hesitantly, 'we could prepare a bit more ground so that it would be easy for you to plant the beans later on and make a second sowing of things like lettuce.'

'If you like,' Florence Moon conceded, getting up and leading the way back to the vegetable garden, 'we'll sow the beetroot first. I don't like it, but it does very well in this soil.'

Rosemary laughed. 'Our first house when we were married had a huge garden,' she said, 'and I grew rows of beetroot. We didn't like it either. I made about fifty jars of pickled beetroot and we carted it round with us wherever we went for about two years. I think it must have been packed up at least three times by removal men.'

Florence wasn't listening. She was looking thoughtfully at the rows of seeds they had planted before lunch. She shook her head sadly.

'It's silly, really,' she said gloomily. 'We'll never eat this lot, Winifred and I.'

'Oh, you can always give it away,' Rosemary told her, startled by her sudden change of tone. 'The shops may be glad of some of it too.'

'People tell me I ought to leave here,' Florence said, nodding towards the house. 'Because of the garden.'

Rosemary, who had quite forgotten the purpose of her visit, looked aghast. 'But you love your garden,' she said. 'You'd be miserable without it, I can see that.'

'Well, my dear, once it starts getting to be a worry—'

'You could cut down on the work, you know,' Rosemary said, giving the vegetable garden a hard professional look. 'You could grass that end and only have about a quarter the size of vegetable plot. And how about a terrace against the south wall, so you could sit there? It would be worth spending a bit to make it all easy to maintain.'

'No, it can't be made easy,' Florence Moon said shaking her head. 'I wouldn't admit it of course, but when the really heavy gardening times approach, like spring when it's all to be planted up and autumn when everything has to be lifted, I almost hate the place.'

'Oh, you mustn't feel like that, Mrs Moon. Look, if we come and live near here, I'll give you a hand. I really do think you'd miss your garden dreadfully.'

She remembered her own father dying of a broken heart when the nursery had to be sold. If only she had been able to persuade him to hang on to it. But he lacked the will, undermined as he always was by the hard and ambitious wife he could not help loving, but who despised his skills and his simple, loyal nature. If Rosemary had been a boy he might have held on for his child's sake, but because she was only a girl neither of them even considered it. It would be different nowadays. But the conventions of the day decreed that both he and she be deprived of a partnership that might have saved him. So he had sold up to please his wife and then she had left him anyway. He had lived long enough to see houses built on his land, while the so-called nurserymen who bought it from him smashed up the greenhouses and used the space to build a shop where they sold potted plants grown in Holland. They say it is impossible to die of a broken heart, but she knew better; she had watched him.

'You keep your garden, Mrs Moon,' she insisted passionately now. 'It keeps you young and alive and in touch with everything that matters.'

Florence Moon was contrary by nature. When friends like Samuel Vereker told her to move into a hotel she naturally argued against it. Instinctively she resisted pressure on her from any side. So when Rosemary Soddie told her to stay here and tried to make out that the garden wasn't really burdensome, she naturally felt strongly that she ought to sell up and that any fool could see that a garden this size was hard work.

'No,' she said firmly. 'I'll most likely give up and go and live in a hotel.'

'Oh, not a *hotel*! Even a little cottage garden would be better than nothing,' Rosemary pleaded.

'Hotel,' Mrs Moon repeated. Then added unexpectedly, 'I could always have an allotment if I wanted.'

'*Allotment*?'

'Yes, there are plenty near here. Full of old folk like me. So there's always somebody around to give you a hand with anything heavy. Then if you want to stop working it, you just give it back to the council. There's no problem about selling it, the way there is with a house. With houses you never know how the market might change, one minute a sellers' market the next minute a buyers',' she concluded, quoting her solicitor in a way that would have astonished him.

Rosemary looked at her thoughtfully. It was a curious predicament that she found herself in, she thought. She could never go along with Claud's plans for ousting Mrs Moon, but on the other hand she couldn't let her end up selling eventually to somebody who wouldn't let her share the garden.

'If you were going to have an allotment,' she said at last, 'you might as well keep part of this garden.'

Mrs Moon shook her head. 'There's no way of dividing the garden,' she said. 'I went into all that once.'

128

'I really meant that the people who bought the house might let you share the garden with them afterwards.'

'Oh, they'd never agree,' Florence Moon said. 'They weren't that sort at all.'

Rosemary suppressed a smile, but all the same she knew it was up to her now to bring reality back into the discussion.

She cleared her throat nervously. It was a long time since she had made such a decision.

'Mrs Moon,' she said, 'if we bought your house, we'd let you come back and share the garden.'

'You mean work it together, like this?'

'Yes.'

Mrs Moon looked at her, nonplussed.

'But you don't want to buy this house,' she said irritably. 'You've just been telling me not to sell it.'

'Yes, I sort of forgot that we wanted to buy it.'

Mrs Moon laughed abruptly, a brief, throaty cackle. 'I like that,' she said. 'I'm forgetful myself sometimes.'

Whatever would Claud have said, Rosemary thought suddenly. She imagined the exasperated expression on his face if he had heard her arguing with Mrs Moon, trying to persuade her not to sell. He had often been exasperated with her, but this would have been exasperation beyond imagining. The enormity of her crime suddenly seemed funny. Besides, Mrs Moon's cackle had set something going. The more she thought about Claud's exasperated face, the more she laughed.

'So,' Mrs Moon interrupted, nodding towards the row of seeds, 'we'll be lifting this lot together in the autumn?'

'Yes, that's settled,' Rosemary said, wiping her eyes. 'And since neither of us likes beetroot, let's get on with planting the onions.'

# Chapter Nine

Jenny Pierce liked and could afford expensive underwear. The fine silk camisole slipped over her head so that her hair, newly washed and unruly, clung to it.

'Look how it stands on end,' Tim said, taking her head between his hands and trying to smooth the hair down.

She grinned up at him.

'Not only my hair,' she commented.

'Oh, Jenny, I do love you. I wish you'd marry me.'

'We'll talk about it afterwards.'

'Bossy boots,' he said, kissing her. A little later, he said, 'Hi, what are these?'

'My latest extravagance. I thought you'd appreciate them.'

'How do they come off?'

'Slowly, for preference,' she told him.

Afterwards, as she lay in his arms on his big divan bed, she said, 'Well, you see work went so well last week that I thought I deserved a treat, so I took myself to Millards – you know, the shop that sells the old-fashioned undies? They're hideously expensive but the materials are out of this world, beautiful lace nighties and things like camisoles and French knickers and modesty vests and liberty bodices.'

'What?'

'They're the things our grandmamas wore, or maybe our mamas. They're all the rage just now.' She laughed. 'I took my mother to Millards once and she just couldn't believe her eyes. She kept saying, "But these things are so dreadfully old fashioned, dear. I wouldn't have thought you young things would have been seen dead in them." '

'How is your mother?' he asked affectionately.

'Fine, thanks. We had a lovely weekend. She asked after you. She always does. She has her eye on you for a son-in-law.'

'Tell her I'd be delighted to oblige any time. How about a spring wedding?'

She shook her head. 'I shan't encourage her fantasies. By the way, she took me to see Aunt Sybil's furniture at the weekend. We spent most of Saturday at the house. It's up for sale and I've got to clear out my share of the loot as soon as possible. I'll show you the list over supper.'

He sat up, astonished. 'Supper? I'd quite forgotten we haven't eaten.'

'I hadn't forgotten. I'm starving. We did things in reverse order this evening. Remember?'

'I'm sorry, Jenny,' he said, getting off the divan. Then he stretched and yawned. 'Oh, what a bore to have to go out,' he said. 'If we were married we could just go and find something in the kitchen.'

'When you say *find*, you mean I'd have shopped for it, washed it, and messed it about and cooked it and—'

'Shut up,' he said, kissing her. 'That's enough women's lib for tonight. I'd have probably seen to all that anyway. It had better be that Greek place, hadn't it?' he added, glancing at his watch. 'They stay open the latest.'

Later over the mousaka, she showed him the list of furniture. 'I'll never get it all into the flat,' she said. 'I suppose I could put it in store for a while.'

'Couldn't your parents store it for you? They've got quite a big house.'

'Yes, but it's crammed full already. Oh, they were so silly,' she exclaimed, putting her fork down and pushing her hair back. 'When my father retired they were supposed to move into something smaller, a country cottage with a small garden and all that. But every time we saw something suitable, they said things like, "But where would we put the tallboy?" '

'It's a nice phrase,' he said, smiling.

'So just because they wouldn't get rid of a single stick of furniture they ended up buying a house nearly as big as their old one, with a vast garden to match. Poor old Pa spends half his life trying to keep it in order and Mother wastes hours dusting and polishing all that wretched furniture.'

'Can't you understand that at all, Jenny? I mean their attachment to things they've had around them for all their married life?'

'No, I think it's crazy to have your life-style dictated to you by your belongings.'

'But, my love, aren't you doing that now? Aren't you reorganizing your life because of Aunt Sybil's furniture?'

She thought about it. 'A little bit, perhaps,' she conceded. 'But if Aunt Sybil's bits and pieces began to get in the way of my life-style, I'd sell them off. I'm not going to let them take control. Besides, I was thinking I might like to move to an unfurnished flat anyway. The furniture only clinches it.'

'There's enough here,' he said, glancing down the list, 'to fill a pretty large unfurnished flat, or a cottage even.'

'I wouldn't mind renting a cottage, so long as it was within commuting distance.'

He shook his head. 'You'll never get a cottage to rent,' he told her. 'You'll end up buying.'

'No,' she said firmly. 'I've quite decided against that. It's too much of a commitment. Besides if I bought a place it would use up all Aunt Sybil's money and I want some left over to have fun with.'

'Buying is a much better investment,' he told her. 'You see, if you rent a place, you're really frittering your salary away and you've got nothing to show at the end of it.'

'But Tim, that's just the point. I don't want to have anything to show at the end of it. I want to use up my life as I go along, not hoard up bits for some unforeseeable future.'

He took her hand, drew it across to him and kissed it.

'Sometimes you scare me,' he said.

'Why?'

'You could come such a cropper.'

'But I won't! Look, if I was buying, there'd be a risk, but I'm only renting, so if it turns out to be the wrong place, I'll pack up and go with a month's notice.'

'That's not what I meant. You know that. I wish you'd let me look after you.'

'You do.'

'Permanently.'

She shook her head. 'Living like we do is so much safer,' she said. 'If it doesn't work out, you just part, in the same way that you can leave a house if it's only being let to you.'

'You mean you only want to rent me?'

She burst out laughing.

'On a very long lease,' she said. 'Don't look so solemn.'

'But it *is* serious,' he insisted. 'You talk as if being committed to somebody is a fearful danger, but I think that it's the people who can't commit themselves, or won't, who are the most vulnerable. It's all right when life's going smoothly—'

'Fortunately my life *does* go smoothly,' she interrupted him. 'I make sure of that.'

He took both her hands in his, turning them over to look at the palms. She had surprisingly small hands. He sighed.

'I wish I could change your mind,' he said.

'You won't,' she told him.

He released her hands as the waiter approached, offering pastry confections stuffed with dried fruit and dripping with syrup.

She shook her head. 'Too fattening,' she pronounced. 'But I'll watch you indulge. I don't think anything would make you put on weight. It's very unfair.'

'But, Jenny, you're no more fat than I am—'

'I soon would be if I ate the way you do.'

'I shouldn't think they're very fattening – they've got fruit in.'

'You speak with the innocence of the naturally skinny,' she told him. 'Anyone can see they're nothing but carbohydrate and sugar. Any more of that and I shan't be able to squeeze into my new clobber from Millards.'

'I'd hate you to split your modesty vest,' he assured her solemnly, scooping up a spoonful of syrup.

She laughed her loud, uninhibited laugh.

'That's better. Honestly Tim, you were getting awfully earnest just now.'

'All right. I'll say no more. But just promise me that if you do settle for anything, even to rent, you'll let me have a look at it first. I'd like to do an unofficial survey for you.'

'Oh, I'd forgotten you're an expert on houses.'

He shrugged. 'Not exactly an expert,' he said. 'I didn't finish the architect's course before I changed to law, you know, but I do know a bit about buildings. I think I'd know enough to realize if you needed a real expert's opinion. And, of course, if you rent and you're on a repairing lease, remember you'll be responsible for anything that goes wrong, so it'll pay you to check everything carefully first.'

She sighed.

'It's a bit daunting,' she said.

'It wouldn't be so daunting if we were in it together. Look, Jenny, why don't we pool our savings and get something between us? Have a trial run?'

'You know what I think about that!' she reminded him. 'If you go through all the hassle of setting up house together, you might just as well be married. It seems to me that women partners have all the disadvantages of being wives and none of the advantages.'

'Ah, so you do concede there are advantages in being a wife?'

She laughed.

'Only compared with being a female partner,' she told him. 'Besides,' she went on more gently, 'it wouldn't be fair on you. You know you won't have much money for two or three years yet. The Bar's unpredictable, we all know that. And I don't need looking after. I'm perfectly happy as I am.'

The coffee arrived.

'It looks even stronger than usual,' she remarked, handing him his cup.

'Thanks. So you're back to looking for an unfurnished flat,' he went on, ladling sugar into his coffee, 'like the one in Victoria where you met your lady with the nesting instinct?'

'Yes. Only please God not at all like that flat. Golly, but it was grim! Still, I'm glad I went or I shouldn't have met Bunty. Or Heather Barnicoat, if it comes to that. Oh, poor Heather,' she exclaimed suddenly, measuring a tiny amount of sugar into her coffee. 'I told you about the evening I spent with her, didn't I? Honestly, Tim, you just can't imagine what her life is like.'

'So you said. But I don't know why you're so appalled, my love. You must have seen family life in the raw before.'

'Mm,' she stirred, pondering. 'I suppose it was because of what she'd given up. You don't usually catch a glimpse of how other people's lives might have been.'

'How would her life have been?'

'Like mine,' she told him promptly.

'And I expect she'd have enjoyed it, as you do yours, if she'd chosen to stay in publishing. But she didn't, and she's probably perfectly happy with the way of life she has in fact chosen.'

'She isn't. She almost cried at one point.'

'Well, don't you ever cry? Everyone has their bad days. I reckon you just happened to strike one of hers. The Barnicoats will settle down happily once they've moved, I expect.'

'Well, it certainly put me off matrimony.'

'Oh, Jenny, really! You might as well say that if anyone met you after a bad day, they'd be put off publishing.'

'No, it's different. I admit there are bad days like black Wednesday when we have our weekly editorial conference. Old Prothers excelled himself last week. He droned on and on about this admiral whose memoirs he's publishing, name dropping left, right and centre, telling us how his lordship and he had had lunch together and the lordship's arthritis was troublesome. Ye gods, so boring and irrelevant.'

'Well, you're proving my point. Outsiders may think your job's exciting, but it has its yawns like every other job.'

'Ah, but I leave it behind at five-thirty. I shut the office door on it, but Heather Barnicoat can't escape. She has to live with the job day and night. It seemed to me that too much depended on her, too many people were draining her. She looked really *worn*.'

'And you don't think there were any compensations?'

'Yes,' she admitted, remembering. 'When she was talking about one of the boys. I can't remember exactly what was in her mind, but certainly something to do with the children and she seemed suddenly radiant. It was odd. Private. I can't explain. But yes, I have to admit that it was maybe a feeling that should be set on the credit side of family life.'

He watched her, loving her honesty, fearing her theories, her way of totting up the pros and cons of different ways of life on some hypothetical balance sheet.

'You used the word *private*, Jenny. Don't you think that all the advantages of being a career girl, the freedom, the money and all that, that you have, are all very clear and visible and therefore enviable? But hers are deeper and hidden, and less tangible. Maybe they have resources, the Barnicoat pair, and the children too, which are far greater, but not on view?'

'Possibly. Certainly the only things on view on Friday evening were chaos and depression.'

'And the occasional radiant look?'

She smiled. 'Maybe radiant was a bit strong. Glowing, perhaps. Anyway, what does it prove? The kids will probably turn out to be selfish little beasts who'll leave home without a backward glance.'

'Like you did?'

'I jolly well didn't. I'm always trotting back to see the aged parents.'

'You know what I mean. You were glad enough to have that kind of family, weren't you? Like Heather is giving hers? You didn't complain that your mother ought to have put herself first and—'

'It's no good,' she interrupted. 'I refuse to feel guilty about the way I live. It's been too good a week at work for that.'

'Why was it so good?'

'John Hooston came up with the last of his manuscript.'

'The chap who wrote *The Ivory Tower*?'

'That's right. That was my first book,' she added, nodding her head with satisfaction.

He laughed. 'You sound as if you'd written it yourself, the way you say *my* book.'

'Yes, it's funny, but you do feel it's your own book in a way, if you've chosen the manuscript and turned it into a book.'

'What's his new one about?'

'It's a historical novel, tracing the life of one of the soldiers in Napoleon's army in Portugal in the Napoleonic War. It sounds unpromising, but it's so real and alive and utterly convincing. You just feel he's got it right.'

'What sort of chap is he?'

'Not particularly striking, just to meet. I suppose it's partly the fact that he was my first author that makes him seem rather special to me. And, apart from anything else, he's a nice person and good to work with.'

'Ah, I smell a rival.'

She laughed. 'I never mix business and pleasure,' she said. 'Besides, I'm afraid it might be a case of baby snatching.'

'Really? I didn't realize he was a youngster.'

'He's about twenty-eight. But a very young and unworldly twenty-eight. I really do mother him.'

'I'd like to see that,' he said, leaning back in his chair and laughing.

'It's true. He's so vulnerable and aware and open to hurt. I feel very protective about him. I want to keep the world away from him so he can get on with writing.'

'Do you ever want to write yourself, Jenny?'

She shook her head. 'Never. I just seem to want to take a manuscript that I admire and have a part in turning it into a book.'

'It's a funny sort of thing to want to do,' he reflected.

'No odder than being in court, which gives *you* kicks.'

He laughed. 'I wouldn't put it quite that way. "I'm here for the kicks, m'lud" wouldn't be the kind of comment that would further the career of a promising young barrister.'

'Tim,' she said suddenly. 'It's awful. We've talked about nothing but me and my work tonight. How did your case go today?'

'Oh, our man got off.'

'Good. I'm glad he was innocent.'

'Oh, no, he was as guilty as hell, but the only evidence was police evidence so the jury wouldn't wear it.'

'Tim,' she said, aghast, 'doesn't it bother you at all, getting somebody guilty off the hook?'

'No. I don't think in those terms. A man must be judged on the evidence. So that's what we look to, not our own feelings about guilt or innocence. Really, Jenny, it's the only way the system can be made to work.'

'Yes, I suppose so. It wouldn't do for me. What are you on next?'

'Armed robbery. This character poured petrol over a night-watchman and threatened to put a match to him if he didn't hand over the keys.'

'Tim!'

'Well, nasty things go on, Jenny. And you did ask.'

'Yuk. I feel quite sick. Publishers may have their funny little ways, but at least they don't go round igniting each other.'

'No igniting took place. The chap wisely handed over the keys.'

'Thank goodness for that. Oh Tim, just look! How's that for bad timing?'

He followed the direction of her eyes. A waiter was preparing to *flambé* something at the next table.

'I don't expect it'll taste much better than if they'd cooked it in a pan in the kitchen,' Tim remarked.

'It's not that. It's just the thought of flames after your awful story. Let's go before he finds the matches.'

As they walked back to his digs, she said, 'Tell me something nice about your work. To make up for that last horror.'

He hesitated.

'Something nice did happen to me, actually, last week,' he said.

'Go on.'

'I had this client to defend. It was a hopeless case. I won't go into details, but he really was pathetic. Anyway, I entered a plea of guilty, but talked at length about the mitigating circumstances. And at the end the judge congratulated me and said to the man in the dock, "You owe to your counsel the fact that you are not being sent to prison." It was nice.'

'Oh, darling Tim!' She stopped and reached up to put her arms round his neck. 'That's lovely. Oh, I am glad.'

They stayed for a while, swaying, then they set off again, walking slowly, his arm around her. She sighed deeply, pressing her head into his shoulder.

'Penny for them,' he said, smiling down at her.

'I'm just so lucky,' she told him.

'We both are.'

They walked for a while in silence, then as they approached his digs, she said, 'I keep thinking how lucky I am compared to poor Heather Barnicoat.'

'Shut up,' he said, rubbing his chin against the top of her head.

'Honestly, Tim, I do wish I'd helped her more. I might at least have given her a hand with the decorating.'

'It's a bit late to think of that now,' he remarked, partly disengaging himself from her in order to find the key. 'Anyway, I'm sure you did help her, just by being there and having a chat. It must get pretty boring having nobody to talk to all day but small children.'

'I hope I cheered her up. At least I did get her to promise to write it all down, all her thoughts and worries, and send them off to her old man in Leicester.'

'That'll be nice for him,' Tim said drily, unlocking the door.

Derek Barnicoat carried Heather's letter round in his pocket all day, increasingly incensed by it. When he had first opened it and glanced quickly through it that morning he had felt surprised, rather touched. It must have been hard for her to write thus, pouring out all her worries about their marriage, admitting to being miserable without him and feeling estranged even when they were briefly together. And the boys not at ease with him as they used to be. Perhaps he didn't realize, she wrote, that he was, well, not exactly more strict with them, but somehow more remote? And with her too?

Her words had moved and hurt him, but as the day wore on he felt more and more irritated by them. And it was a very wearing day, too, beginning with being asked to sacrifice his one free period to take a lesson for an assistant English master who was off sick. He didn't mind that, but he had meant to use the time preparing a lesson for the Middle IV, who were easily the most difficult lot in the whole school. Since their lesson wasn't properly prepared they naturally behaved even worse than usual and very nearly succeeded in getting him to lose his temper. It mortified him to find that kids could still play him up. Then what should have been the best part of the day, a double period with the Upper VI, turned sour because they wandered in saying they were sorry but they hadn't had time to do their essay for him. It was their offhand manner that did it. So he really let fly at them, asking stupid rhetorical questions such as 'Did they think it was a school picnic or A levels they were preparing for this term?' and other feeble sarcasms, so that they naturally grew sullen, this group of kids who were usually so friendly. He went on to make the same mistake with the Upper V in the afternoon, resorting to filling them with foreboding about failing *their* exams in his efforts to get them to work a bit harder. It was against all that he had ever preached about helping the young to see public exams as an incidental part of the process of learning, not to be fussed about. Do the work for its own sake, he'd always said, and the exams will fit into the scheme of it all. He was sure that that was right and it had always worked well before. He realized he was inducing panic into them now because he was nervous of not getting good enough results in his new school, and he knew that he was being stupid.

The day ended with a rehearsal for the school play, which he was producing. Half of the cast forgot about it and went home after school; the rest didn't know their words. Altogether it was a rotten day and by the end of it he only remembered that he had had a letter from Heather which had hurt him and made him angry.

But after he had gone back to his digs and done some marking and re-read the letter, he found it less of a grouse than he had thought. Poor old Heather, it was an honest letter really, affectionate and sad. And she was worried too about James, who'd been off school. A healthy James was pretty demanding, he reflected, but an off-colour James really was the end. He could imagine the chaos. In his own weariness at the end of a frustrating day, he understood her weariness and anxiety. He felt his anger drain away. Instead he felt worried and a bit guilty about Heather.

Mrs Peck called him down to supper; he joined her in the neat and tidy dining-room which smelled of furniture polish and disinfectant. Food smells never got the upper hand in Mrs Peck's house.

She asked him about his day, as she always did, as she arranged the dishes on the table, waiting on him, handing him the gravy. She had a way of doing all this which was somehow intimidating. She might seem to be waiting on him, but it was with a deliberate subservience of manner which somehow put him in the wrong.

'I'm afraid I give you a great deal of trouble,' he said, as she cleared away the first course.

'It is what I am here for,' she corrected him, as he had known that she would.

'And how is Mrs Barnicoat?' she enquired as they ate their apple pie and custard.

She always asked kindly after Heather. It made him feel ashamed and a bit hypocritical because Heather never enquired after the health of Mrs Peck, indeed she showed no signs of being kindly disposed towards his landlady at all.

Suddenly he felt a need to unburden himself to Mrs Peck.

Suppressing a momentary flicker of guilt at his disloyalty, he said, 'Well, I'm afraid she's getting a bit depressed by the situation.'

'Oh, I'm surprised to hear that, Mr Barnicoat. I should have thought she would have had more spirit.'

'Yes, come to think of it, she does tend to give in rather easily to these emotions.'

'She must learn to count her blessings,' Mrs Peck said, putting down her spoon and fork neatly side by side and wiping her mouth firmly on her napkin. 'More apple pie, Mr Barnicoat?'

'Yes, please. Well, it isn't always easy, you know. She finds the boys are quite a handful.'

'Oh, you don't need to tell me about boys, Mr Barnicoat,' she said with her knowing, dismissive little laugh. 'I know all about you boys.'

Then she cut sharply into the pie and went on severely, 'All the same, she must pull herself together and tell herself she's a very lucky woman. Knowing you, as I have been privileged to do, I know she has much to be grateful for.'

'Thank you,' he said, accepting the pie at the same time as the compliment.

She handed him the custard.

'But you see,' he said in mitigation of Heather's ingratitude for being married to him, 'I'm not there to give her the support she needs just now. And this being separated is going on for much longer than we ever intended, as you know. It's going to be a year of living apart. It's a long time.'

'Others have accepted it, Mr Barnicoat. I lost my own husband after five years of marriage. But I count my blessings. He was a wonderful man and we had five very wonderful years. Boys can manage without fathers. When my son was five years old, I said to him, "You're the man of the house now," I said, "You're my husband now as well as my son." '

She took a long drink of water and then added, 'And he was. Though I say it myself, my son was one of nature's gentlemen. People used to stop me in the street and remark upon it.'

He felt awkward somehow, chewing noisily away at the pastry while she said these things. A bit clumsy and rough, he felt, as he had often felt at his mother's immaculate table. But he enjoyed the sensation, all the same; it was as if he was regaining some adolescent sensibility lost during his marriage.

Mrs Peck poured the coffee and sipped hers, as she always did, with her little finger delicately crooked.

'I think you must be firm with her, Mr Barnicoat, very firm.'

'You think so, Mrs Peck?' he enquired earnestly. 'I do value your opinion very much.'

She beamed at him, her face alight with pleasure. 'Well, sometimes we older women do acquire a little wisdom,' she said almost coyly.

'I'm sure of it. Sometimes, Mrs Peck,' he ventured to go on, 'you remind me very much of my own mother.'

'There is no greater compliment any young man could make me,' she said, evidently moved. 'So I will say to you what I would say to my son: it is a great mistake not to be firm. I'm afraid my son has made that mistake.'

She paused, the eyes suddenly hard behind the glinting spectacles. 'What my daughter-in-law needs,' she said, fiercely, 'is a good hiding.'

He looked at her, startled.

'Oh, I mean it, yes I do. Many's the time he comes in and there's no meal ready, because she's only got in from work five minutes before him. Now I always had everything ready for Mr Peck. A man must have his comforts, he's the breadwinner, after all, I always say.'

She looked at him knowingly. 'He'll see it in time, my boy will. He'll be back home one day, I shouldn't wonder. Underneath, you see, he likes things done properly, as all gentlemen do.'

Afterwards he went back to his room to write to Heather in a rather different frame of mind. He smoothed out the letter and read it again. The words now seemed petulant and unfair. He had every intention of replying very firmly. And comprehensively, he thought, taking a piece of scrap paper and beginning to make notes of all the points he wanted to make. He'd settle this once and for all.

He began by listing all the matters she had raised in her letter, though, he realized now, she didn't really express herself in a very orderly way. The same point found its way into different paragraphs: he drew red lines with his marking pencil to link them, trying to clarify her arguments for her, as he would a VI-form essay. Automatically he corrected her punctuation too. Her spelling wasn't faultless either.

She began by saying she didn't really want to write all this down; she had so wanted to talk to him about it in the Easter holidays, but there'd been no time. Well, he thought in exasperation, making notes on his scrap paper, hadn't he explained to her at the time, and hadn't she seemed to understand? He had had no option but to go on the school cruise when the head asked him if he would take the senior master's place. It was short notice, of course, but obviously he couldn't refuse the only request of this kind that the head had yet made. She had agreed with his decision. And it wasn't his fault that when he did get back home they had guests to stay for the whole week before he had to go back to school. Hardly a moment alone, together, there'd been, and at night they were both too exhausted to do anything except flop into bed and sleep. So of course there was no time or privacy for talking. The cottage was just too small for visitors, that was the truth. When his cousins had asked to come and stay she should have refused.

Why did she want to talk about it all anyway? He didn't agree that their marriage was in some sort of peril. He made a note. Peril in Her Mind Only. He didn't hold with this modern craze for talking everything over, or *through*, as the jargon now had it, as if to give spurious authority by changing the preposition. Only the other day, Mrs Peck had said that people talked too much about their feelings nowadays, and that in her view a few inhibitions and a bit of self-control didn't come amiss. He went along with that. Stiff Upper Lip, he jotted down.

But if she wanted to have this soul-baring session, so be it. She said she was trying to be fair and that she understood how much the new job mattered to him, but she was desperately unhappy because he seemed so remote and she and the boys missed him so. Well, it was hard on him too, wasn't it, he thought, suddenly clenching his fists. He had to make the best of things up here, didn't he, without his family? Besides, other people were worse off. It would have been much worse for her if she'd married a sailor, for example. Or he might have died, like Mr Peck. Think of the widows, he'd tell her, he thought, jotting the words down.

And it was absurd to talk about his drifting away from them. Quite absurd to suggest he was returning to his bachelor days, with Mrs Peck as some sort of mother substitute. It made her worry that he shouldn't really have married, she said. Really, what rubbish. And this about his being less spontaneous. However did she expect him to behave spontaneously that week in the tiny cottage with the boys all over the place and the Ant's bed in the sitting-room? Oh, how he had longed for the peace and quiet of Mrs Peck's house.

Not of course that he'd say that. No, he could see that wouldn't be very tactful. But he would say that he was grateful to Mrs Peck and her care of him. Heather should be grateful for it too. If she loved him. She should be solicitous of his needs. Yes, he would say that. Surely he couldn't be expected to object to the fact that he was well cared for here? Better looked after than he ever was at home, come to that. He wasn't complaining about home, of course, just being fair to Mrs Peck.

As if on cue, there was a knock at the door and Mrs Peck appeared with a mug of Ovaltine. 'A different drink tonight,' she said. 'We must ring the changes.'

He thanked her and she put the drink down on the table beside him.

'Still working?' she remarked. 'Oh, you do work hard. We must keep your strength up, mustn't we?'

'You spoil me,' he said, smiling up at her.

'It's my pleasure,' she said, smoothing her apron.

★ ★ ★

The chairman of John Baynes, building and civil engineering contractors, fidgeted impatiently with the elaborate brass ink-stand on his huge desk, as he waited for his call to Ethiopia. Then he sighed deeply and leant back in his great leather chair, alternately drumming on its polished arms with the soft pads of his little pink fingers or tapping the edge of his desk with his beautifully manicured nails. He was a restless, paunchy little man and as he sat in his high-backed chair at his vast desk surrounded by acres of gleaming mahogany he had the look of a rather feverish small boy in a disproportionately large four-poster bed.

That was how Claud Soddie pictured him, as he answered the summons to the telephone in Ethiopia.

'Sorry to keep you waiting, sir,' he said breathlessly, wiping his face with a handkerchief which he then used to grip the telephone, for the temperature was well over a hundred degrees and any exertion brought him out in a sweat all over.

'That's all right, Claud. We've just been having a board meeting this morning. The opening of the northern office was the main item on the agenda. We missed you, needless to say.'

'Yes, I'm sorry I couldn't be there. Everything in order? I think Mattinson should have been well briefed.'

'Oh yes, I must say I congratulate you on the way you managed to get things done over here somehow or other.'

'Well, I do have the odd spell in the Leicester office, you know, and I've got some very good chaps up there. But all the same I'll be glad when I'm permanently back.'

'I'm sure you will. I've no worries. It was just that I felt that the northern office at the moment was a bit like an army without a general, and I wanted to confirm direct with you that everything will be ready for the opening.'

'Certainly. We'll set up on the twenty-fifth of next month, sir.'

'Good, that's what I wanted to hear. So long as you're happy that everything's under control.'

'Yes, I am. I'm far more worried about things out here. I'm afraid we had a real bombshell this morning.'

'Good God!' the little chairman exclaimed, misunderstanding. 'Anyone hurt?'

'Not *literally* a bombshell,' Claud reassured him, and then added ruefully, 'I'm not sure I wouldn't have preferred the real thing. No, I heard just a couple of hours ago that the man we'd appointed agent has changed his mind and isn't coming.'

'Why ever not?'

'Probably realized what a thankless task he was undertaking and thought better of it. Probably wise, too, from his own point of view,' he added with an abrupt laugh.

He sounded harassed; the chairman could detect it. He didn't want that. He set great store by Claud Soddie. He wanted him back in England, but he knew he wouldn't hand over unless he was sure he was leaving everything in order. Meticulous was Claud Soddie, a compulsive worker, too. Compulsive workers are very profitable to a firm, they can be relied upon to see a job through to the end, always put work first, are loyal enough not to question top policy decisions which are sometimes made for not particularly laudable reasons. Yes, he reflected, the limitations of compulsive workers like Claud Soddie are as valuable as their capabilities.

'Leave it to me,' he said reassuringly. 'I'll see what I can come up with. Don't overdo yourself, that's the main thing. You ought to have a holiday.'

Claud Soddie was not reassured. 'Thank you, sir,' he said. 'One day, perhaps.'

'It shouldn't be difficult to find a mere agent? I mean one hears of all these eager young chaps in our industry, itching to travel. We've had a perishingly cold spring here this year; you'd think they'd jump at the chance of getting a bit of sun.'

The chairman did not travel. His idea of Saudi Arabia or Ethiopia was that it must be just like Croydon only warmer. He had a vague notion, Claud had come to realize, that the site was dotted with engineers lounging about in deck chairs.

'Now you just let us know what you want and we'll get on

with advertising. Who's that chap in Personnel? Summerton, isn't it? He'll see to it.'

'I've rung his department already this morning. But it takes time, you see, sorting out all the applicants, following up references, interviewing; you never get anyone in less than a couple of months. And we need somebody *now*.'

'Of course you do, my dear chap. I still think you'd be better to get one of our own men to come out.'

'Oh, I know that,' Claud said rather more impatiently than he usually spoke to the chairman. 'But who? You see it's not a job that's going to lead anywhere. As you know, we're pulling out of this area. Whoever we appoint will just have the thankless task of clearing up and then clearing out. We've nothing to offer afterwards, not as things are at the moment. The place is inhospitable and the climate awful. It's one of those jobs where a chap'll be lucky to escape without doing his career any harm and there's no chance of doing it any good.'

'You don't, I hope, intend to say all this to your likely candidates for the job,' the chairman asked him drily.

'You know me better than that.'

'Don't forget the old stick and carrot, eh? Well, Claud, pop in and see me whenever you're back.'

'Yes, sir, I'll do that.'

'You were having problems about a house, weren't you?' he said, remembering suddenly.

'Yes. We thought we'd bought one but then the old lady who was selling it changed her mind.'

'Ah, one hears that everywhere now. People stuck in these wretched chains of house sales. But you got things shifted?'

Claud laughed. 'I didn't,' he confessed. 'My wife did. This'll interest you, sir. I asked her to go and lean on the old girl – I'd have gone myself but couldn't get back home. She was very unwilling, mind you. I had to talk her into it. But she went up there and at the end of the day the old lady agreed to sign on the dotted line. Very impressive. I couldn't have managed it better myself.'

'Probably your wife did it better than you could have done, you know, Claud.'

Claud laughed. 'Could be,' he said.

'You know, I always say, put a woman in charge and she'll be as tough and unscrupulous as any man. We underestimate these ladies, Claud.'

'Yes, you may be right. I must say I was surprised, pleasantly surprised.'

'And you've sold your own house?'

'Yes. I told Rosemary to get in touch with the solicitors about it straight away. Everything's on the move now.'

'I'm delighted to hear it. Good luck to you. Remember me to your good lady.'

'Thank you, sir. Goodbye.'

'Goodbye, Claud.'

# Chapter Ten

He was called out of a lesson to take a telephone call in the school secretary's office.

'Mr Barnicoat?'

'Speaking.'

'Browning of Browning & Samson, solicitors, here. We have heard from Mr Blunt, the Soddies' solicitor, that they are ready to go ahead with the sale of number 10, Wellington Square. You remember we were negotiating the purchase for you several months ago? Of course I couldn't say if you were still interested; you may be pursuing another property now.'

'Oh, yes, we're still interested. It's marvellous news.'

'Good. Then you would like me to inform them that you want to go ahead with the purchase?'

'Yes, please. Do that. As soon as possible.'

'I'll check the contract and then of course there will be the new date to insert. I take it you would like possession as soon as possible?'

'Oh yes. Apart from anything else we have these people, the Armstrongs, wanting our cottage.'

'Ah, now I was going to ask you about your own sale. You are sure the Armstrongs are still interested?'

'I think so. Anyway there's no problem. We had queues of people after the cottage when we advertised it.'

'Good. But I'm glad you have the Armstrongs, for I believe it is less easy to sell than it was last year.'

'Well, if there's anything else, perhaps you could ring me in the evening at my digs? I must go now, I'm in a class.'

'I'm sorry to interrupt you at work, Mr Barnicoat. I did try to contact your wife at home but there was no reply at various times this morning. And I felt it was urgent, so I made use of this number you had given me in case of emergency.'

'Oh, you did right. I'm most grateful.'

'I felt it was as well to give Blunt's an answer as soon as possible. Evidently their clients are eager to sell and we don't want them to accept some sudden offer from somebody else.'

'Good God, no!'

'May I say how pleased I am that it has all worked out, Mr Barnicoat?'

'Not half as pleased as I am, Mr Browning.'


He didn't ring Heather when he got back to his lodgings. She hadn't replied to his letter or rung him. Let her be on tenterhooks about the house for a few hours more, he thought meanly.

He meant to ring and tell her about the house straight after supper, but decided to finish his marking and preparing first. It grew late; in fact when Mrs Peck knocked at his door, he thought she must be bringing his hot drink, but it was only to tell him that Heather was on the telephone.

He picked up the receiver. 'I was just going to ring you,' he said, feeling suddenly guilty. 'I've got some news for you.'

'Oh.'

She didn't sound very interested.

There was a silence. He didn't break it. Let her apologize first, he thought childishly; she'd started it all.

'Derek,' she said, her voice unsteady. She was obviously upset. So she should be. She'd upset him, hadn't she?

'Derek, I'm at the hospital. It's Jonathan. He's in intensive care. And the doctor thinks you should come home for the weekend.'

Everything went out of focus; he felt suddenly weak.

'Jonathan?'

'Yes, it's some sort of stomach trouble.'

'But I thought it was James who was ill?'

152

'Oh, that was nothing, just a fever, but perhaps it did distract me from realizing about Jonathan. You know, he's always quiet and undemanding, and James had this temperature of a hundred and three, so I suppose I just didn't take as much notice as . . .'

'Oh Heather, my darling, of course you did everything you could. Look, I'll come home now.'

There was a choking sound. 'I thought, I thought you wouldn't be able to get away before the weekend.'

'I'll manage it. Where are you?'

'I'm ringing from the hospital. Sister's been very kind and let me use her phone. I went to the public box, but I hadn't any change and . . .' her voice broke again.

'Go home now. I'm on my way.'

'There's nothing you can do tonight, really, you needn't rush. They've told me I should go home. You won't be able to see him tonight.'

'Silly girl. It's you I'm rushing to. You go to bed now and I'll creep in beside you sometime in the early hours of tomorrow morning.'

There was a pause, then she said, 'Oh Derek, you don't know . . .'

'I'll try not to wake you up. Now tell me how you are getting home from the hospital.'

'Sister's arranging a car. Everyone's been so kind.'

'Off you go then. Sleep well. Try not to worry. Tell me all about it tomorrow morning.'

He rang off and snatched up the local telephone book. Thank God the Headmaster had an odd name. There just couldn't be many Dodworthys in the book. There was only one.

'Oh, yes, Barnicoat?' he sounded surprised. 'What can I do for you?'

He explained briefly and began to outline what his various classes could do.

'Don't worry,' the headmaster interrupted. 'We'll sort something out. And it's lucky you've so many Vth and VIth – they'll be glad to get on with revising at this stage. Give me a ring and

153

let me know how things are at home. Otherwise forget about school and concentrate on your wife and son.'

Mrs Peck was less understanding: she seemed put out by his sudden departure and said what about his meals. He told her he might be back late on Sunday night, and requested a key. Then he pushed a few clothes into a case and ran out to the car.

Short of petrol, he noticed; better fill up on the way to the motorway. The route took him past the Dursley roundabout. He'd fill up at the garage where they'd asked about The Limes. That awful weekend. He should have taken Heather somewhere really nice. She deserved it. Should have told Mrs Peck where to get off.

The same attendant was on duty.

'So The Limes is sold,' Derek remarked, amazed at how calm and normal his voice sounded. 'I see the boards have gone.'

'Yes, at long last. People who bought it are going to make it a bed-and-breakfast place. Good position on the main road.'

'Yes, it makes sense. Nobody else would want to live there, I suppose.'

'You'd be surprised how many people used to ask us where they could stay. Going up to Scotland, you know, or down to Cornwall, looking for somewhere cheap to break the journey.'

'Well, thanks; must be on my way.'

'Go carefully, they forecast snow.'

'It's cold enough.'

'You can say that again. More like January than April.'

The snow began to fall as he reached the motorway. He could hardly believe it, thought it was a trick of the light, making rain look white. But it was no trick; first it was sleet, then it thickened into huge blobs which landed in fat little stars on the windscreen. He peered through it, trying not to think about Jonathan, just concentrate on getting there safely, drive well, main thing. Concentrate on driving. If only he hadn't written that damned letter. If only he'd written it but then not posted it. Or if he had to post it, why the hell hadn't he sent it second class? Might have been a chance of overtaking it then.

The snow was no longer falling, but lay deep on the side

roads after he left the motorway. He had to drive very slowly. There was a full moon. Everything was very still. He was the only moving thing in this quiet, white world. It was two o'clock in the morning when he parked the car outside the cottage, shutting the door as quietly as he could. All the same the noise of it seemed to echo up the village street, and the click of the gate was loud in the stillness. Even his footsteps falling softly on the snow-covered path made an alien sound, intruding into the silent world of the moon and the snow and the pine trees at the bottom of the garden.

He let himself into the cottage. There were no lights on. He washed and changed in the bathroom, which was a lean-to off the kitchen; probably against building regulations, young Armstrong had said. They wouldn't allow it now. The door into the sitting-room was slightly open. He peered in. The Ant was fast asleep in his cot. He could see him clearly in the moonlight, lying on his stomach with his bottom up in the air, as he always did. Derek turned away and crept up the creaky, semi-spiral staircase.

Heather was asleep. She must be exhausted. Perhaps she'd taken a sleeping tablet. He slipped in quietly beside her and lay, grateful for the warmth of her body, very still until he fell asleep.

James was astonished to see him the next morning. He stood in the bedroom doorway and demanded accusingly, 'Whatever are you doing here? Have you been redundanced?'

'Daddy's having a long weekend,' Heather told him calmly. 'Isn't that a lovely surprise?'

'He'll be able to go and see Jonathan, won't he?'

Heather seemed to think for a moment. 'Yes,' she said. 'That's a good idea. We can both go and see him while you're at school.'

'When's he coming home, Mum?'

'The doctor isn't sure yet.'

'I miss him, in a way,' James remarked, puzzled by this discovery. 'When will the Ant be big enough to play properly?'

'Oh, in a year or two, but Jonathan'll be back before then.'

He marvelled at her. What a double life she had to lead, hiding all the worry, cheerfully parrying questions. He helped her get the boys ready and prepare breakfast.

The snow was lying all round the cottage. James was over-joyed, longing to get out in it. She wrapped his scarf firmly round his neck, wiped his nose, still red from his cold, handed him his gloves.

'Got your dinner money?' she asked.

He tapped his pocket, then he hoisted up his satchel and set off up the drive, looking suddenly very small in the outside world.

'Now tell me all about it,' Derek said, as they turned away from the window. 'We'll sit for a minute before we go to the hospital.'

'He started being ill about four days ago,' Heather began, sitting down at the kitchen table, drawn and tired, Derek noticed, now that James was out of sight. He pulled his chair up close to hers and took her hands in his.

'He kept being sick and having diarrhoea,' she went on, 'but I didn't really worry at first. I was more worried about James at the time. Then it just went on and on, even though he'd had nothing to eat. Just a little sip of water would make him sick. So on the third day I got the doctor.'

'I wish you'd told me.'

She shrugged and looked at him miserably.

'I didn't want to worry you. There was nothing you could do.'

'Just talking would have helped.'

'Besides . . .'

'I know. I'm sorry.'

'It doesn't matter now,' she said quietly. 'Anyway, I saw straight away that the doctor took it seriously. He came back again in the evening. He said I must try to get him to drink because he was in danger of getting dehydrated. But it was hopeless. I sat up with him all that night, trying to get him to take sips of water, but he just couldn't keep anything down. He had a dreadful night, poor little boy. It was so awful having no idea what was wrong with him. Dr Bates had told me that it wasn't poisoning, but you know how you go on worrying. I even went out to the garden shed to see if by any awful chance we'd put weedkiller into a lemonade bottle and he'd drunk it without my knowing.'

He could imagine her, creeping out, distraught, in the middle of the night, hunting among the jars and bottles. It was dreadful that she hadn't rung him. He put his arms around her. 'He lay so still,' she whispered, 'quite, quite still, with his eyes shut. He looked like marble.'

He said nothing, only held her closer to him.

'By the morning, he was more restless and felt hot. He had a temperature and I began to think he'd caught the fever that James had, but then James hadn't been sick with it. Anyway, when the doctor came he said the temperature was due to dehydration and he must go into hospital. And he said they'd have to do tests in case it was gastro-enteritis.'

She paused and shook her head. 'It was funny really,' she said. 'You know how kind Dr Bates is? Well, I could tell he didn't want me to be upset because of Jonathan having to go into hospital. He kept reassuring me that it didn't mean there was anything ominous, and so on, but honestly I was so relieved, that he was going to be in expert hands. I just couldn't go on with this dreadful fear that he'd suddenly get much worse and I wouldn't be able to save him, you know? So really I took him into hospital very cheerfully.'

'I'm sure you did, my darling. And kept smiling for the sake of the other two. What happened to them, by the way? Mary to the rescue?'

A flicker of a smile. 'As always,' she said.

'You've helped her too quite a lot in the past,' he reminded her.

'That's what she said, though I think the balance must be a bit in her favour at the moment! Anyway, she was marvellous and had the Ant all day and collected James after school with her three. It was his first day back at school actually and I didn't want him to be upset. He was still a bit convalescent and very snuffly.'

157

'So what happened at the hospital?'

'Well, they explained that in case it was gastro-enteritis Jonathan would have to be in an isolation ward until they knew the results of the tests. That means that everyone who goes in to see him has to wear a gown. I had to, too, of course, and so will you today. It must seem very spooky to him, lying there with all these white-robed figures milling around. They look a bit sinister, rather like the Ku Klux Klan, you know.'

'Yes, but not to him. He doesn't know about such things. It's in your mind, not his.'

'Yes, I suppose so. He doesn't seem to pay much attention to anything actually. Even when they had trouble setting up the drip he was incredibly good about it. Almost too good really. It didn't seem natural. They couldn't find a vein to put the needle into. Apparently when you're dehydrated the veins tend to collapse and then, of course, being so little, his veins are tiny anyway. In the end the registrar paediatrician came and fixed it up. He's very nice. Dr Mackenzie, he's called. I felt Jonathan trusted him more than the nurses, I don't know why. He just seemed happier with him, more relaxed. Not that he shows much reaction to anybody really. Perhaps he just liked the idea of a man looking after him. And, come to think of it, Dr Mackenzie does look a bit like you. Anyway, he got the drip set up without any more bother.'

'How does it work, this drip?'

'The idea is that it gets fluid into his body without having to go through his digestive system. So his stomach and everything will get a complete rest for about thirty-six hours. The solution's in a tank above his head and it goes down in controlled amounts to a glass bowl, and from there down a tube into a needle they call a cannula which is inserted into a vein in his left hand.'

'Poor little kid.'

'Well, he's been very passive. The nurse, who stays with him and keeps a check on the drip, says we're very lucky. Some children keep pulling the needle out and have to be strapped down, which must be dreadful. We just explained to him that he must keep still and he did, though really I don't think he has enough energy to move about anyway. But you'll see. So I stayed for the rest of the day and then in the evening I rang you. That's all really.'

He held her very close. He kissed her.

'Shall we go to the hospital now?' he asked.

'Yes. We'll deliver the Ant to Mary on the way.'

A thaw had set in; the roads were slushy as they drove the five miles to the hospital. Piles of dirty snow lined the roadsides, thrown up by cars and lorries.

Despite all Heather had told him, he had not expected Jonathan to look like this. There was something monkey-like about the shrunken little face; it might have been the head of a very old man. He seemed shrivelled and looked much smaller. His eyes were sunken too and looked somehow flat, not just dull but physically flat. He looked at his parents without a flicker of interest. They spoke briefly to the nurse. They sat down by the bed. Derek picked up the hand that didn't have the drip; it was very small and dry. The skin felt loose over the bones.

'Well, we'll soon have you home again, old chap,' he said.

'Oh.'

Even to produce that tiny sound took a great effort. He seems out of this world already, Derek thought with horror.

'It's been snowing,' he went on. 'Did you know that? Fancy, snow in April! It's still lying here round the hospital. There's a lawn under your window. We could make a snowman there later on. Do you remember the one we made last year? And the one we made when Mummy was away having the Ant? Do you remember you and James and I made a snowman in front of the sitting-room window? And we gave him a hat and a scarf? He was really great. He lasted a week, do you remember? Then he just got smaller and smaller every day until he disappeared.'

He stopped. Jonathan was getting smaller every day, melting like the snowman, the childish flesh shrinking away. Mustn't think like that. Jonathan's eyes were closed. It was impossible to tell if he was asleep or not. His breathing was so shallow, his face so white and he lay so still. He knew what Heather meant now. Like marble. Marble death. Don't think like that. It's the awful stillness of him. Being active is part of being young and alive. When any of the boys had been ill before, they'd always been so restless. He'd never known them to lie as still as this unless they'd been asleep. A kind of resignation, a giving up of the spirit.

The registrar paediatrician came on his rounds and after checking the drip and talking to the nurse, beckoned Derek and Heather outside into the corridor.

He was a tall, gentle-looking man. 'We don't have the results of the tests yet,' he told them, 'but we shall by this time tomorrow.' He spoke softly with a slight Scottish accent. 'Myself, I doubt if it's gastro-enteritis, but we have to make sure.'

'And if it's not?'

'We'll talk about that tomorrow when we have more facts to go on,' he said. 'Meanwhile he's perfectly safe on the drip. It's going very well and you've no cause to worry. Just keep him as happy and relaxed as you can. That's a very good little boy you've got there, haven't you?'

He was gone before they could ask any more questions.

They stood for a moment together in the corridor.

'Well, he was very reassuring, wasn't he?' Derek remarked.

'Yes.' Heather paused and then added, 'But he would be, wouldn't he?'

Since that was exactly what he himself had been thinking Derek didn't reply. 'Let's go back to the ward,' he said.

All day long they sat by the bed, reading aloud, telling him bits of news from home, making up stories for him. It was hard to tell if he was listening, as he lay there, inert, his eyes closed. He seemed unaware of them, unaware of the drip, unaware even of the cannula, thrust like a thorn into the back of his left hand. Derek had a feeling that his son would rather have been left undisturbed, but instinct told him to go on pushing life at him, to refuse to leave him in peace to drift away.

Heather went home for a while in the evening. When she

came back at seven o'clock they sat one on each side of the bed until Jonathan sank into a deep sleep. There was nothing they could do. Heather was looking desperately tired and ill. He was not surprised when Sister said to him, 'I should take Mrs Barnicoat home, I think. The best thing she can do for Jonathan is to take good care of herself now.'

Heather had left a meal ready prepared for them. He looked at the food on the table but all he could think of was the little body lying on the bed, the feel of the dry hand, bony inside the loose skin and he knew that he couldn't eat. They glanced at each other, and then Heather began to clear away the food and they went upstairs. In bed she broke down for the first time and sobbed. He didn't try to stop her or find reassuring words; he shared her fear too totally for that. He held her closely to him until, frozen as they both were by fear, they seemed to begin to warm each other. Afterwards he thought that it was strange that they should have made love at such a time. It was unlike anything they had ever known before. Something profounder, simpler passed between them, as body reached out to body, passionately giving and receiving comfort and strength, fighting back at despair with the power of human love. But he saw that she was stronger the next morning; she seemed calmer, more ready for anything the day might bring.

Jonathan was no longer attached to the drip. He looked different. He was restless now, twisting and turning on his bed.

'We've just had a bit of a struggle with him trying to get him to take ten millilitres of fluid by mouth,' Sister explained to them quietly. 'We had to force it down, I'm afraid.'

'Oh, dear.'

'Well, it's pretty nasty, you know. It's a solution of dextrose and saline. None of them ever cares for it. But he must take it every hour. Oh, here's Dr Mackenzie to have a word with you.'

Back in the little alcove in the corridor, the registrar told them that the tests were negative.

'So that danger is ruled out,' he said. 'Tell me, has Jonathan suffered some stress recently?'

They looked at each other.

'Yes,' Derek said. 'We've been separated for about nine months now.'

A shutter seemed to pass over the doctor's face: surprise instantly veiled.

'I don't mean that kind of separation,' Derek explained hastily. 'I just mean parted, you know. I've had to move for my work and the family have stayed behind here because we couldn't get a house. It hasn't been easy and, yes, the boys have felt the strain, I'm sure. So has my wife.'

'And would you say he's a sensitive boy? One who doesn't show his feelings easily?'

'Oh, yes,' Heather said. 'He bottles things up. Just the opposite of his elder brother who lets everyone know what he thinks.'

The registrar smiled. 'It's easier for the ones like that,' he said. 'Now I'm fairly sure that tension is at the bottom of all this. It could be that some mild infection started off the diarrhoea and vomiting, but then instead of just getting over it as he normally would, the tension prolonged it and he developed a kind of reflex vomiting whenever he drank even water. Maybe subconsciously he was asking for extra love and attention because he felt insecure. It's hard to tell with children – they react in ways adults find difficult to understand.'

'So what do you think?' Derek asked. 'I mean, what do we do now?'

'We'll keep a close watch on him. I think we'll leave him in that little room for the rest of today. The less upset he has the better. You just keep him as happy and relaxed as possible. He'll have to go back on the drip unless he takes his ten millilitres of fluid every hour, so anything you can do to help with that is very useful. Of course children are funny. Some will take medicine better from a parent than a nurse. Some make much more fuss with their mothers than they do with us. But I'm sure you'll work out the best way with the staff here. What about your other children?'

'A friend has the little one and the other's at school, then he'll go back to her house at teatime.'

'Well, remember they need you too,' he said gently.

'Yes, they do,' Heather said with sudden conviction. 'I felt very torn before my husband came back, not knowing whether to stay with Jonathan or try to keep things as normal as possible for the others by being at home. But I think I'll go home now and let Derek stay here with Jonathan.'

'That's a wise decision, Mrs Barnicoat. And you know sometimes sick children seem to be almost too close to their mothers. They seem to sense the anxiety that's in them. Fathers can be more casual somehow. Well, I'll see you tomorrow then.'

After he had gone Heather turned to Derek and said, 'I'll go home now. The Ant's beginning to be a bit unsettled and I think James will be thrilled if I pick him up from school. He's still not quite right. I'll try to keep things as normal as possible at home and you stay here with Jonathan.'

He put his arms round her. She spoke matter of factly, but he knew what it cost her to leave Jonathan when he was so ill.

'I'll explain to him,' he said. 'It'll make another topic of conversation.'

She smiled. 'Yes, it's heavy going sometimes, isn't it? I'll come back about eight then.'

He was startled, when he went back into the ward, to see that Jonathan was lying on his stomach, kneeling up, his bottom in the air. It might have been the Ant.

'They do that sometimes,' the nurse said quietly, seeing his expression. 'Little children do. As if they're trying to get back into the foetal position, when they're distressed. It's very awkward, if you're trying to keep them on the drip.'

So it was normal. It horrified him all the same, to see Jonathan lying there like that as if he was regressing into infancy.

He sat down by the bed.

'Here,' he said cheerfully but firmly. 'I don't fancy talking to your bottom. You just turn over and let me see your face.'

Jonathan rolled over. His face was flushed.

'Where's Mummy?' he asked.

'She's gone to look after the Ant. We left him with Mary when we came here. We took his Teddy too. And his bowl and his cup.'

Suddenly he thought of something.

'Do you remember how you taught the Ant to drink?'

A flicker of interest passed over Jonathan's face. He opened his eyes. Teaching the Ant to drink had been one of the great achievements of his life.

The nurse noticed the change. She glanced at Derek.

'You tell nurse what you did,' Derek said.

'The Ant,' Jonathan said slowly, 'couldn't drink, and Mummy couldn't teach him, so I said, "It's easy. You put your cup to your mouth and let your top lip paddle." '

'Can you show me?' the nurse asked.

Derek propped him up and the nurse held the spoon, with its ten millilitres of dextrose and saline that he must have, up to his mouth.

'Like this,' Jonathan said. 'Just let your top lip paddle. It's easy.'

He slurped his lip in the liquid and they watched as the muscles of his throat moved. The spoon was empty.

'That's very good,' nurse said. 'Would you show some of the other nurses later on, so that they'll be able to teach the babies? We do have a lot of trouble teaching them, you know. They'd much rather go on sucking their bottles, because it's easier.'

'It's not very nice stuff. Haven't you any proper water?'

'Sorry. That's all we've got today.'

Jonathan sighed. 'All right,' he said. 'I suppose I'll get used to it.'

One by one at hourly intervals during the day, members of the hospital staff came in and requested a demonstration and Jonathan, quite unsuspecting, showed them. How easy it is to deceive children in small ways, Derek reflected as he watched each time the gentle movement of the throat and the emptying of the spoon. But in the bigger things they see so easily through our adult deceptions.

By the time they left him that evening, Jonathan was looking, though still very pale and ill, somehow back in this world. There was even perhaps, Derek thought, a tinge of colour in his cheeks, but he didn't dare say so to Heather in case he was imagining it.

The next morning when they arrived, he was sitting up in bed. 'I'm hungry,' he said. 'Did you bring me anything to eat?'

They stared at him, dumbfounded, then Derek managed to say, 'What do you fancy, then?'

'Sausages.'

'You can have milk today,' the nurse interrupted, 'mixed with water. But tomorrow you can have lovely things like jelly.'

The paediatrician came in early that morning.

'We can hardly believe it,' Derek told him as they talked in the usual alcove in the corridor. 'I mean this time yesterday he couldn't take a sip of water and now he's requesting sausages.'

The paediatrician smiled. 'Children are like that,' he said. 'They sink down very rapidly. It can be very alarming the way they decline, especially for their parents. But then, you see, they recover quickly too. He'll bounce back, you'll see.'

'You don't think it's just a passing improvement and he'll relapse again? I mean it's permanent?'

'Oh yes. He'll improve rapidly now. We'll get him on to a light diet tomorrow. He might even have a little something tonight. We'll see how he goes on. I should think you'll be able to take him home on Monday or Tuesday. Keep him as relaxed as you can, that's the main thing. And plenty of fluids.'

'We're so grateful to you . . .'

He dismissed their thanks. 'I shan't be in tomorrow,' he said, 'but I'll check him on Monday.'

Heather went home and Derek spent the rest of the day playing snakes and ladders and reading aloud to him the same story out of his favourite book. He revelled in having his father's undivided attention. His eyes were brighter and there was colour in his cheeks again. He requested bacon and eggs at tea time but only got more milk. That evening, for the first time he didn't want to be left.

'We'll be back tomorrow morning,' Derek said firmly, and

propelled Heather out of the ward.

'Shall I have to go on being nice to him, Dad, when he comes home?' James asked them that evening when they got back.

'Aren't you always nice to him?'

'No. But you see when he was ill, Mum said I had to be nice to him so he'd get better. And I was. And he got worse and had to go into hospital. It didn't do much good all that being nice to him.'

He paused and then added, 'I don't think I'd do it again.'

All the same he asked that night if the Ant could be moved upstairs to share his room.

'I miss Jonathan's noises,' he admitted.

After he had taken the cot upstairs and settled the boys down for the night, Derek rang the headmaster.

'Stay at home for Monday,' Mr Dodsworthy said. 'Oh, and you might as well stay for Tuesday since the governors have so unpredictably given us the day off. Then you'll be sure of bringing your boy back home from hospital yourself. We're managing very well here. We'll see you on Wednesday morning.'

'It's very good of you. I should like to stay to settle him in. I'm really sorry about it all.'

'Nonsense. These things happen. You helped us out with the education cruise at Easter. We owe you a good deed or two. Besides,' he added, 'I've always found that the best teachers are the ones who care a lot about their own families. The other sort are a bit theoretical, you know.'

Derek thanked him and slipped out to buy some wine while Heather was cooking.

'Just think, we can have the sitting-room to ourselves again,' she said, 'now that the Ant's vacated it.'

'I'll make a fire.'

'Oh, it's not worth it. We never have one now you're away.'

'Well, I'm not away, silly, and of course it's worth it.' He kissed her quickly. 'I'll go out and get the fuel.'

He rummaged around the shed finding kindling and logs and the remains of half a sack of coal. By the time she had brought in their supper on trays he had a good fire roaring up the chimney and the wine was warming on the hearth.

'Let's just ring the hospital first,' Heather said. She spoke to the night sister. Jonathan had eaten a bowl of cornflakes and was fast asleep.

'My goodness, but that's given me an appetite,' Heather said, watching as Derek filled her glass. They drank to their son's health.

'It seems weeks and weeks,' she said. 'I can't believe he's only been in hospital for four days.'

'I've rung the head and he says I can stay until Wednesday. It was his idea. I didn't ask.'

'That's lovely. You'll see Jonathan safely home. I think that matters. The doctor said we must try to keep him feeling as secure as possible.'

'We will, my darling. And anyway, now that we know we've got the house and it's all going to be all right, I shall be able to come home at weekends and not have to househunt and—'

'What house?'

'Wellington Square, of course. What other? Oh, my God, I forgot to tell you.'

He stared at her, disbelieving.

'Derek, what is it?'

'I must be mad. I quite forgot.'

'Tell me.'

'The solicitor rang. It must have been on Wednesday. He rang me at school. He'd tried to ring you here but there was no reply.'

'That's right. I was out at the hospital all day.'

'Apparently the Soddies can have the house they wanted after all, so everything's moving. I can't think how I forgot to tell you.'

'Because it wasn't important,' she said, 'compared with Jonathan.'

He thought of the little figure, pale and still on the bed, felt again the cold fear. No, nothing mattered compared with that.

'We'll have to tell the Armstrongs,' Heather said. 'Won't they be thrilled?'

There were freak snowstorms in the week before they went on holiday. Bunty woke one morning early, with the brightness of its reflected light shining in through the window. Country born and bred, she had always loved the snow. She got dressed quickly and went upstairs to look at it before it was all spoiled.

This was the day the baby would have been born; how different her life would have been. She stood at the top of the area steps and it was so beautiful, even this mean London street, that her eyes filled with tears. It was not like the snow of her childhood, it was not thick and challenging, there were no drifts. It just lay like a delicate and cold shroud, over everything, so that the outlines were all recognizable but somehow everything was changed. A woman, making her way cautiously along the pavement, looked at her curiously, as she stood there, a small, neat figure gazing intently out at the world. It was a childish little face, she observed, but there was suffering in it, and resolution.

'I'll ring the travel agents,' Christopher said, 'and see if the insurance covers delay through snow.'

But the snow had all gone by the end of the week.

'A clear evening sky,' Christopher said, interrupting his packing on the eve of their departure, to peer up through the window. 'And the forecast's good. Where did we put the weighing scales?'

'Weighing scales?'

'You know, the bathroom scales we were given for a wedding present.'

'Oh, yes, they're in a box in the bedroom cupboard. We didn't leave them out for fear of rust, you remember?'

He ferreted around in the overflowing cupboard, found the scales and proceeded to weigh his luggage carefully.

'It's well underweight,' he said with satisfaction. 'How about yours?'

Hers, as she had feared, was over the limit.

'You can just give house room to two pairs of my shoes,' she told him, laughing. He took them with feigned reluctance. Then he closed her bulging case for her and tied on the labels.

'Not bad,' he said, glancing at his watch. 'Just gone ten and everything ready for the morning. I'm off to my bath.'

He was pleased with her and pleased with the success of his plans for this holiday. It had given her something to look forward to. She was taking more interest in life now, he noticed. It was high time she got back to normal. Of course, he reflected tolerantly as he went into the bathroom and turned on the taps, he understood her disappointment over the baby. After all, it had been disappointing for him too, especially being a boy, like that. But he had accepted it. One had to accept these things. No good moping. Better luck next time, that had been his motto. He climbed into the bath and began to scrub himself vigorously and systematically.

Despite the good forecast it was raining when they set off the next morning. They stood for a moment at the bottom of the area steps while she put on a headscarf and he turned up his coat collar. Then they took up the luggage again and were just turning towards the steps when they heard the telephone ringing behind them.

'Shall we go back and answer it?' she asked.

'No,' he said. Then he hesitated. 'Well, perhaps we'd better. It might be about a house.'

He put down the cases, found the key and opened up the flat. But the telephone had stopped ringing before he could get to it.

# Chapter Eleven

'Good Lord, I didn't know you were back among us,' the chairman said, as Claud followed him into the lift.

'Just for a few days, sir, to try to get an agent for the Ethiopia job.'

'Really? Looking for an agent out there, are you?'

'Yes. If you remember, we talked about it on the telephone when you rang me. The agent I thought was coming out changed his mind, so I'm looking for another at short notice.'

'Ah, yes, of course.'

He had forgotten all about it, Claud realized. Just as well he hadn't depended on offers of help from him.

'People are so unreliable nowadays,' the chairman said testily. 'You can't depend on anyone any more. Well, I'm very sorry. That puts you in rather a hole, doesn't it?'

'Yes, it does. So I decided the best way was to fly back and try to arrange something myself.'

'Well, good luck with it all,' the chairman said benignly by way of valediction as Claud got out on the fourth floor and he himself continued on his way up in the lift which would take him to the lonely eminence of the top-floor office, where his vast desk and elaborate brass inkstand awaited him.

Claud walked down the corridor to the room which he used when he was in London. He made a few phone calls, asked a secretary to ring his wife and tell her he was back in England and would be home that night. Then he asked to be put through to the tendering department.

'Bill,' he said, 'can I have a word with you?'

171

'Of course. I'd no idea you were back. What can I do to help?'

'It's an off-chance, I know, but is there anyone of your lot might conceivably be persuaded to fly out to Ethiopia now? And I mean *now*. Anyone barmy enough?'

There was a pause.

'I doubt it, Claud. I very much doubt it.'

'It's a real crisis, Bill,' Claud persisted.

'You know I'd help if I could,' Bill said, 'But I just can't think of anyone. Well, there is one young chap . . .'

'Go on,' Claud encouraged him eagerly.

'He did well out in Nigeria as sub-agent on that big mountain reservoir contract, but I don't think he'd want to go. He specifically joined me because he didn't want to work abroad any more.'

'It's worth asking,' Claud said. 'I've known people say that they're longing to get back to England, and then when they actually come back they soon get disenchanted.'

'Well, there's a lot to be disenchanted about in England now.'

Claud laughed, then went on more seriously, 'Look, if your young hopeful can be persuaded to go out for a couple of years, you can certainly have him back at the end of it. We shall be pulling out once we're shot of this contract. It's a dead-end job.'

'I'll sound him out. I'll send him up to you, shall I, if I think there's any hope?'

'Thanks. I'm here all day. I'll be leaving for Leicester tonight. And Bill . . .'

'Yes?'

'No need to paint a gloomy picture of things out there in Ethiopia. Forget the dead-end job bit.'

Bill laughed. 'What do you take me for?' he asked. 'I know the drill.'

Bunty stood at the kitchen sink and began to sort out the holiday washing. There seemed to be an astonishing amount of it, considering it had been created by two people who had only been away for a week. It was not so much dirty, she thought, looking at the great heap on the floor, as crumpled and sandy. Some of it she would take to the launderette, she decided, picking out the sandals and flip-flops and knocking them together over the sink to get rid of the sand. It was adhesive stuff; she took a wet cloth to the sandals and rubbed hard while the rubber flip-flops bobbed about in the water. Then she carried them into the sitting-room and ranged them in front of the gas fire to dry.

The letter was still on the table. Even the sight of it brought on a sudden feeling of panic. It had arrived that morning. It seemed that the solicitors had been trying in vain to ring them, and had therefore written to let them know, as a matter of urgency, that the cottage was now available. Christopher had read the letter out to her, then he had seized her round the waist and danced her round the flat, whooping with joy, telling her that everything had come right in the end, just as he had said it would, hadn't he, all along?

Dismayed by the prospect of having to face it all again, the cottage with the apple tree, the kindly Barnicoats with their three little boys, she had made a poor attempt at seeming pleased, but Chris, late for work and delighted with life, hadn't noticed the effect of the letter on her. Even now, hours later, just seeing the envelope there on the table sent shivers of fear through her.

It was cruel. She wasn't ready yet; she needed time to build up her new strength. Because it had done her good, that holiday. Everyone had said it would, but she hadn't really believed them. Already it seemed a long time ago, she thought, as she dunked Chris's maroon-coloured shirt in the sink and watched the water turn pink, that week among the rocks and cliffs with always the sound of the sea tumbling and breaking in the background. It had been quite different from anything she had imagined. She could still remember the shock of the first sight of it. They had arrived in darkness the night before so had seen nothing as they were decanted from the coach straight into the hotel. But the next morning they had emerged from its luxurious stuffiness into a fresh world of pink cliffs and ancient rocks towering out of the nearby sea. Timeless, they seemed, and indestructible; she looked at them with awe, and the row of concrete hotels suddenly seemed a very temporary aberration.

They walked for miles each day along those cliffs and sands. Once they were out of sight of the concrete blocks they saw almost nobody and there were no more man-made things. They walked hand in hand and she thought they were back as they used to be a year ago. What had happened in between was something which couldn't be changed now, just accepted. It belonged in the past. It was immutable. It was no good reliving it, as if by going over it again and again, she could somehow alter it. For the first time since she had lost her baby she had a feeling of acceptance, or at least that acceptance was a possibility. She knew it was a feeling that she must cling to. She must try to bring it back home with her, not lose it when she returned to the familiar London things, the same old flat. It was a germ of survival; she must cherish it, nourish it.

But now, before she had had time to build up that little strength, this challenge had been thrown at her. She simply could not face the memory and pain of the cottage. But she couldn't tell poor Chris, not after all his care of her and that expensive holiday which had helped to heal and strengthen her, though not quite in the way that he had imagined.

She must get on with the immediate things, she thought, removing the maroon shirt from the pink and gritty water. She would sort out the clothes for the launderette and do the shopping while she was about it. Determinedly she sat herself down at the table, pushed the solicitor's letter out of sight behind the terracotta lamp from the Algarve and began to write a shopping list.

'Come in and sit down,' Claud said, after they had exchanged introductions. He liked the look of this young man and did his best to put him at his ease.

'Incredibly awful spring you're having in England,' he

remarked jovially. 'Maybe you think there's something to be said for missing the full rigours of the English summer if you can?'

The young man laughed and agreed.

'Well, now to business. You've had experience of working for us abroad?'

'Yes, two years in Nigeria under Mr Medway.'

'Yes. I've had a word with Mr Medway and the African department that you've had dealings with.'

He smiled approvingly as if what he had heard had been very satisfactory. The young man waited, hanging on his every word.

'And you'd like to work abroad again? You enjoyed it?'

'Oh, yes I enjoyed it very much. And I prefer being on site actually to being in the office, but domestically we felt it was time to be settled.'

'Ah well, you know in this profession you have to keep these things in proportion.'

'I appreciate that.'

'Well, as no doubt you've been told, there's a great opportunity out there for the right person. So I'm looking around and I've made a few enquiries and it seemed to me that that right person, able and deserving of promotion, might just possibly be yourself.'

He went on to explain what the job entailed, painting a rosy picture. The young man listened very attentively.

'But it isn't just the job,' Claud concluded, 'it's what could follow from it. There are great opportunities for the sort of chap who shows what he's made of by going out there at short notice. We shall no doubt soon be looking for a contracts manager for the whole area and then the area will probably expand as works grows, so the job will expand with it. Now I'm not making any promises, nobody knows how things will turn out in this uncertain profession of ours, but naturally the man on the spot, the man who has proved himself, will get that job. And later he'll be in line for one of the overseas director-ships and finally, who knows, he may be sitting in my chair?'

He smiled disparagingly. 'If he's fool enough to want it,' he added.

Christopher Armstrong listened to him, stunned. Was he really in this office on the fourth floor being offered these prizes? He was nervous, excited, apprehensive and hopeful all at once.

'I'd jump at it, sir, really I would,' he said enthusiastically. 'The problem is we've just heard we can buy a cottage we've wanted for months and thought we couldn't have. It fell through last summer and we've just heard we have the chance of buying it. It would be very difficult to go abroad at this precise moment.'

'I understand. We all have to make these decisions. And of course buying a house can seem the most important thing in your life, I don't doubt that.'

He paused and looked hard at the young man.

'But do bear in mind that these chances are rare. Opportunity doesn't knock twice, not in our line of business, it doesn't.'

He let the words sink in and then added, 'And of course if you are seen not to be mobile in a profession which requires mobility a black mark does tend to go up against your name.'

He smiled as if to soften the threat.

Then he sighed and went on, 'Naturally we shall have no difficulty in finding somebody else who'll take this job and all it has to offer, but I felt you deserved the opportunity.'

There was in his voice a note of disappointment that a favour offered by the firm was being so ungratefully rejected. The chairman himself could not have improved upon the performance. It filled Christopher Armstrong with guilt and shame.

'It's very good of you to consider me, sir,' he burst out. 'Please don't misunderstand me. I do appreciate the trust you have shown in me. It's just that I can't say immediately. I'd need to ask my wife what she feels.'

'But of course, my dear chap. I don't expect an answer this afternoon. Heaven forbid! I'm not unreasonable, I hope. Tomorrow will do.'

Christopher sighed with relief, like one taken back into the fold.

'Talk it over with your good lady this evening,' Claud suggested.

'Yes, sir, I'll do that. Thank you.'

'Look here, why not go off early this afternoon? Give you time to think about it. I know it's come as quite a surprise to you.'

'That's very good of you, sir.'

'And don't forget what I said,' Claud went on, holding out his hand. 'The opportunities are boundless for the right man.'

He shook hands so vigorously that it somehow seemed that they were clinching the deal. Then he walked across the room with Christopher and opened the door for him.

'Pop in and let me know what you've decided first thing tomorrow,' he said.

'Yes. Thank you. I'll come up at nine, shall I?'

Still bewildered, he found his way back to the lift and down to his own department. Distracted as he was and fearful of telling Bunty, he didn't get much work done. In the end he decided to do as Mr Soddie had suggested and go home early.

Bunty came back laden. She dumped the sailing bag full of clean, warm clothes down in the bedroom and decanted the shopping over all the available surface space in the little kitchen. But all the time, as she tipped the groceries out of paper bags, fought her way into the contents of plastic containers, rolled chicken pieces in flour, she was arguing with herself. What were the alternatives to the cottage? Even if she could bring herself to tell Chris, did she really want them to stay here and go on looking for another cottage? It was crazy. Of course they must go ahead with the Barnicoats' cottage. But oh, not yet, not yet.

She poured oil into the frying pan and added the pieces of floured chicken, poking them about as they frizzled. She was surprised to hear somebody coming down the area steps, shoes on metal rungs. She heard a key turn in the lock.

'Something smells good,' Chris said, coming into the kitchen.

'You're very early,' she said, as he kissed her.

'Well, yes, I am, aren't I? I'll explain about that later.'

She was too absorbed in her own anxiety to notice that he sounded guilty.

He waited until after supper. Then he said, 'Well, there's been a development. There's something we must talk about.'

'Development?' she repeated sharply, fearing a sudden visit to the cottage.

'Don't be alarmed. Nobody is going to make us go or anything like that.'

'Go where?'

He explained about the job abroad, going through all his carefully rehearsed arguments about why they should accept this opportunity which had been so unexpectedly offered to him.

Her reaction astonished him. She didn't seem to care at all, she scarcely heeded his excuses. In fact she interrupted them to say, 'But of course we'll go if you want to.'

'But the cottage,' he said. 'We've only just heard about the cottage.'

'I expect we'll find something else when we get back. Something is bound to turn up.'

'But you've always wanted the Barnicoats' cottage,' he objected, baffled by her. 'I thought you loved it.'

She shrugged. 'Yes, I did once,' she said. 'But I've got over it, I suppose.'

She couldn't explain. It had all been spoiled, but reasoning would not comprehend it. Only experience did that.

Her relief at being spared the pain of ever seeing the cottage again was so great that it seemed to set the seal on her new-found strength. It would be marvellous to leave the flat with all its reminders. It was amazing how everything had worked out. She felt a great surge of confidence, she who had thought she was an unlucky person, unloved by the gods.

She asked him more about the job and he told her, taken

aback by the shrewdness of her questions from one who had always taken everything on trust.

'It's not just this actual job,' he explained. 'It's what it may lead to, the opportunities that will come afterwards. The opportunities are boundless for the right man.'

'Is that what he said? I mean are those his very words?'

'Yes, I suppose so.'

He hadn't realized that he'd been quoting.

'If the job's already well underway, what happened to the last agent?'

'I don't know. He didn't say.'

'It just seems odd that it's happened so unexpectedly. I mean you'd think they'd have somebody next in line?'

'I suppose the next in line wasn't suitable to take charge. It isn't like having understudies in a play, you know,' he added defensively. 'You can't plan ahead too far in our profession, you never know where the next job's going to be.'

'No, of course not.'

She paused and then went on, 'Yet they can promise you all these things if you take this job? As if the future was all mapped out?'

He shrugged.

'I'm only telling you what he said.'

She wasn't as convinced as he was that the job was so marvellous. It all sounded just a bit too good to be true. And the short notice, that had a certain air of desperation about it. But she didn't say so, not wanting to spoil it all for him. He deserved to take what he saw as his great chance, so she would not carp. Let him enjoy the moment.

Besides, she realized suddenly, when the let-down came, if it came, she would be able to help him, support him. It wouldn't be too terrible, for she was stronger now. Nothing could ever hurt as much as losing the baby had done, not loss of job or home or anything. It had given her a curious strength. She was just sorry that he was quite so carried away by this offer. He shouldn't be so trusting. For the first time she felt older than he was, more wary.

She had been wrong, she reflected, to look back on their early married life as a time when they'd been interdependent. It hadn't been so. She had been too dependent on him, too beholden, too inclined to seek in him the father she had not known. She shouldn't have put such a burden on such young shoulders. It had made him try too hard to take charge of both their lives. Now there would be more equal sharing. She knew it. They would support each other as independent adults, who could manage without the other if they had to. Their dependence on each other would be of choice, not necessity. Freed at last of her childish dependence on him, she knew that she would never look to him as she had once done, which was just as well now that she had come to realize that he wasn't as omniscient as she had once supposed.

'We'd better answer that letter now,' she said. 'It's only fair to let the Barnicoats know as soon as possible.'

'Yes, of course. They'll have to find someone else to buy the cottage. After all, they're buying a house somewhere in the Midlands, aren't they?'

'Yes,' she said. 'In Leicestershire, where he works.'

'Your very good health, my dear,' Claud Soddie said, raising his glass to his wife. 'You're looking remarkably well, if I may say so.'

The red velvet dress suited her, he noticed; it went well with her pale skin and dark hair. Almost Spanish, she looked. Handsome.

She smiled back at him, accepting the compliment gracefully.

'Welcome home,' she said.

'Oh, it's good to be back,' he told her. 'I'm sorry I couldn't come home yesterday, Ro. I just had to stay in London today and get this young chap fixed up to go out to Ethiopia. It was a vital day's work, that was.'

'So you needn't go back? To Ethiopia, I mean?'

'No,' he said definitely. 'I'm quite determined to leave the rest of them to get on with it now. I've done my bit out there, I reckon. Oh, a few phone calls maybe, but there's no reason why they shouldn't manage without me. I can't tell you,' he went on with anticipatory relish, 'how I'm looking forward to being able to concentrate on my new job at last.'

She smiled up at him, enjoying his enthusiasm.

'And thanks to you, my dear,' he said, 'we'll be in our new home on schedule too.'

He raised his glass to her again.

'I must congratulate you,' he said, 'on doing a very good job on Mrs Moon. A very good job indeed. I couldn't have done it better myself.'

She did not reply.

'I was just saying,' he said as Simon came into the room, 'what a good job your mother has done on Mrs Moon.'

Simon went to the bookshelves, took out a book and went out again without answering.

His father shrugged.

'Boarding school would improve his manners,' he announced. 'Now that we know we shan't be here next term, I think we might consider sending him away to join his brothers.'

'No,' she said. 'He will be staying on here. He can board with Mr Francis.'

'Who?'

'Mr Francis. He teaches economics and he and his wife take in the odd boarder, mostly those whose parents have had to move for one reason or another when the boys are in the middle of exams.'

'Well, I'd have thought you'd have waited for me to decide.'

'There's nothing to decide. He obviously can't move in the middle of his exams. So there's really nothing to discuss.'

He began to say something, but thought better of it. Instead he lay back in his big leather armchair, closed his eyes and relaxed. Rosemary looked at him. Was this the moment, she wondered, to talk to him about what she and Mrs Moon had arranged about the garden? No. He wasn't going to like the idea; she would let him enjoy his first few days at home in peace, before she broke the news.

# Chapter Twelve

'I don't believe it, I just don't believe it,' Derek said, shaking Mrs Peck's telephone, as if by so doing he could unscramble Heather's words and rearrange them into a more acceptable message.

'You'll have to, darling. I'm sorry to ring with such awful news. I couldn't take it in either, at first. At least they let us know promptly.'

'But they were so keen, the Armstrongs. I mean they just loved the cottage.'

'Oh, they still do, they make it quite clear in their letter that it's only because he's going to work abroad. Hence the change of plans.'

'But they said they weren't going to work abroad any more. They wanted to settle down and have a family and all that. She told you.'

Heather sighed. 'I know. I'm as shattered as you are, but there it is. Apparently with all the government cuts there is less work at home for engineers.'

'Well, I suppose we must just try to think positive. There were lots of other people who wanted the cottage when we advertised it last year. Didn't you keep a list?'

She laughed. 'I threw that out ages ago. Part of the tidying-up campaign. I think it would be simpler if we put another advertisement in the Sunday paper. Like last time.'

'Can you see to it?'

'Yes, I'll use the same wording as before. After all it brought them in in droves.' She hesitated. 'I suppose we'll have to tell the Soddies, won't we?'

Derek groaned.

'Must we? Already?'

'Well, they'll be wondering why we don't go ahead with the contracts now, won't they?'

'But if we tell them we can't sign yet, what's to stop them selling Wellington Square to somebody else?'

'Oh, she wouldn't do that.'

'*He* might.'

'I don't think she'd go along with it. I got to know her a bit when I went to see her about carpets and everything, and I think she's got more character than shows at first sight. Besides, they must appreciate the way we hung on when their purchase was held up by the old lady. I mean we didn't rush off and buy something else, did we?'

He laughed. 'We did our best, if you remember. Cast your mind back to The Limes and The Old Rectory.'

'Yes, but the fact is that we didn't buy anything else. We waited for their house, and I think they'll be grateful for that and give us a bit of time now that we've got a problem.'

'I hope you're right. Maybe I just don't have your touching faith in my fellow human beings. Years of teaching have made me cynical.'

'Well, let's not worry about it, until we've seen what our advertisement produces. Oh Derek, doesn't it make you wonder how anybody ever synchronizes buying and selling a house?'

'I must say I sometimes wish I'd never taken this job.'

'Rubbish,' she said sharply.

'When I think of all the trouble it's caused – not just the cottage, but Jonathan, and between us . . .'

'But you enjoy the job, don't you? You were ready for a move. You know you were.'

'Oh, the job's all right. It's marvellous. But the family's paid a price for my job satisfaction, hasn't it?'

'Worth it, my darling, so you just shut up about the job. Now I'm going to go and send off that advertisement and then I'll blitz the house. Oh Lord, we shall have to keep tidy again ready for showing people round. That's the painful bit.'

He heard her laugh, he heard Mrs Peck's drawing-room door open.

'Well, this call's costing the earth,' Heather said. 'Good-night, darling.' She made a kissing sound down the telephone.

He smacked his lips noisily back. 'I love you,' he said.

Mrs Peck crossed the hall. He heard the kitchen door shut behind her.


'I want to see one of the partners immediately,' Claud told the receptionist in the estate agent's office. 'Soddie's the name.'

She was going to ask if he had an appointment, thought better of it and rang through to the office of the senior partner, Maurice Freeman.

'You can go straight in,' she said, getting up and leading the way to the inner sanctuary.

Maurice Freeman was a morose-looking man at the best of times, and these were not the best of times for estate agents. When Claud told him that the purchase of his house was delayed, he pulled down the corners of his mouth and looked even more lugubrious than usual.

'I'm sorry to hear that,' he said, shaking his head gloomily. 'Very sorry. But not altogether surprised. It's happening all the time, all around us. Delays, housing chains held up because purchasers can't sell their own houses. What's the trouble in your case?'

'The Barnicoats who are, as you know, buying our house, have just informed us that they can't go ahead yet as the people who were buying their cottage in Surrey have let them down.'

'The old story. Transactions are taking at least twice as long as they used to. Fortunately Surrey is easier than here. They'll sell in time.'

'Well, I'm not prepared to give them time.'

'I'm afraid there's nothing I can do to help you, Mr Soddie. It's up to the Barnicoats' agent.'

'No,' Claud corrected him impatiently. 'I want you to find me another purchaser.'

Maurice Freeman looked at him, surprised. 'But the Barnicoats haven't gone back on the purchase,' he pointed out. 'They still want your house, don't they?'

'As far as I know, yes.'

'Then my advice to you would be to wait.'

'It's all very well, but I want to get settled into my northern office.'

'They waited for you while you settled for your house up north,' Maurice Freeman pointed out.

'Yes, I appreciate that. All the same, business is business and I have my own interests to consider. In my view one can't mix sentiment with business and the sale of one's house is a business transaction, after all. If someone else came now and made an offer I couldn't afford to refuse it.'

'I think it is very unlikely that such a person will appear at the moment. You must understand that the housing situation has completely changed in the last few months. We're in a buyers' market now.'

Claud glanced at his watch. 'Well, now, look here,' he said, 'I want you to put the house on the market again.' The agent shook his head. 'Surely you don't have scruples about it?'

'It's not that,' Maurice Freeman told him, with his gloomy, deprecatory smile. 'It's simply that the partners had a meeting last week and decided to take on no more houses. We've got too many on our books already.'

Claud looked at him in astonishment. He had not expected this.

'It's something that has never happened before,' the estate agent told him. 'But we feel that there is absolutely no point in taking on any more until the ones we have already get moving. You're luckier than most vendors in that you have a potential purchaser who definitely wants your house and owns a cottage in an area where sales, though slow, are not nearly as difficult as they are up here. You would be unwise to risk losing him.'

He got up and held out his hand.

'I'm sorry I can't be more helpful' he said.

'Well, I'll give it a month,' Claud said, 'and see what they can come up with in that time. By the way,' he added, as he made for the door, 'No need to mention this visit to my wife if you happen to be in touch with her. I don't want her worried, you know.'

He made his way downstairs, puzzled to find that his disappointment at the outcome of the interview was modified by something that felt strangely like relief.

Abstracted, he did not reply to the receptionist's greeting, but hurried past her to the street door. She shrugged. 'Well, be like that then,' she muttered to herself. 'Well named, you are.'

Her employer, following his client down the stairs, heard her. He looked at her morosely, smiled his lugubrious smile and shook his head.

'There's a nice man inside,' he told her, 'trying to get out.'

'Not putting up much of a struggle, if you ask me,' she said, watching as the subject of their remarks got into his car and drove quickly away.

Jenny Pierce rolled up the tape measure and stood staring around the room disconsolately. It was no good. There was no way Aunt Sybil's furniture would fit in here. It was a nice flat. It suited her. Originally a vast Victorian drawing-room, it had been partitioned, when the house was converted into flats, to make a sitting-room with a bedroom and bathroom off. She shared the use of a kitchen downstairs, but rarely exercised her right to it, preferring to eat out. An electric kettle and toaster seemed to cover all her other culinary requirements.

She wandered back into the bedroom. It had fitted cup-boards down the entire length of one wall. That had been one of its attractions for her when she first came to look at the flat. The bed took up most of another wall, which was broken by the door into the sitting-room, the third wall had the bathroom leading off it, and the fourth was almost entirely taken up by a huge Georgian sash window. There was nowhere to put Aunt Sybil's pretty little kidney-shaped dressing table or the beauti-ful wardrobe. It was the same in the sitting-room, which had no wall space for the desk or the piecrust table or indeed any of the furniture, apart from a chair or two. For some reason she hated the idea of putting it all in store.

But it wasn't just the furniture. All the measuring up was only a distraction. Something to do, to stop her thinking. Try not to think about it, Jenny Pierce, she told herself; try to suppress the misery and the rage. Tim will be here soon, cling to that thought.

Part of herself still couldn't believe it. Yet the scene re-enacted itself quite clearly in her mind. She felt again the chill of the freezing cold conference room as she sat facing the baronial fireplace. Down at her stared the massive pair of oil paintings framed in gilt, of a nameless lady and gentleman, presumably Frobisher ancestors, once described to her by Andrew Bligh, the editorial director, as ruffly Elizabethan.

Around her the meeting had droned on. It always surprised her how much her male colleagues seemed to enjoy the sound of their own voices. They each said what needed to be said in about five minutes, then they waffled on interminably about matters of monumental insignificance, raising non-urgent problems for desultory discussion. Andrew was a good editor but he was no use at controlling a meeting and was quite incapable of persuading his colleagues either to stick to the point or shut up.

She had amused herself by staring at the two anonymous forebears of the chairman who looked so disapprovingly down at her, and carrying on imaginary conversations with them. She wondered idly what they made of her, Jenny Pierce, and if they were as cold in their silks and satins as she was in her Laura Ashley pinafore dress and lacy camiknickers from Millards. She should have dressed more warmly for the editorial scheduling meeting, but had quite forgotten, in her excitement over the progress of John Hooston's book, to dress for the arctic rigours of the conference room.

Her own books were last on the agenda. Prothers was carrying on about his admiral, agonizing now over a sub-title for the autobiography. The only moment of light relief was when he solemnly asked the assembled company what they thought of 'Pro-consul of the Western Seas' as a suitable sub-title for the admiral's memoirs.

When it came to her turn she had two books to report progress on, one at the proof stage, the other ready for publication next month. Then she began her brief report on John's book, intending to give some idea of its schedule to the production and sales department. She had hardly got launched when Andrew Bligh interrupted her. 'I'd hoped to have a word with you before this meeting,' he said, 'concerning this book. The chairman only told me yesterday that he regarded it as insufficiently commercial.'

The words were clear enough, but their meaning didn't sink in. She thought it was a question of how many copies should be printed.

'We printed three thousand of his last book,' she said, 'and they sold out in fifteen months. I think we should print at least five thousand this time. Keep the price as low as possible. Hooston's ready to reach a wider market in my view.'

'It isn't a matter of how many we print,' Andrew interrupted her gently, 'but of not printing it at all.'

Even then she didn't understand. Vague fears of delay, of printers' strikes, even of unexpected paper shortages, chased each other across her mind.

'The chairman has vetoed it,' Andrew said.

It was suddenly very quiet in the conference room. Her colleagues, silent and embarrassed, gave her about as much support as the chairman's ancestors, who continued to gaze disapprovingly down at her. After what seemed an hour's silence, Andrew said, 'I should like to talk to you about it afterwards, Jenny. I'm sorry I didn't manage to do so before this meeting.'

She would have liked to get up and go there and then but the rest of the meeting had to be got through. Then she stumbled out after Andrew and followed him along the winding corridors of the old building to his room.

She had always liked him; he was funny and kind. He was also loyal to the firm. He simply handed on the chairman's views to her without comment. It was maddening.

'But Andrew, *you* passed it. It got official authorization from you. I thought that was all that mattered. I never even warned John . . .'

'The chairman takes a real interest, Jenny. He has a right to intervene. You have to remember it is a family business still. The family fortune is involved. And for the past few years, as you know, it has been very hard to make a profit. In fact, we've made an alarming loss.'

'But why choose to axe *this* book? You know it's one of the best on this list. You said as much to me yourself.'

'It isn't a question of literary quality, Jenny. The chairman feels we have to go for the best sellers, spend a lot on promotion and measure the sales in tens of thousands. We need safe books . . .'

'But it *is* safe. We won't lose on it. His last book sold out. It would have sold more copies if we'd printed more. This one will sell out too.'

'No, Jenny, we don't mean safe in that sense. If our policy is to spend huge sums on promotion, we have to be sure that the books will sell in huge numbers. The Hooston book simply isn't in that category.'

They talked long after everyone else had gone home. He didn't dispute any of her claims for the book. Yes, he agreed, the book was of real worth. Yes, it captured the period. Yes, it was entertaining and vivid. He had no doubt that the chairman had enjoyed the synopsis. But no, it was not commercial. Commerciality seemed to be all that mattered. She gripped her hands together as she remembered. How could they, how could they? What was the point of publishing if you couldn't turn a worthwhile manuscript into a book you were proud to have on your list? Meanwhile even the loyal Andrew admitted that they were publishing books they wouldn't have given shelf room to ten years ago.

Most dreadful of all, she had to tell John. In all their discussions about the book, it seemed that nobody had given a thought to its author. That was how much they cared. It shocked her. It was like casually sacking a good employee, that was how rejection would seem to John. He had thought it was all settled. Tomorrow she must write him a letter that, however carefully she phrased it, would damage him. He would have his three years' work flung back at him for no reason that could possibly seem in any way valid to him. And because it would make no sense to him it would shatter the frail confidence that he needed for his next book. It was more than this present book that they were destroying.

She paced the room. Unaccustomed self-doubt began to nag. She should have realized it would happen. She didn't doubt her ability to do that part of her job that involved recognizing literary worth, or working on a manuscript with its author, but perhaps she wasn't up to that part of her job that involved making market judgements. Not up to her job, she, Jenny Pierce not up to her job! The words kept going through her head. That was it, she thought in despair, that was why she had misled John Hooston, and tomorrow she had to write and tell him so.

What would she say to him? She was too hurt and bewildered to help him as she should. She tried to get a grip on herself. She needed to talk to somebody else about it before she wrote. It should have been Andrew Bligh, of course, but he had been no help, refusing to talk in other than commercial terms. Maybe he felt too guilty because he hadn't put up more of a fight for the book on her behalf. Maybe he had to consider his own career, for the trade was in recession and nobody's job was safe. Whatever the reason there'd been no help forthcoming. Tim would be better at helping her to clarify the real issue before she wrote to John. Thank God for Tim.

She glanced at her watch. Gone eight. Then she remembered. Usually he came here on Wednesdays, but last Monday she'd suggested he didn't come, as she had various chores to do. She couldn't even remember what they were now. She sat on the bed in sudden despair. If only she hadn't been so stupid and told him not to bother to come. Or if only they were always together, not just by special arrangement. Oh, please let him forget what I said, and come just the same because it's Wednesday.

As if in answer to her prayer, the doorbell rang. She rushed to answer it and, expecting Tim, was taken aback to find her landlady, Mrs Hogarth, standing on the threshold.

'Can I have a word with you, Miss Pierce?'

She sounded apologetic.

'Of course,' Jenny said, recovering herself with great effort. 'Come in. Have a drink.'

She liked Mrs Hogarth, a tiny cockney lady of immense wealth, whose father had bought up a great deal of property in London, including this house, when it was going cheap during the war. Much of it had been bombed but he had done quite well out of the compensation. The rest had been worth a fortune when things settled down in the post-war years.

She followed Jenny into the sitting-room and perched on the edge of a chair, her eyes darting about the room. Her sharp little face bore two circles of rouge, one each side of the great beak of a nose which was heavily coated with white powder. Her short hair, dyed a strong shade of black, grew spikily upwards. Bedraggled but cheeky, she had the look of a weather-beaten old starling.

'I'm not sure you'll want to give me a drink when you hear what I have to say,' she said, looking mournful but sounding cocky.

Jenny laughed.

'You should know me better than that,' she said. 'Here's your usual,' she added, handing her a glass.

'Well, I'll get it off my chest. The family's persuaded me to sell up and move out into the country, though what I'll do in Birmingham I'm sure I don't know.'

She drank half a glassful in one gulp.

'So you want me out?' Jenny asked directly.

'Oh, I wouldn't make you go, dear. I'd sooner sell the place with you in it. But of course it would be easier to sell with vacant possession. I'd get a better price. But there's no hurry, dear.'

'It's all right, Mrs Hogarth. Honestly, it's no bother for me to go.'

All the same, this second blow of the day shattered her more than she'd expected. It was one thing to choose to leave her home herself, in her own time. It was quite another to be asked to quit. It brought home to her the fact that it wasn't her home at all. She was only here on sufferance.

'There'd be no hurry,' Mrs Hogarth went on. 'Though I know the Porters on the ground floor want to go anyway and the Taylors in the attic are leaving in two months to go somewhere foreign. She did tell me where, but I forgot. The people in the basement, you know, the ones with the funny name I can never get my tongue round, well, they're off in August, so it seems a good time to sell up in a couple of months. But only if it suits you, dear. I'm going to go and see them all this evening.'

'So you're doing the rounds? Poor Mrs Hogarth. It must be awful. But don't worry about me. I was thinking of moving, truly I was. I'd like something bigger and unfurnished anyway.'

'Oh, that does make me feel better. You've lifted a weight off my mind, dear. Well, I don't mind a top up, thanks. Just to celebrate.'

There was a ring at the doorbell.

'You've got visitors,' Mrs Hogarth said. 'I'll drink up and be off.'

'It might be Timothy,' Jenny said, making a great effort to control her voice. 'You've met him, haven't you?'

'Oh, I know your Timothy. The lawyer chap. A bit of all right, he is. But I'm not staying all the same.'

It was Timothy.

'I'm just off,' Mrs Hogarth told him.

'Don't let me drive you away.'

'I was going anyway, dear. I've got calls to make. I must admit,' she said to Jenny, 'that I came to you first because I knew you'd be the easiest to deal with.'

'I'm glad someone finds her easy,' Timothy remarked.

'Get away with you. She's the pleasantest lady I've ever had for a tenant,' Mrs Hogarth told him. 'Well, I'll leave you two young things to get on with it,' she said, and winked.

'What was all that about?' Tim asked, when she had gone.

'She wants me out in a couple of months,' Jenny told him bleakly.

'What you need is a good lawyer.'

'No.' She shook her head. 'It's probably all for the best. I needed an incentive to get out and find something else.'

'You don't sound as if it's all for the best.'

She shrugged.

'Well, I'd sooner it had been my own choice. And to happen now – just when I needed to be able to shut my own door behind me, have my own refuge . . .'

Suddenly, to his amazement, and her own dismay, she was in his arms, crying hard. At first she was furious with herself for breaking down, then she relaxed, giving way to tears. She let him take her over to the big armchair by the gas fire, and nurse her, like a child, on his knee, comforting her. Slowly messily, she told him what had happened. He listened to her incoherent tale, stroking her hair, wiping her eyes with his handkerchief.

'And I'll have to write to him and tell him tomorrow, Tim. It's that that I can't face. I just don't know how I'll begin to tell him.'

He thought for a while.

'Jenny,' he said, 'he'll obviously be very shocked and disappointed, but I don't think he'll be as shattered as you imagine.'

'He's not very confident, Tim, and one thing I do know is that it takes confidence to start a book – I mean it's a huge undertaking and it's something nobody actually *has* to do, so he could just back away from it, if he lost courage.'

'I think you underestimate him. If he really is the writer you say he is, he'll dredge up the courage from somewhere.'

'Do you think so? Really?' she asked uncertainly. 'I mean you're not just saying that to cheer me up?'

'Of course I'm not. In a way I think it's worse for you, than it is for him. After all, his task was to write the book and he's done that. Nobody can take that from him. Certainly Frobishers can't, even if they have reneged on publishing it. It's done. He's done what he had to do. But your job is to turn a manuscript into a book and you've been prevented from fulfilling that.'

'Yes,' she said slowly, 'Yes, that's true. Oh Tim, you do understand everything so well.'

'Not really. It's just that you were too close to see clearly. Too involved. Tomorrow you'll see it differently.'

'I only know that I felt like giving up. I still feel partly to blame. And just the thought of going into the office tomorrow makes me feel weak at the knees.'

'Of course you won't give up. You're in the right job, Jenny.'

'Thank you.'

She nestled up against him.

After a while she said, 'I'd like to stay here like this for ever. Don't let's go out. We could have supper here.'

'What have you got in the cupboard?'

'We can have toast, marmalade and coffee.'

He laughed at her.

'Breakfast at this hour?'

'Well, why not? I'll go and fill the kettle. You pull the table up to the fire and find something to drink with this banquet.'

'Don't you ever use the kitchen?' he asked. 'The one downstairs?'

'No. I've always reckoned that by the time you've bought all the ingredients it's just as cheap to eat out.'

'Rubbish,' he said, kissing her.

'Maybe in my next flat,' she conceded, as she went to fill the kettle in the bathroom, 'I'll have a kitchen.'

They put it all ready on the little table; bread, marmalade, Dubonnet and chocolate biscuits.

'There's muesli if you want it,' she said. 'And we can toast the bread.'

'I'd quite forgotten,' he said suddenly. 'I've got some cheese.'

'*Cheese*?'

'Yes, in that carrier bag I dumped down when I arrived.'

'Why?'

'Well, as you know I wasn't going to come to see you tonight, as you'd said not to. But I was feeling angry with myself so I went for a walk. I passed a late-opening grocer's and bought a few bits and pieces I needed. Then I realized I'd been walking in your direction, so I decided to come on and see you just the same.'

'You didn't walk all the way?'

'No, I took a bus for the last part.'

'Why were you angry with yourself?' she asked, plugging in the kettle.

He hesitated.

'Oh, just something,' he said.

'Go on.'

'I did something stupid in court. And was reprimanded. It wasn't nice.'

'Oh Tim, darling. I'm sorry. Tell me about it.'

'I forgot to apply for bail on behalf of my client. You're supposed to apply after the hearing but before the court rises. I simply forgot. I don't know why.'

He went back to the chair and slumped down in it.

'The judge rose,' he went on, 'and was half-way to the door before I remembered and in a panic I shouted, "M'lord, bail, I wish to apply for bail." The judge turned round and walked slowly back to the bench. The officers followed him. He sat down, the whole court sat and I was the only one left standing there, wishing the ground would open and swallow me up. I began trying to make my application but the judge stopped me and said, "When the court has risen, application of this sort must be made to me in my private room." Then he paused and added cuttingly, "The time will no doubt come when you will learn to do these things properly." Then the court rose for the second time and went out. It was a total humiliation.' He covered his face with his hands. 'And I'll have to go into that court again tomorrow. And I just feel I can't face it, ever again.'

'How beastly of him. Which judge was it?'

'No, Jenny,' he said wearily. 'He was right. Things must be done correctly in court.'

It was her turn to comfort him. She stood behind his chair and gently removed his hands from his face. Then she took his head in her arms and carried it to her breast. 'I'll think of you going into court tomorrow morning and facing them all. Because you will,' she told him softly, her cheek against his. After a while she moved round to face him and held his head a little away from hers, so that she could look into his eyes. 'And I'll tell you something, Tim. Everyone will have forgotten all about it in a week. More important scenes will be enacted there.'

'Thank you, Jenny,' he said, almost inaudibly.

Then he put his arms around her waist as she leaned over him and drew her gently down towards him.

Across the room the kettle began to boil.

She sighed.

'And it's not the sort that turns itself off,' she said.

# Chapter Thirteen

The weather was perfect at half-term. Heather spread a rug under the apple tree and they sat and ate a picnic lunch under the blossom. The Ant ran about naked, staggering and falling occasionally and shouting with laughter.

'He ought to have his knickers on,' pronounced Julie, Mary's prim five-year-old.

'Boys don't wear knickers,' James corrected her.

'Knickers, knickers, knickers,' shrieked the Ant and fell over.

They were interrupted by the arrival of the man from the estate agents to put the FOR SALE board up.

'I think it's *horrible*,' James said. 'People will think *we're* for sale.'

'I wouldn't buy you for tuppence,' Derek told him. 'Come on now, you and Jonathan, and I will help to put the sign up. You carry the hammer, Jonathan, and James, bring that stake that I put ready. Are the rest of you coming?'

He led them away like Pied Piper, James and Jonathan and Mary's three children who were staying while their parents went away for a long weekend.

Heather stayed on the rug with the Ant, momentarily sleepy, on her lap. Absent-mindedly she stroked his head, warm and sweet-smelling, and sighed. She had wanted to avoid this, the children having to live in a house with a FOR SALE board up. Herself too. There was something forlorn about a house with a board up. But it had to be. After the Armstrongs had let them down – no, that wasn't fair – anyway, after they hadn't bought the cottage, plenty of people had come to look, after seeing the advertisement in the Sunday paper, but none had made an offer. People just weren't buying any more. Everything seemed to have gone into reverse since last year. So they had put the cottage into the hands of agents, and now the board was going up. Ah well, she thought, smiling down at the Ant, at least one of the family is sleeping through it all.

'Do you know what he said?' Derek asked, coming back with the children. 'That's the last board they've got. All out.'

'I can believe it. The whole neighbourhood seems to be for sale. Chorfield is sprouting FOR SALE signs like a plague of triffids.'

Derek came and sat with her, leaning back to back. Jonathan climbed on to his knee and requested Ride a Cock Horse.

'All right, but quietly, mind,' Derek said. 'The Ant's asleep.'

'When do you have to go away?' Jonathan asked.

'Do you want me to go already? I've just got home.'

'No, but I like to know how long we've got.'

'A whole week. I don't go back until a week on Sunday.'

Jonathan sighed contentedly. His cheeks were a good colour, his father observed, and his face had lost that anxious look.

Jonathan sighed again.

'Everything's nice,' he said.

Later they took the remains of the picnic to feed the ducks. The children climbed the fence and ran ahead.

'Take care of the Ant,' Heather called out. 'Don't let him go too near the pond.'

James and Jonathan took a hand each, lifting him up by the arms now and then, and swinging him.

'He was right,' Derek said. 'Everything's nice.'

She laughed. 'It was lovely the way he said it, wasn't it? But actually everything's far from nice, now we can't sell.'

'Oh, I don't know. It's better than it was before, when we thought we'd sold but had nowhere to go. I think I'd rather have it this way round.'

They leant on the fence, watching the children throwing bits of bread into the pond and the ducks diving and thrashing about in the water.

'Don't fight, you lot,' they heard James shout at the ducks.

'He's the one to talk!' his mother commented.

'My only worry,' Derek said, 'is if the Soddies decide to sell to somebody else.'

'They wouldn't find that easy nowadays.'

'It just needs one offer.'

'I still don't think she'd do it.'

'He might. He's the unknown quantity.'

'They're bound to give us a bit of time. Anyway, we may sell the cottage straight away now we have a board up and the estate agents have sent details off to all their clients.'

'I found their fulsome description of our humble cottage too embarrassing to read.'

'It's a jolly good little cottage,' she told him. 'It deserves every excessive adjective.'

'And gets it.'

They heard a car draw up at the gate and a door slam. They looked at each other and then watched as a tall man got out and walked round the car to the passenger door.

'Customers,' Derek said, awe-struck.

'You show them round,' Heather told him, 'while I stay out here and keep an eye on the kids.'

Then she stood, transfixed, watching as the pair came through the gate and down the path, the girl, tall, elegant and beautifully clad, leading the way.

'A *rich* customer, too,' Derek murmured, even more awe-struck.

'That's no customer,' Heather told him. 'That is Jenny Pierce.'

The children were still playing by the pond at five o'clock. Heather stood pressing her spine against the warm frame of the open door and watched them. From within she could hear Derek expounding.

'This isn't a load-bearing wall,' she heard him say. 'So you could knock it down if you wanted to extend on this side. Or put in a reinforced concrete beam.' Heather smiled to herself as she listened to him unconsciously quoting Chris Armstrong.

Poor Derek, she thought idly, shaking her head over him. There was something rather touching about the determined way he was treating Tim and Jenny as purchasers. Jenny had explained the minute she arrived that she and this Tim were only calling in for a moment on their way down for the weekend with her parents. But having got it into his head that they were customers, Derek had insisted on showing them round the cottage, relentlessly going into every irrelevant detail. To be fair, Tim did seem very interested in all of it and certainly Jenny could be heard exclaiming at the prettiness of this, that and the other as they did their tour. But she knew Jenny would never buy. It was just that she had somehow or other failed to communicate this vital piece of information to Derek. It was altogether a ridiculous situation, and she only hoped he wouldn't explode with rage when the truth finally dawned on him.

The children were beginning to straggle back by the time Derek emerged from the cottage. She could see, by one glance at his face, that he was full of groundless hope.

'Well, I think it's a perfect cottage,' Tim said, ducking his head as he followed Derek out through the back door.

'Good. I must say we've been very happy here,' Derek enthused. 'And I'm sure that whoever follows us will be, too.'

'Yes,' Jenny nodded. 'I'm sure you won't have any trouble selling it.'

'What?'

'I mean I'd buy it myself, if I was looking for something to buy. I suppose you wouldn't consider letting it? I'm looking for something to rent.'

'Rent it?' Derek repeated, stupefied.

Heather was so afraid that disappointment would make him brutally frank about what he thought of this suggestion that she cut in quickly.

'I wish we could help, Jenny,' she said, 'but you see, we have to buy our next house, so we must have the money from this one.'

'Of course,' Jenny said. 'I just thought it was worth asking.'

'Oh, that's all right,' Derek assured her, but couldn't resist adding, 'Actually it does say FOR SALE in quite large letters on the board.'

The four of them walked together up the brick path.

'It's a lovely cottage you've got,' Tim said, glancing back as they reached the gate.

'Yes,' Derek agreed briskly. 'And the sooner we can get shot of it the better.'

'Derek, what a thing to say,' Heather exclaimed as the car drew away.

But it was true. The cottage into which they had put so much time and love and energy was now a burden to be got rid of. In the following week, however, neither the FOR SALE board nor the estate agent's prose produced any serious purchasers. Many came to look, but none stayed to buy.

Rosemary Soddie was having breakfast when the telephone rang. She took her coffee with her when she went to answer it.

'I have Mr Soddie on the line,' the receptionist of the Bull Hotel, Hexbury, told her.

'Thank you.'

She sipped her coffee and waited. Then, 'Hello, Claud,' she said.

'Sorry to ring you so early, Ro, but I thought I'd better get in touch before I go to the office. I've decided to come home by train this weekend. I hate long drives. Can you meet me at the station? I'll catch the six-thirty. I'm afraid I don't know what time it gets in.'

'That's all right. I'll look it up.'

'Thanks, Ro. I must say it's a whole lot simpler than it used to be getting home from abroad, eh? By the way, I heard yesterday that things are going really well in Ethiopia now. Getting young Armstrong out there was the best thing I ever did.'

'Good. And how are things going at the new office?'

'Very well.' He sounded enthusiastic. 'We're getting a proper switchboard installed today. Yes, things are shaping up. All we

203

need now are a few profitable jobs to justify our existence. I must say I'm really enjoying it. At least I would be, if we could get the house settled. I suppose there's been no more news?'

'No. I'm afraid not. The poor Barnicoats are still trying to sell.'

'Well, don't get too sorry for them. Spare a thought for us.'

She laughed. She was relieved that he hadn't suggested putting the house on the market again and trying to find another purchaser.

'It's not their fault,' she said. 'The people who were buying their cottage let them down. You remember?'

'Oh, I know that. People do behave badly nowadays. In the old days if you said you wanted to buy a house you went ahead and did it.'

'Apparently he was offered a job abroad and he felt he ought to take it.'

'Any old excuse. It's like the chairman was saying the other day, nobody is reliable any more. Look, Ro, why don't you ring Mrs Barnicoat and see if you can't lean on her a bit? See how the land lies. Maybe they ought to drop the asking price for their cottage?'

'We can't expect them to drop their price unless we drop ours, can we?'

'Really, Ro, we have to have the wherewithal to buy Mrs Moon's house! I only meant, well, try your hand with the Barnicoats. You did a good job with Mrs Moon after all.'

'All right, I will. I think I'll ring Mrs Moon as well to let her know why we can't sign yet.'

'Is that wise?' he asked, alarmed.

'Of course,' she said evenly. 'We're friends and I did promise to let her know exactly what was happening.'

'All the same, we don't want to alarm the old girl into selling to somebody else.'

'She isn't easily alarmed.'

Impressed by the new firmness in her voice, he didn't argue. 'I leave it to your judgement,' he said. 'I thought of calling on her myself, but you know her better than I do.'

'Yes, that's true.'

'How's Simon?'

'Busy revising for end-of-term exams.'

'A levels, isn't it?'

'No, that's next year. These are just school exams.'

'Oh, yes, of course. Well, wish him luck all the same.'

There was a pause, and then he added, 'Remind me of what subjects he's taking.'

'Economics, history and maths.'

'Of course. It comes back to me now.'

'By the way, I had a word with Mr Francis – you know the one who teaches him economics and says he can have Simon as a boarder if we've moved by next term – and explained that I may still be here, if the house isn't sold, so Simon will stay with me.'

'Good Lord, Rosemary, you're not seriously thinking that we shan't get moved up here by next term?'

'It could happen. The hotel's comfortable, isn't it?'

'Well, it's all right for a few weeks. I couldn't stand it for more than that. We must move soon, Rosemary, really we must.'

'I hope so,' she said, thinking of Mrs Moon and their plans for the garden. 'Oh, I do hope so.'

'That's the spirit,' he said, pleased at the conviction in her voice. 'I hate living in hotels. Well, I suppose I'd better be making tracks and you'll want to get on with ringing the Barnicoats.'

'All right. And, Claud . . .'

'Yes?'

'I'm glad you want the Barnicoats to have the house. I mean I'd have been sad if you'd suggested trying to sell it to somebody else.'

He was touched. It was generous of her. He did not spoil the effect by admitting that he had tried to do just that.

'Thank you, darling,' he said. 'Goodbye.'

'Goodbye, Claud.'

205

Mrs Florence Moon was incensed. At this rate there'd be no sharing of the lifting of potatoes, no harvesting together of carrots and onions, no drying of herbs, no gathering of apples and pears. And all the other plans that she and Rosemary had made would come to nothing.

'I'm old, Samuel,' she told her lawyer, 'so I want things *now*. When you're young you can wait for things, you can afford to be patient. I can't.'

She lashed out at a harmless dead nettle with her stick. 'This hold-up that's stopping the sale, Samuel. It's a wretched nuisance. You must sort it out.'

'But I've told you, Florence, there's nothing I can do. I only called to talk about investments.'

'Oh, those,' she said with contempt.

'You must consider your finances, Florence. When the house is sold you will have a large capital sum, tax free, since this is your only residence, which we must consider investing.'

He spoke with relish. He understood money. 'I think you should invest in property. I know the market is very flat at the moment, but we must consider the longer run. Bricks and mortar hold their value. That's what I'd invest in.'

'But I'm getting rid of my bricks and mortar, Samuel,' she reminded him in exasperation. 'You've spent the last five years telling me to get rid of my bricks and mortar and now you say this!'

'I didn't mean you should keep this house, of course, Florence. I had in mind investments in such property as holiday flats. Or perhaps a unit trust that specializes in property.'

'It's all a bit hypothetical, isn't it, since I haven't sold yet and haven't acquired this fine capital sum for investment?'

'You will sell in time, my dear. So you must plan ahead what to do with the money. This is a house of great character, somebody will want it.'

'Mrs Rosemary Soddie wants it and she shall have it,' she told him fiercely.

'But as you know, their own sale is held up.'

'Well, I held up theirs, didn't I? So it's up to us to sort things out now. She told me last night that they could go ahead immediately but their people can't buy because they've been let down themselves.'

'That's right. People of the name of Barnicoat, Mr Soddie's solicitor told me.'

'Really? I didn't catch the name on the phone. Barnicoat's a Cornish name. I knew some people once called Barnicoat, lived near St Ives. They grew mimosa outdoors. Think of that! And the house had a splendid pittosporum hedge all round. Of course they don't get the frosts down there. Variegated it was.'

She smiled, glad to think that her friend Rosemary was selling to such people.

'Apparently Mrs Soddie seems very keen on waiting and letting them have the house. She feels she owes it to them.'

'Of course she does. She told me as much last night. We had a long talk about it. There must be a solution, Samuel, if only we could hit on it.'

She set off suddenly round the garden, her head swivelling, her stick thrashing, still limping a little. Despite all this it was quite hard to keep up with her. Samuel Vereker was relieved when she came to rest suddenly by the rose pergola.

'I have it,' she said.

'Florence?'

'What we must do is this.'

She looked up at him, a battered little old woman with triumph in her eye.

'Yes, Florence?'

'I will buy the Barnicoats' cottage.'

He stared at her.

'You?'

'Why not? Then they can buy the Soddies' house and the Soddies can buy mine. There, it's all settled. I can't think why you didn't suggest it earlier.'

'But, Florence, you don't want to go and live in a cottage somewhere you've never even seen . . .'

'Oh, Samuel, don't pretend to be so dim-witted. Of course I

207

shan't live in it. I shall let it or leave it empty, until somebody wants to buy it. It doesn't really matter what I do. Just so long as I've bought it, I'll get all those house sales moving.'

Samuel Vereker used his most damning phrase.

'It's very unorthodox,' he said.

Florence Moon shrugged.

'Never mind that,' she said. 'Just go and arrange it.'

'But I've never heard of anyone doing such a thing,' he insisted. 'I mean I've often known of these housing chains, everyone held up because one sale doesn't go through, but I've never, never known the first one buy the last one in order to resolve it. Never.'

He sounded so shocked at the idea of doing something that he had never heard of anyone else doing before, that she said more gently, 'There are always surprises, Samuel, even at our age. We should be glad of it. And,' she went on more briskly, 'don't forget you have just this minute been telling me to invest in bricks and mortar.'

'But I never meant that you should rush into a wild scheme like this. I had in mind property investments, managed for you.'

'Well, I mean it, Samuel, and if you don't want to be involved I shall take charge of the purchase myself. Mrs Soddie will tell me about these Barnicoats, no doubt,' she went on, warming to the idea, 'and I'll get in touch with them—'

'It's all right, Florence,' he cut in, horrified. The idea that anyone, let alone Florence Moon, should even consider buying or selling their own house without benefit of a solicitor had always filled him with a very special kind of dismay. 'If you must go ahead with this scheme, I'd far rather you left it for me to deal with.'

'Very well then, that's settled,' she said, smiling with sudden glee now that she had got her own way. 'Off you go back to the office and see to it.'

Then her expression changed and she added with sudden ferocity, swivelling her head about, 'Just look at that. Do you see what I see?'

He looked around, baffled. It was always difficult to follow her line of vision.

'Something wrong?' he hazarded.

'An *invasion*,' she said. 'You can't call that a mere infestation, can you? Colonies of them.'

The roses were indeed crawling with greenfly. Every stem was thickened with little green bodies, as if covered with thick lichen. The new shoots were drooping, sucked of all vitality.

'We'll soon sort you lot out,' Florence Moon told them furiously. 'Just you wait, my lads.'

She wheeled off in a great rage towards the house, accompanied by her solicitor.

'I'll give them a dose of the new systemic stuff,' she told him. 'Much more effective than the old poison. That just killed the ones it happened to hit. The new sort gets into the sap, so when they stick their beaks in, wham, they're done for.'

'I'll be on my way then,' he said, raising his hat to her, 'to pursue the purchase of the cottage. I'll speak to both the other solicitors and I'll arrange for a valuation. You'll have to decide how much you're prepared to pay, Florence.'

'Oh, I'll leave all that to you,' she said, more interested now in spraying.

He hesitated, hovering nearby as she filled two buckets from the outside tap in the yard and then slopped two measurefuls of evil-smelling brown liquid into each. 'They won't like this,' she pronounced. 'This'll make 'em skip. Carry the buckets down for me would you, Samuel? I'll bring the spray guns.'

Regretting not having made his departure while the going was good, he obligingly picked up the buckets while she selected, from a fine array of devices for spraying, two implements which took her fancy. One was a modern plastic gadget, the other a very old brass one which her husband had always used. Holding one under each arm she set off for the rose pergola, followed by her ancient solicitor weighed down by buckets.

At the pergola he put them down with relief and stood rubbing his elbows. He made a last attempt to interest her in the transaction she had just entrusted to him.

'Florence,' he began, 'about the valuation of the cottage . . .'

'I've said you can see to it all,' she told him absently, distracted by greenfly. 'Don't forget to send me your bill, will you?'

He hesitated for a moment, then raised his hat again and left her, pausing only to say, 'Now don't overdo it will you, Florence? All this spraying, I mean.'

She didn't bother to reply. She thought it a foolish request. She could never understand why people made such a fuss about spraying. She liked everything about it, not just the sense it gave her of slaughtering the enemy, but the smell and even the sound of it. She listened now, head on one side, to the gentle sucking sound as she pulled out the plunger and drew the liquid up into the long brass barrel, followed by a very satisfactory hissing noise as she took aim and pressed the plunger so that the pesticide sprayed out over the roses, falling among them with a patter like soft rain, making the leaves rustle as they were tossed about by the fine jets of liquid. With relish she imagined the terror she was causing to the invaders, as she repeated the process again and again, rhythmically dipping the nozzle into the bucket, drawing up the fluid and shooting it out in all directions, often spraying herself copiously. She did not mind. Life was good. Tonight she would ring Rosemary Soddie and tell her that all was well; meanwhile there was nothing she enjoyed more than going into battle with the aphids. Florence Moon sighed contentedly and gave herself up to the joys of spraying.

She was wearing the same red velvet dress, Claud noticed. The one that made her look Spanish.

'It reminds me of last time we were celebrating,' he remarked, as he raised his glass to her, 'when I got back from Ethiopia and you'd fixed Mrs Moon.'

'We celebrated a bit too soon, didn't we?' she said, smiling.

'I don't think anything can go wrong this time. You've done very well, Ro, the way you've managed Mrs Moon.'

'I didn't manage her. I just told her what the situation was for the Barnicoats. It was entirely her own idea to buy their cottage.'

He shook his head. 'Well, anyway, you leant on her very successfully the first time, persuading her to get out like that. Nothing like a bit of personal pressure on these occasions. Here's to the old girl, anyway.'

There was a pause and then she said, 'Claud, Mrs Moon and I are probably going to start a small nursery garden together.'

He stared at her, astonished.

'What did you say?'

'Concentrating on herbs,' she went on. 'There is, you may remember, a big walled garden that would be ideal.'

'I don't understand,' he said.

'I didn't say anything to you before,' she explained, 'because of course we were suddenly held up by the Barnicoats not being able to buy. But when I went to see Mrs Moon about the house we decided that's what we'd like to do. So I stayed there an extra day and we went to see the planning people to make sure there'd be no difficulty. But it seems it would be quite simple, subject to a very few regulations, like not putting sign boards up in a residential area, and so on.'

'Sign boards? Rosemary, I'm baffled. What are you trying to tell me?'

'I'm telling you that Mrs Moon and I will be in partnership.'

'But you don't know a single thing about business, or about running a nursery garden. You couldn't possibly contemplate such a thing. I don't know what's got into your head.'

'Actually, Claud, I do know quite a lot about herbs. And I've a small library of books on how to grow them. I'm not worried about my theoretical knowledge, and I feel fairly sure that the practical side will come back to me.'

She spoke firmly; she knew for certain that the skills learned in her youth were still in her.

She'd taken leave of her senses, he thought. Suddenly it occurred to him that perhaps it was her age.

'Have you thought of seeing the doctor?' he asked.

She didn't reply.

'Well, anyway, I can't have it, I'm afraid. You should have consulted me first, you know.'

'You weren't there.'

'No, well,' he hesitated, grew defensive. 'Look here, Ro, I know I'm away a lot. But it's a bit hard to be reproached just because I've always worked hard for you and the boys. I've tried, striven, yes, striven, to give you all you need, a nice home in a pleasant area; anything you've wanted, I've tried to give you. Within reason.'

She shook her head slowly. 'No, Claud. You've worked for work's sake, and your own. I don't blame you, indeed I respect you for it, but don't say it was all for us.'

'Well, anyway, it comes to the same thing.'

'Not quite. I accept your need for work, you must accept mine.'

'I've never forbidden you to work. In fact, if you remember when you were depressed a few years ago I suggested you might find a little part-time job or do a voluntary task once a week or so. Be fair.'

Ah yes, she remembered. When the boys had first gone away to school and she had felt no longer needed, Claud had made this suggestion about a little job, implying it must be something trifling, that even she could manage. It had destroyed her last vestige of self-confidence. But, oh, it was a different thing when a stranger, from whom you expected nothing, made you a gift of trust and hope, assumed you were competent, believed in your skills, took them for granted.

'But this would involve serious things, Rosemary, like money. What do you know about it? I don't expect you've given a thought to raising capital.'

'Yes,' she said, 'I have. We have agreed that Mrs Moon will finance the stocking of the herb garden. It is in fact very well stocked already, lots of old bushes which we could take cuttings from. She has more than enough equipment, everything we need. And two fine greenhouses, one at least thirty foot long; indeed both are commercial sized. And heated too.

We could expand to other plants later, but the thing is we can just start small and see how it goes, feel our way.'

'Have you considered the risks? Does the expression risk capital mean anything to you?'

'There's very little risk involved. Mrs Moon is quite happy to invest in the scheme and I shall provide the labour and organization. If we need it and can afford it, we may get in paid help later, but only if the thing grows.'

'And what about your own labour? Your own time is valuable too, you know. You should cost it out.'

'But the value of my time never worried you when I was cooking and dusting. So why should you put a price upon it now, just because I'll be doing something I enjoy?'

There was silence. Then he tried another line of attack.

'And what about the rest of us? Have you considered that? You have a new home to make for me and the boys. Running that would be enough for most women. No, the more I think about it the more I think it's a scatterbrained idea, and you risk coming a fearful cropper. I can't have that, Rosemary. No, for your own sake, I can't allow it.'

She looked at him directly.

'I am going to do this, Claud. I am certainly not going to let Mrs Moon down.'

'Explain to her that you acted in haste.' He laughed. 'You'll most likely be surprised to find she's very relieved to get out of the whole thing.'

'No.'

'I mean it, Rosemary. I really cannot allow it.'

She looked at him hard.

'In that case you can go and live up there alone. I shall stay here with the boys. Then Simon won't need to go and board with Mr Francis.'

He turned away from her gaze, began to pace the room. He couldn't think what had come over her, couldn't make it out at all. From the moment he'd got home from abroad he'd noticed a change in her. She even looked different, firmer, her expression was less vague, her voice brighter. Everything about her was somehow more alive. A dreadful thought suddenly struck him. He stood by the window, horrified, not able to turn to look at her. Was it possible that she was having an affair? Was it one of those things you imagine only happen to other men's wives? Could it have been going on all the time while he was away? Here? He cleared his throat. He said nothing. Oh God, he didn't want to know. He suddenly realized that if she was having an affair he didn't want to know about it. That was something they'd always taken for granted, the faithfulness of the other. Work and Rosemary, it had been like that for him all their married life. In that order, maybe, but never, never a thought of anyone else. But he couldn't not know. Yet he couldn't bring himself to ask.

'Rosemary,' he said, 'I can't help feeling that someone has been, well, *influencing* you.'

'Yes,' she said.

'May I ask who?' He gulped in an undignified way as he took a deep breath and added, 'And how, exactly?'

There was a pause, and then he heard her say softly, 'An old woman stepped into my life, and redeemed it.'

Whatever he had expected her to say, it was certainly not that.

Astonished, he turned to look at her, relief overwhelming him, for he knew that it was the truth that she was telling him, he never doubted her word.

'It will be all right,' she told him confidently. 'There's nothing for you to worry about. My running a nursery garden, Claud, doesn't threaten you in any way.'

'No,' he agreed, 'No. I understand.' Then he added humbly, 'Perhaps I might be able to help you?'

'Oh, yes,' she said, magnanimous in her new-found power. 'You can help me with the accounts and all sorts of things like that.'

She moved towards him as she spoke and suddenly he was across the room to her, had her in his arms, clutching at her in his relief. It was the first time in years that he had seized her in an impulsive embrace. As they clung together, she said again, 'It's going to be all right.'

214

Unable to speak, he rubbed his chin against the thick, dark hair.

'You'll have your job and I'll have mine,' she told him. 'It'll all work out quite smoothly.'

She knew, of course, that it wasn't strictly true. He would try to reassert himself, re-establish their old pattern; nobody could change the habit of twenty years of married life quite so easily, certainly not Claud Soddie. But she also knew that her determination to run a nursery garden that her father would have been proud of was formidable and that it would grow, as the garden would grow. So it was with total conviction in her voice that she said once again, 'It's all going to work out, Claud, when we move, I promise you. I know that it will.'

'It's odd to think we don't know the person who's buying the cottage,' Heather said, as they washed up after lunch. 'I'd like to know her, or at least meet her.'

'I can't say it bothers me, so long as she pays up,' Derek replied. Then, seeing the look on her face, he added, 'But I know what you mean. Though it isn't as if she was going to live here, is it? The couple who're renting it are the ones who matter really, and you've got to know Jenny and Tim quite well.'

'Yes, and I do like them both very much. I have a feeling that they'll get married pretty soon.'

'You always want people to get married,' Derek remarked thoughtfully, rubbing away at a tablespoon with a damp tea towel. 'I suppose it's because it's been so nice for you being married to me.'

'And I shouldn't be surprised,' she went on, ignoring the interruption, 'if they don't buy the cottage from the old lady in the end.'

'Well, they'll be sitting tenants, so they'll have first refusal.'

'Fancy the old lady being so rich that she can buy a cottage just like that. I didn't realize there were people as rich as that still around nowadays.'

'Oh, the rich, like the poor, are always with us. Where does this bowl go?'

'Inside about ten others under the sink.'

He knelt down and there was much clattering of glass, and some mild swearing.

'Never mind,' she told him, 'think of all the cupboards we're going to have in the kitchen at Wellington Square.'

He got up and kissed her. 'I think of nothing else,' he said.

'Liar. But isn't it lovely to think that after next week we'll have room for everything? And next term you'll be living near school and have no more long journeys home at weekends?'

'And no more Mrs Peck. Do you know, I think she was quite pleased to see the back of me? Odd really. She rather went off me towards the end.'

She laughed, amused that he didn't realize that he had become a less compliant lodger. Let it rest. Water under the bridge.

'All part of experience,' she said vaguely.

'What?'

'Oh, moving and things. Just look at that place the boys have made on the side lawn.'

It had begun with the tent. It was a very small one, so they had added a clothes horse with a blanket over it, and were busy now extending to one side by covering a framework of brushes and sticks with an old sheet.

'Yes,' he said, leaning over her and looking out of the kitchen window. 'Home-making is a pretty strong instinct, isn't it? I like the extension on the side.'

'Talking of extensions,' she said, 'did you realize when you were telling Jenny and Tim about the things they could do to the cottage that you were quoting Christopher Armstrong? All that technical stuff about extensions and what not?'

'Pretty impressive, wasn't I?'

'I have reason to suppose,' she mimicked, 'that this is not a load-bearing wall. Of course you could build on to the west side and—'

'Shut up.'

'And how about a reinforced concrete beam, or RCB as we call it in the trade?'

'I told you to shut up,' he said, taking hold of her.

'All quotes from young Armstrong,' she went on, laughing. 'And the water table, as we knowing ones refer to the village pond—'

He covered her mouth with kisses, pressing her back against the wall, but still she couldn't stop laughing.

They didn't hear the sound of the gate clicking open, or the footsteps on the path. They heard nothing until James flung open the back door and shouted, 'There's a man.'

There was indeed, a yard or two behind him, a young man standing looking very embarrassed.

They sprang apart, guiltily.

'I am sorry to disturb you,' the young man said, 'but I have come to take our board down.'

She couldn't think what he meant. To make it worse there was something so immaculate about him, standing there in his good blue suit and shiny shoes talking about his board that she battled in vain against continuing laughter.

Fortunately Derek understood.

'That's quick,' she heard him say. 'Usually you estate agents like to leave your boards up as long as possible as an advertisement, don't you?'

'Yes, but I'm afraid times aren't usual just now,' the young man explained. 'We have so many houses on our books that we've run out of FOR SALE signs. We need this one for another property.'

'Well, help yourself,' Derek said.

The young man hesitated.

'I didn't realize it was still *in situ*, as it were,' he said, glancing down at his feet, 'or I would have come dressed for rough work.'

'Never mind,' Derek told him. 'We'll take it down for you, won't we, boys?'

'Oh, *please*, yes,' Jonathan said. 'I want to take it down more than anything.'

'Me too. Shall I get a hammer, Dad?'

'Yes, and bring a spade and fork. The ground's quite hard round the stake.'

The Ant tried to join in. Heather scooped him up. He arched his back and tried to break away. 'Not with those bare toes, you don't,' she told him, holding him firmly. 'You don't want a fork in them, do you?'

'Yes,' he said.

She stood holding him and watched as Derek and the boys collected up the tools and set off purposefully down the uneven brick path. Derek had laid that path one Sunday after a late party the night before. More spirit than level, he had said of it afterwards. Young Armstrong was going to take it up and relay it. She wondered idly what the next owners would do with it, and the cottage too if it came to that. And the next, and the next. The estate agent's car was parked by the gate. The young man opened the boot and stood observing his client's efforts on his behalf. Heather too watched as the three of them struggled briefly with the stake, Derek loosening the ground around it, the boys taking it in turns to knock it sideways with the hammer. Then triumphantly they uprooted the FOR SALE board, carried it through the gate and dumped it in the boot of the estate agent's car.